By The Way

D1570351

Other books by Caperton Tissot

Pirates on the Saranac, 2019
(A children's story)

On Thin Ice: The Life of a North Woods Caretaker, 2018

Kicking Leaves: The Contrarian Life of a Yankee Rebel, 2018

The Beat Within: Poetry Another Round, 2017

Adirondack Flashes and Floater: A River of Verse, 2014

Saranac Lake's Ice Palace: A History of Winter Carnival's Crown Jewel, 2012

Adirondack Ice: A Cultural and Natural History, 2010

History Between the Lines: Women's Lives and Saranac Lake Customs, 2007

Books available at your local bookstore and on Amazon.

More information and contact at
www.SnowyOwlPress.com

By The Way

Short Stories
by
Caperton Tissot

*For friends and family whose kindness
and generosity put wings on my recovery.
Thanks to your support, the days flew by.*

"No man is wise at all Times,
or is without his blind Side."

- Desiderius Erasmus
1466 - 1536

Contents

Lockjaw

"Did you see that?" Emma yelled to the two other wives walking toward her on the lakeside trail.

"See what?" they called back as they came closer.

"That powerboat over there," she said, pointing across the lake. "It just ran over a swimmer!"

"What boat? That one in the distance?" asked Ali, a tall, sturdy blond.

"Yeah, that bright blue one by the far shore. Somebody was swimming near our dock and that boat ran right over him... or her," said Emma, who had lingered behind her friends to study a small wildflower. She had been hurrying to catch up when they turned around and started heading back.

"Oh, come on, Emma. We were watching and we didn't see anything," said Joan, a deep-voiced brunette of medium build who took each step with care, as if she were balancing an imaginary plate on her head. Medium applied not only to her build, but to her haircut, her dress, and, one might even conclude, her mind. Nothing about Joan in looks or speech stood out from the crowd.

"The sun was in your eyes. I was shading my face when I looked out and spotted the swimmer. That boat ran right over him."

"Are you sure you weren't seeing a loon which dived underwater? From so far away, how can you be certain? A loon

1

flapping its wings could be mistaken for a swimmer," suggested Ali.

"Huh. I don't know. Maybe. You all didn't see anything?" Emma asked again.

"No, we didn't. I think your imagination got the better of you," declared Joan.

Emma said nothing more. *Why does everyone doubt what I say? It's really annoying. Of course, I could be wrong, but it did look like a person in the water. I'll wait and watch the papers. If anyone is reported missing, then I'll speak up.*

Emma was used to being talked over by those who always "knew better". Maybe it was her soft voice or her reticent manner. But she remembered when she was at a party a couple of weeks ago and had mentioned that heavy rain was predicted two days from then. A couple of men immediately pulled out their devices, checked their own weather sources, and proceeded to set her straight. No rain predicted. As now, she had wondered if she was mistaken, but she had been pretty sure she was not. She had gritted her teeth and said nothing. It poured rain two days later. *My revenge,* she had thought with a smile on her face.

The day of the boat sighting was warm and clear, and the three women had taken advantage of the sunshine to walk along the lake trail. But then, after an hour, Joan, always with food on her mind, said, "Hey, let's head back and get a bite to eat at Jill's."

It was customary for Emma, Ali, Joan, and another friend, Tina, to meet for lunch every week. Tina was unable to join them for the walk, but planned to come for lunch. The three women drove back to Jill's Cafe on Main Street in the village. Finding a table, they had just put in their orders when Tina arrived. She was dressed in a bright, loose-flowing dress, but looked a bit pale. She told them her husband, Josh, was going on a business trip. She had said goodbye and left him packing his bag. Later on, their caretaker Jim would drive him to the airport. Josh was a historian at the Radiman American History Museum in the next town over, and he often traveled for his job, so, at the time, no one thought much about it.

Jill's Cafe was in the village of Lockjaw, named after the first settler in the region who had moved back east from out west in 1850. Taken by the beauty of the forest and lakeside location, he established a homestead. He was said to have brought along a "pile of gold," which was used to bring in workers, construct a railroad, and build an elaborate house on the lake, along with a hotel and country store a couple of miles away. When asked how he made the money, he typically responded with silence. In fact, he had been a rather shy fellow, thus acquiring the nickname of Lockjaw. He didn't talk much, but was educated and a prolific writer. However, before any of his writing could be published, he died unexpectedly, less than a year after his wife.

As far as anyone could tell, he took his riches with him. No will, no money. What happened to his gold remained a mystery. Had he spent it all or hidden it away?

His house, inherited by his daughter, had undergone multiple restorations over the years, but always remained in the family, eventually coming into the possession of Emma, his great-great-granddaughter.

The settlement he founded was named after him, and in 1893, the village was officially incorporated as Lockjaw. For many years after Lockjaw's founder had passed away, the village appeared to have inherited the habit of its taciturn founder. Residents were short on conversation: one or two words sufficing in lieu of sentences. Lockjaw was a pretty place to live, but had a rather somber undertone.

Now, years later, modern life replaced the somber... but also replaced the pretty. Once upon a time, a person walking along Main Street could have nodded a hello to families sitting on front porches, to children roller skating along the empty streets, and to couples out for an evening stroll. There was a time when wisteria wound its way up the low-slung wood homes and lilacs flourished in yards enclosed by white picket fences. Back then, tall pines rose to lofty heights, as if protecting the village from the elements. That time was no more.

Now, up and down Main Street, sprawl, like an epidemic, had crawled into the village, scarring its once lovely downtown. Trees were rare. Chain burger shops, auto dealerships, gas stations, banks, restaurants, and parking lots crowded both sides of the street. Renouncing tradition, once somber residents had become a garrulous lot, the loudest ones dominating.

Emma, however, was a holdover from the past. She enjoyed listening to others, rarely feeling the need to join in the conversation. Time spent outdoors had taught her to listen, not expound. She wasn't exactly lockjawed, but neither was she outspoken. Unlike Emma, Ali, Joan, and Tina, newcomers to the area , were competitive talkers.

Ali, a charge nurse, worked night shifts at the local hospital so she could be home for her kids when they returned from school. She was an efficient, well-organized woman, and responsible to a fault. While she carried out every last detail of her job as both nurse and mother, she spent little time pausing to hold a frightened patient's hand or to cuddle her children through childhood traumas. When her husband, a bank officer, came home in the late afternoon to take over from her, it was to an immaculate house and kids running wild.

Joan was a stay-at-home mom whose husband, a project manager, was often away on business. She was "correct" in everything she did. Her loudly-voiced opinions lined up precisely with whatever the majority believed at the moment.

Tina, independently wealthy, was childless by choice. She spent a good part of her days sitting at her sewing machine or hand quilting unusual fabrics. Her creations were abstract. Shells and pieces of glass were often woven into the designs. Many hung in art galleries, a few in museums.

The women chatted over lunch, but rarely went deeply into any subject, having almost come to blows over politics a year ago. Ali, a committed conservative, had shouted everyone down. The meal had not ended well. Now, they carefully avoided such flareups and kept conversation light.

For days after thinking she saw the swimmer, Emma watched the papers. Her husband Ted, the editor of the local newspaper, had a sterling reputation for keeping all reporting to important information only. There was no gossip in his paper. But at home he relayed to Emma all kinds of things that never appeared in print: snowbirds were coming back from the south, camps along the lake were opening up, Joe's dog had been hit by a car, Ruth Stack had emergency surgery for appendicitis, Josh's powerboat was getting a new paint job...

"Wait," interrupted Emma. "Didn't he just paint his boat last year? I remember you went over to celebrate the new do-over with Josh. You told me Tina was the one who wanted a new look."

"Guess Josh didn't like blue after all. I don't know why he wastes his caretaker's time like that."

"Blue. Did you say it was blue?"

"Yeah, a lovely deep blue. Looked good to me, but Jim says his boss didn't like the color, so he's doing it over."

5

Should she tell Ted about seeing a blue boat seemingly running over a swimmer? Emma wondered. She did not. Understandable. Ted was for facts, not speculation.

Two weeks later, the women gathered for lunch again. Tina was not there. No explanation. Down to only three, conversation lagged. They missed Tina chatting about quilt designs and galleries. It filled the empty spaces.

When another two weeks passed and Tina still didn't show up, the women began to speculate.

"I talked to Tina today. She said Josh was still away and that she was too busy to join us. That seems odd," said Ali as she attacked a large, onion-slathered hamburger.

"I hope nothing's wrong," chimed in Joan, who was struggling not to spill her taco onto her lap.

"Makes you wonder," commented Ali.

"Maybe they're not getting along," Joan replied, scooping tomato and cheese off her skirt. "Maybe he didn't leave for business reasons."

"I guess they have their moments like everyone else," offered Emma, who was sitting back in her chair, sipping a glass of wine.

"Nonsense," declared Ali. "Those two lovebirds? They're the perfect couple."

Emma said nothing. She was, as always, overruled by the loudest mouth. She seethed inwardly, tired of being contradicted. *Though, maybe I am wrong, maybe they get along better than I think.* But Tina had made comments before that left Emma suspecting all was not well in Shangri-La.

"So, let's talk about something else. Guess what I'm doing now?" said Joan who had finally gained control of her lunch. "Genealogy. Everyone's into it, so I thought I'd give it a try. It's really fun. I found ancestors I didn't know existed. I'm trying to learn more about them. The research is full of surprises."

The next day, Emma went for a long walk along the shore, as she often did. She enjoyed her solitary outing with no one talking and disturbing the peace. She felt lucky to live by the lake, to be surrounded by the woods, and yet be only a couple of miles from the village center. There were few homes along the shore to mar the view. Tina and Josh lived around a peninsula out of view. A dozen camps lined the far end of the lake, not far from a public dock. Other than that, it was mostly wild. Some might think her walks were lonely, but not to Emma. Birds were always chirping, lively leaves fluttered in the wind, chipmunks scurried along the ground, flower blossoms popped up in unexpected places, and the breeze sang in the trees. In fact, she sometimes felt more alone around others who constantly talked over her, causing her to doubt herself. Old feelings of anger about those times came rushing back. *Too much brooding*, she thought. *I need a project. Maybe, like Joan, I should try genealogy.*

The following week, she began tapping into the internet in a search for ancestors. Time on the screen was a bit boring until she came across a startling piece of information. All of her great-great-grandfather's writing had, at some point, been turned over to the local library. *What am I doing sitting in front of my computer when his actual papers are right here in the village?* She wasted no time in getting herself to town.

When the librarian, Marion, was asked for Lockjaw's papers, she was surprised. "You know, his notebooks have laid around here untouched for years. Then, a couple of months ago, Josh from the museum was in here looking at them. And now, you come along as well."

Marion, a stooped woman with her hair pulled back in a tight bun, led Emma down to a basement room protected under lock and key. Opening the door and switching on the light, Marion pointed out stacks of dusty file boxes on rows of shelves... some with no lids, all overflowing with yellowed papers. "Let's see. At least four of these contain Lockjaw's papers," she said, as she started reading the labels. "Ah, here they are. You can take them to the corner desk over there and read all you want. However, nothing must leave this room. Also, I would prefer you put on gloves to protect anything you touch. Here, I keep extra pairs for you visiting scholars. When you're through, just come get me."

Scholars! Nobody has ever flattered me like that before, thought Emma. From that moment, the two women began to bond.

Marion, on her way upstairs, paused at the lower step and looked back, "I hope you find something interesting. It would be fun if you dug up a scandal in those forgotten papers."

And so began many days of poring over old, yellowed pages owned by her ancestor. Much had to do with surveying, land purchases, and related finances. Occasionally, she found short descriptions of the abundant wildlife in the days before the settlement had grown. It broke her heart to realize how much wilderness had been lost to development. It was on the third day that she discovered something curious.

She was reading through a flimsy notebook dated shortly before his death. One scrawled page explained how he thought it was time to write a will, leaving his daughter the gold he had managed to hang on to. He had written: "I don't trust the bank, so I will store it safely away near home, but in a place where digging will never find it. I'll let my daughter know the location, but shall not mention it in the will."

At that point, to her great dismay, she saw that two pages had been ripped out. Had Lockjaw done that, afraid the document might fall into the wrong hands? Or, had someone ripped those pages out more recently? But the only other person who had ever bothered to look at these pages was Josh. Surely a historian would never do such a thing.

Several weeks passed before Tina, slightly overweight and dressed in a brightly-colored flowing dress, showed up at the women's lunch group. She was clearly upset. When her friends pressed her, she finally broke down. It turned out that Josh had not gone away for business. He had moved away for another woman. Her friends, eager to hear more, pushed her for the details.

"One night, several weeks ago, he told me he was leaving to live in California. I was shocked. The next morning, he insisted I meet you for lunch as usual. He didn't want a scene. He would pack, take a last swim, and be gone when I got home." Tina related, tears running down her cheeks. "I'm sorry. I thought I could handle seeing you all, but here I go, breaking down again," she said in a quivering voice.

"Make sure the bastard pays you alimony," Ali burst out. "The dog!"

"No, there's no need for alimony. My father insisted I sign a prenup before we married. He never did trust Josh. He said if we ever broke up, he wanted to make sure Josh wouldn't get any of my inheritance."

Ali and Joan, showing little sympathy but a lot of curiosity, quizzed Tina at length. She tearfully tried to answer their questions. *They're heartless,* thought Emma. *Leave the poor woman alone.*

Finally, Emma spoke up, "I'm just so sorry to hear all this. It has to be very hard for you right now. Will you be okay out at the lake by yourself?"

"I'll be okay with Jim doing all the outside maintenance. I guess the inside maintenance... I'll have to do myself. Somehow, I have to find a way to keep going, not break down like I am now." Smiling through her tears, she continued, "I feel like a knife is ripping me apart."

Ali was immediately ready with suggestions: yoga, meditation, Tai Chi, soothing music, the right herbs. "Maybe let her be," said Emma. "She needs sympathy, not advice."

"Nonsense," responded Joan who could be counted on to go right along with Ali. "She needs our help and guidance."

Does she? wondered Emma.

Despite the strong opinions of her lunch friends, Emma still found them good people and fun to see, on occasion. For their part, they viewed Emma as a quaint local. In their eyes, she lacked sophistication and was too stuck in the old ways. On the other hand, her friendship made them feel as if they were part of the inner workings of the village.

Other than lunches with them and her genealogy work, Emma was happy to spend her time walking in the woods, studying the different mosses, searching for tiny woodland plants, and listening to the birds flitting through the trees. Then there was the lake. She loved to hear the waves lapping at the shore, watch the ripples in the sand under the shallow water, and see the ospreys soaring overhead, occasionally diving at the flash of a bass to scoop it up in their fearsome claws. These moments brought balance into her life, reminding her not to let the little things get her down.

One day, when she was standing on the shore by her house, she looked down and saw broken snorkel equipment. The previous day's storm had washed it up. *Now, why would that be here?* she wondered. *I wish I could tell my friends about it, but they'd just pooh-pooh my suspicions.*

That evening, she began to wonder about a lot of other things besides the snorkel: the swimmer, the repainted boat, the missing pages and Josh. *Could there be a connection? I should read more of Lockjaw's papers. Maybe I missed something.*

The next day Emma was back at the library. Marion was there at the front desk, welcoming her with a big smile. "Could I take another look at the files?" Emma asked.

"Of course," Marion replied, reaching into the drawer for a key to the downstairs room, "I thought you'd be back for more. There's a lot there to read. Can't be done in a few sittings, that's for sure."

Emma spent the next several days at the library. Marion seemed glad to see her. The two chatted and their friendship grew. On the fourth day, as she turned the pages of yet another old notebook, Emma suddenly let out a cry of astonishment. She had found a map of the lake with a black dot on it... and the dot was near the shore of her home! As she was by herself in the downstairs archive room, there was nobody to see her jump up in excitement. Probably a good thing. *I've got to share this with someone,* she thought, *but with whom?* She was sure her lunch friends would write her off as silly if she ventured to voice her concerns. Besides, it would upset Tina even more. And, as much as she loved Ted, she did not think she had enough facts to persuade her skeptical husband. As the paper's editor, it was natural he was like that, but Emma needed someone more sympathetic to hear her out. *Ah, Marion. Maybe I can talk to her.*

She seems to believe in me. Maybe she can help make sense of all of this. She put the file boxes away and on the way out, stopped at the front desk.

"I'm through for now. But I've found some curious stuff. Would you be interested in having lunch together tomorrow so I can share it with you?" she asked. Marion, delighted, said yes.

The next afternoon, Emma and Marion sat down for lunch at Jill's Cafe. It was a good place to meet. Carpeting and well-separated tables insured that conversations were not easily overheard. Emma had arrived early and selected a table in the far back next to a pine-paneled wall hung with sports posters. Marion joined her at the wooden table, pulling out one of the mismatched chairs (the latest trend in modern dining) to take a seat.

"I'm really curious about your research. What did you find?" asked Marion, before they had even looked at their menus.

Emma immediately launched into the subject, telling first about the map, then about the ripped-out pages, then about the other things she thought might have some connection to Josh's disappearance. The waitress returned three times to take their order before they remembered to look at the day's specials and make a choice.

Marion, a widow, lived a less-than-adventurous life. The prospect of solving a mystery made her shiver with excitement. After Emma described all of the details to her unusually eager listener, the two began to speculate on how the disparate parts of the story could be related. They did not lack for imagination.

"Do you actually think Jim could have killed his boss?" asked Marion.

"Well, if you add my seeing a boat running over a swimmer to the torn-out pages about the location of the gold, it sort of points in that direction," said Emma. "Josh probably took Jim along in

12

the boat to help him pull up the heavy box, promising a cut of the treasure. Then Jim decided he would rather have all the goods instead."

"Wow! A real murder right in our town and the clue was hidden in the library all these years!" said Marion, her eyes sparkling. "But wait, you said at the time that you weren't actually sure if the boat ran over a swimmer or if it was a loon. What makes you so sure now?"

"Let's think about it. Josh had little money of his own. Most of his and Tina's income came from her inheritance. He had plenty of motive to go after the gold for himself... and remember the snorkel I found? That's just what he would have used to search the lake bottom."

"True. Oh, and you told me that he left her for another woman. He probably couldn't have done that without extra money. Yes, it's all beginning to make sense," said Marion.

"That's right."

"But if Josh tore out the pages with the directions to the gold, why did he leave the map with the x on it?"

"I think maybe he never read that far. The map was on the next to the last page of the notebook."

The women were both silent, thinking while they munched on their sandwiches.

Then, Marion went on musing. "So, you think Josh took Jim along because the box was too heavy for one person to manage alone? But if that was the case, why did Jim think he could go back later and pull it up by himself?"

"I'm not quite sure about that part but he must have had some kind of plan. Maybe using a block and tackle?" speculated Emma.

"I bet once he thought he could be financially independent, he planned to live like a jet setter with his girlfriend," said Marion.

"Yeah, something like that," agreed Emma.

"So, the x is not far from the end of your dock?"

"That's right. That's part of what got me thinking about all this. Why the snorkel washed up on *our* beach."

"So, when he told Tina he was going for a last swim before he left, he foretold his own doom," said Marion, eyes wide with excitement.

The two animated women continued whispering conspiratorially, their eyes lit in a fever of excitement. They ordered a round of wine to top off the hard work they had put into figuring out what happened.

"There's another thing," said Emma. "If Josh's girlfriend wondered why he never showed up, she couldn't very well call his wife to inquire."

"Yeah," said Marion. "Now, what's next?"

"At this point," replied Emma, "I think I had better tell my husband what we've come up with. While he sometime jokes about my speculations, he can also be sympathetic. No doubt, he'll know what to do."

That evening, Ted had just sagged his weary body into a chair on the deck. Emma brought him a glass of wine and sat down to join him in watching the sun go down.

"I've something I need to share with you," she began.

Ted braced himself. "I'm listening. Go ahead."

And she did, sharing the entire scenario that she and Marion had worked out.

Ted was quiet for a full minute before speaking. "Interesting," he finally said, while gazing across the lake as if looking for the blue boat. "But, what about the body? Wouldn't that have floated to the surface by now?"

14

"I've been thinking about that, too. Haven't you noticed that there's often a boat out after dark with a search light going along the shore? Maybe that's Jim searching for the body," she replied, as she stood up to better survey the golden lake reflecting a setting sun.

"Or maybe it's just the locals out hunting bullfrogs for their favorite dish of frog's legs," Ted mused.

"Hmm," Emma responded.

"And don't you think those pages could have been torn out of the notebook by Lockjaw himself?"

"Yes, I guess it's possible. But, on the other hand, maybe they weren't," she responded.

"And that dot on the map... could've marked good fishing," Ted continued. "That happens to be an excellent spot to catch fish."

"Uh-huh," she replied. "But there's also the snorkel."

"Oh, Emma," responded Ted with a sigh. "Do you know how many people go snorkeling in this lake? It could have come from anyone. And, by the way, how can we make a serious report to the police if we don't have a body and Josh's girlfriend never came looking for him, nor made a missing person's report."

We? Sounds like he's coming around, Emma noted with relief.

Ted continued, "You don't even have a witness to the crime. Only your distant sighting, which you weren't sure enough about to report to the police in the first place."

"But there *is* a witness. Jim!" Emma exclaimed.

"Wait. First you think he's the murderer, then you call him a witness?"

"Well, why not? He's both!" she replied.

"If Jim found that money, I doubt he'd stick around very long. Would you like me to go interview him and ask if he happened to have murdered his boss?"

"Well, obviously not. But you're clever at talking to people. Maybe you could casually stop by when he's outside and ask how things are going and such. Then you could casually ask if he plans to stay on working for Tina. That could be a clue."

"That's a lot of casual. I don't know that I can pull it off, but it seems the only option right now. I'll give it a try the next time I see him."

The following day, Ted came home with shocking news. Jim had been sawing down a tree on Tina's property. When it fell, it killed him. It also killed Ted's plan to have a talk with Jim. Emma and Ted did not discuss the subject any further that night.

The next morning, after Ted had left, Emma poured a second cup of coffee and carried it down to the lake. The mist was beginning to rise, the day warming up. Pulling off her sweater, she sat down on the wooden dock, dangled her legs over the edge and listened to a loon hollering in the distance. Waxwings chirped in the cedars along the shore. The lake, still as a mirror, breathed serenity. Reflecting on the last several weeks, she struggled to make sense of it all. *Should she put in a report? What to do?*

Then she remembered the owner of a lakeside resort telling her about the chaos when one of the guests had gone missing, presumed drowned. A search had been initiated involving helicopters roaring overhead, firetrucks grinding large ruts in the dirt road to the resort, and dozens of volunteers' cars parked askew all over the lawn. People had tramped through the grounds, grinding garden plants underfoot, and tracking the outside inside on their countless trips to the bathroom. Fences were dismantled to allow an ambulance access to the lake. Trucks had arrived with food to feed everyone. Tables had been set up down by the docks, blocking access to the resort's boats. Garbage cans had been brought in; power boats had zoomed every which way. There were drag nets and divers roiling up the lake, while two-way radios had kept up a constant barrage of crackling voices.

Do I really want all that? she wondered. *This peaceful spot forever tainted by such an intrusion? Perhaps the mystery is best left buried in the annals of Lockjaw.*

She stretched her arms into the warm morning air, then laid back on the dock and watched the clouds sail by. A passing breeze whispered through the leaves. In the distance, a dove was cooing. She took a deep breath, exhaled slowly... and basked in the sunlight.

Pea Soup

"His favorite is pea soup with ham. I'll make it every day of the year if it keeps the judge happy," Betty Abel schemed aloud as she dished up yet another meal of rice and beans for her husband, Walt. "You know what Judge Norman did today?" she went on. "Bought 100 ferns for his garden. Said they were extremely rare and imported from a jungle somewhere. It must have cost him a bundle! I saw them… they just looked to me like asparagus gone wild. The man has so much money he doesn't know what to do with it."

"Surely he'll leave it to his sons," replied Walt as he wheeled up to the table for supper.

Betty untied her apron, hung it on the back of her chair, smoothed her dark cotton skirt down over her stout figure, and took a seat opposite her husband.

"I'm not sure. He's not so pleased with them," she said. "Norman may be a judge, but it's Mary's fortune which has let that family live lavishly. It just doesn't seem fair when I work so hard and we have so little. Mary had so much… yet never worked a day in her life. Nor do her wayward sons ever have to worry about going without."

"Now, Betty, don't be jealous."

"And when I think of my teenage nephew… it's just not right," continued Betty. "Judge Norman sentencing him to two years behind bars for selling drugs. He was only trying to buy a present for his parents. Maybe he shouldn't have done it… but he was so young. His heart was in the right place. What does the judge know about that? He's as hard as New Hampshire granite. Seems like he was carved right out of a quarry."

"Maybe he was," agreed Walt. "His family goes way back in this community."

"Here I am, the one who cleans their house, and I nursed Mary through her last years. Her sons did not. Yet, they will get to inherit a bundle and I will get nothing. Nothing."

"Oh Betty, be grateful for all we have: your good health, no medical bills, a nice warm apartment, food on the table. We get by nicely with my disability, my VA benefits, your job. And you'll soon be getting social security."

Maybe you can get by, she thought, *but I'm getting weary of running back and forth between two needy men. I'm looking for a change.*

It was early morning at the Whitney house when the phone rang. "I'm coming, I'm coming," muttered Norman, as he tied his robe tighter and shuffled over to the telephone.

"Hello?"

"Dad, it's me, Nathan. Just called to see how you're doing."

"Not dead yet, if that's what you want to know, but I'm thinking about it."

"Come on, Dad, that's no way to talk. How about Rosaline and I come visit? You going to be around?"

"For you, maybe. Not for that darkie. She'll never be part of this family!"

"Sorry, Dad, she already is and it's time you wake up to how lucky I am that she's my wife. Couldn't be a better soul in the world than my Rosaline." Nathan heard the usual click as his father hung up on a changing world.

19

So much for family, thought Norman. *One son married to a darkie, the other son gay. How lucky can a man be?* He headed for the kitchen. Thanks to Betty setting the timer the night before, the coffee was hot and ready. *At least somebody cares about me. I've had a successful career. You'd think the boys would appreciate that fact. But no, they have to rush off and drag our name through the mud. It's humiliating. Mary never could see the error of their ways... kept trying to defend them. Maybe it's best she's at peace now. She couldn't have kept up a front forever.*

Norman poured his coffee, found a plate of Danish and orange sections wrapped in plastic, and carried it into the dining room. Seating himself at the head of the table, he gazed upon the portrait of his darkly-robed father, who, like Norman, had also been a judge. Ignoring the TV, he reached for last evening's paper. *Can't stand all those biased newscasters pitching their slant on the day's events.*

An hour later, he heard the click of a key in the lock, the door opened and Betty entered, her dark hair plastered down by rain, tan coat dripping onto the polished floor. "Did you find your breakfast alright?" she asked, as she slipped off her coat and hung it to dry.

"Yes, it was fine, but my appetite was spoiled by Nathan. He called and threatened to visit with his wife."

"Now, now. Don't be too harsh on the boy. Give him time. He'll grow up. You can't mix oil and water like you can't mix black and white. That marriage will never last," she said.

"I hope you're right. I fear Nathan takes after Mary too much... both so vulnerable to honeyed words... and I'm sure that woman used a few to snag him." Norman couldn't bear to say her name. He carefully refolded his newspaper, laid it on the table and stood up. He was a tall man, his body strung taught as a wire. "At least I

20

don't have to worry about Jack tainting our bloodline. Guess that's one blessing."

Betty secretly welcomed the harsh words spewing from beneath Norman's carefully trimmed mustache.

Love had slipped out the window of this dark house two years before in 1996, when Mary gave up the long struggle, bowing to the ravages of disease. But Betty wondered if Mary had actually bowed to something else. *After all*, she thought, *the old vulture wasn't exactly the cheeriest bird in the Whitney flock. Norman and Mary had been together so many years. How had she withstood his crankiness, his constant criticism, his constant pecking at her sons? Had it finally worn her down before her time?*

At Nathan's apartment on the outskirts of Boston, a spirit of peace filled the rooms. Nathan's wife Rosaline, an immigrant from Haiti, had brought with her the warmth of island life. She filled Nathan's needs in a way that society, country clubs, fancy schools, and the study of mathematics had never done. He had tried his best: good grades, becoming a professor in the local college and a village volunteer, but still, he had felt empty. Then he met Rosaline. She never asked about family or position. She fell in love with him for who he was. It was mutual. When she did learn about his parents, she tried to visit. She especially liked his mother. But the doors to the family compound did not easily swing open to the likes of her. Nathan, a slight blond-haired man, was delighted with Rosaline, his beautiful woman with a wonderful head of curly black hair and soft features that easily broke into smiles. She was a violinist, had a scholarship to study music, and dreamed one day of joining the symphony.

"Don't be misled by my family's wealth," he had told her. "My father has plans to cut my brother and me out of his will. He's not happy with us."

"Oh, Nathan, that's because of me, isn't it?"

"No, love, it's because of him. He grew up in a very exclusive society. Mother did, too, but she found her way out. He loved her deeply, came close to following her lead… but then she died and he turned back."

"Nathan, I don't care. We have each other. We'll get by. He may have cut us off, but what does he have left? Certainly not joy."

"Misery. Misery coming down from a long line. But mother loved him, and my brother and I do our best to stay loyal for her sake."

Nathan's older brother, Jack, lived with his partner, Russ. They were inseparable. Jack was blond-haired, handsome, and affectionate. He could easily have been mistaken for Nathan's twin, except that he was shorter.

Jack had begun teaching English at a local high school in a small Massachusetts town outside of Boston, but was let go on a trumped-up pretext when they learned that he was gay. After that, he became a technical writer for an appliance manufacturing company. Hardly an inspiring job, but it paid the bills. What he dreamed of doing was writing. Words, he believed, were the stepping-stones to enlightenment. However, words alone would not support them, so, for now, he wrote down his ideas in notebooks. It was Russ who made sure those notebooks were kept in a safe place until the day Jack could put them all together and publish. Russ worked as a chef at the hotel down the street.

Their social life was somewhat limited. Step outside of convention and friends can be hard to find. However, they often visited Nathan and Rosaline. The four enjoyed simple pleasures:

taking long walks, picnicking along the Charles River, visiting museums, and enjoying free outdoor concerts. They each struggled with exclusion, in his or her own way.

Their father was aging fast, his heart not good, his blood pressure high. The family lawyer, Joe Flack, had for some years urged him to write a will, but Norman had resisted. He didn't feel his sons deserved the inheritance Mary had brought to the family, however, there was no one else to leave it to. He certainly didn't want to contribute to all the "do-gooder" charities who grovelled before him begging for money. "If people lived the way they should, they wouldn't need all the handouts," he often muttered, like a sort of mantra. "They won't find me wasting the family fortune on them."

But, on one of his occasional visits to the house, Flack finally persuaded him to get on with it and write the will. "You might remember what Mary wanted," he had ventured to remind Norman.

"And what would you know about my beloved Mary's wishes?"

Picking his words carefully, Flack replied, "I only know what she said when you all visited my office a few years back. 'Don't forget our boys when you make out your will.'" Norman remembered very well. He only wished there had been no witness to those words. Much as he had loved his wife, they had disagreed about the boys' lifestyles. Now that Mary's wish was being openly acknowledged, he felt a certain guilt about not complying.

"Alright. Write it up, let them inherit. At least I won't be around to see the mess they'll make of their fortunes, just as they have their lives." And so, a week later, the will was written, signed, and filed.

Maids know a lot about their employers' private lives. Ears held to closed doors are very helpful in this regard. Betty, no exception to this practice, was well-informed. She knew the will was written and what it said.

Betty had had to fight hard for every penny she earned, but she had not given up on her dreams. Her husband, Walt, had been a construction worker who was crippled long ago when a crane dropped an air conditioner on him. He was a cheery sort and joked, "Didn't help me a bit, my legs are hot and dry all the time."

Betty lived in the hope that their lives could change... that she could stop working so hard, that they could afford an electric wheelchair, move to an apartment with a ramp to the outdoors, and buy a handicap van. Somehow, Walt always managed to stay in a pleasant mood. Fortunately, they had a good TV. He watched a lot, and especially liked movies of all kinds. In the evenings, Betty joined him. Her favorites were murder mysteries.

Mornings, when Betty arrived for work at Norman's home, she would immediately begin picking up: empty whiskey glass by the armchair, magazines on the floor, cigar wrappers and ashes around his desk, pens and scraps of paper scattered about. She was a meticulously neat housekeeper. Trash barrels were set out on the sidewalk every Tuesday night, sidewalks swept clean every Wednesday, laundry done on Thursdays. Nobody could accuse her of slovenly habits.

"Now, don't go throwing everything out," Norman barked at her. "I need those notes I wrote; they belong on my desk. And the cigar bands? I'm collecting those. Be sure you put them with the others in the lacquered box in the den."

"Of course," she would reply. "I'm only throwing out trash."

"You do a good job, Betty, but you get a little carried away with picking up." Yesterday, he was about to change his socks when the phone rang. He took the call in the den. When he returned to his bedroom, Betty had already scooped up his socks and thrown them in the wash. "Lord woman, you are such a neat-nick."

But despite this irritating habit, Judge Norman was appreciative of her good care. Lunch was always ready at exactly 12:15, dinner at 7 p.m. sharp. She knew each piece of silverware, what it was used for, and how to place it on the table. She was also an excellent cook. Meals were served on the proper gold-rimmed porcelain she pretended to admire, wine poured at the perfect temperature. When the phone rang, Betty had the protocol down pat. Picking up the receiver, she would respond to each caller by name so Norman would know who it was and decide if he wanted to talk to them. Looking in his direction, she would watch for him to signal whether or not he wanted the call. If yes, the phone was brought to him; if no, she explained he was out and to please call back another time.

Norman had few visitors. Since his wife was gone, the light had gone out of his life. Velvet curtains covered the windows from outside intrusions. Shielded inside, he resorted to reading: *The Fall of the Roman Empire, The Education of Henry Adams,* biographies of past US presidents, and, occasionally, in need of escape literature, he turned to spy books, especially Robert Ludlum's *Bourne Series.* Sometimes, he wrote letters, though not often. Betty mailed the few envelopes she was given. None were ever addressed to his sons.

Norman's one indulgence was gardening. Not flowers, but a variety of ferns. And he only went out to work in his garden on cloudy days. "Suits my mood better," he explained. He would dig and putter around for an hour or so at a time, lingering over rare species and ripping out others that looked just as good but were deemed "weeds." Once a week, on Wednesdays, he would cut some of his ferns, bring them indoors and give them to Betty. She would arrange them in a vase on the front hall table. She did a nice job fixing them, but was way too eager to throw them out when they showed the first signs of wilt. "Betty, doggone it!" he would bellow. "Why are you always throwing everything away? Those ferns still had life in them!"

It was a sunny afternoon several days later, just the kind Norman disliked, when he opened his mail to find a letter from Nathan: subject line: *What now in the world?* It read as follows:

Dear Dad,

I am writing rather than calling so you'll have time to quietly reflect on our good news. (*Uh-oh,* he thought.) We are delighted to announce that Rosaline is pregnant. (*For God's sake! Delighted?*) The baby is expected six months from now. As you can imagine, our baby may well be coffee-colored. a perfect symbol of the beautiful uniting of black and white. We are thrilled. You may not be. (*That's an understatement if ever there was one,* reflected Norman.) However, with time, I'm sure you'll come to appreciate this joyous occasion which we hope to share with you when your grandchild is born. Congratulations, Granddad. (*Granddad! Never!*) Jack has accepted our request that he be the godfather. May this family finally come together in peace.

Affectionately,
Nathan

Norman sat quite still. *It has come to this, has it? Just what I feared.* It was 4 p.m. when he finally stood up and stormed into the hall. "Betty!" he bellowed. "Bring me a whiskey! I know, I know, the sun hasn't crossed the yardarm yet, but I have!"

A few minutes later, Betty scurried into the room with his drink on a silver tray. "Is everything alright?" she asked softly.

"No, everything is not! *That* woman is pregnant!"

"Oh my," murmured Betty. "That *is* too bad."

"It's more than too bad, it's a disgrace!"

"What are they going to do?"

"Do? Probably celebrate! Nathan's actually happy about it. Where did we go wrong? We gave our sons everything a person could want. Spoiled, they are! Rotten oysters!"

"Yes, and rotten oysters don't produce pearls," Betty commented.

"They certainly don't. You'd think my boys would appreciate good family genes and an excellent education. It's those damned liberal colleges that led them astray!"

"Oh, Judge Norman, you're so right. Too much education does something to folks. They seem to lose their way." Norman wasn't quite sure how to take that. "And to have good health as your sons do… not everyone is so lucky. How I wish I could have mine back."

"I thought you were doing alright."

"I used to be, but now the doctor has diagnosed me with a serious heart condition. I take lots of pills, but they cost so much I can't always afford them. And Walter often has to see the doctor." Betty looked down at the floor, pulled out a handkerchief and wiped her dry eyes.

"That's exactly what I mean. They are very lucky and don't even realize it," said Norman.

"Will there be anything else?" asked Betty.

"No. That's it for now, but make sure to serve me wine at dinner tonight."

Several days passed with no further incidents. Betty powdered her face each morning to cover her healthy color. It went unnoticed until, one day, when the doorbell rang. Betty answered it to see Jack standing there. "Good morning, Jack," she said. "Does the judge expect you?"

"He does not. If he had known I was coming, he would have barred the door. Now Betty, I'll just go to the den and wait for him there."

"Oh, Jack, I'm not supposed to let anybody in without his permission.'

"I'm not anybody. I'm his son, born and raised in this house. I don't need to stand on an invitation." With that, he smiled at Betty, walked past her into the den and settled himself in a leather armchair. Betty followed. "How are you doing Betty? It's good to see you again. You do look pale, though. Are you well?" Jack asked.

"Not so much. It's my heart," she replied, holding both hands to her breasts and letting out a long sigh. "I tire easily nowadays."

"You've been very good to us all these years, Betty. Sorry to see you're not well."

"Thank you, Jack," she responded, giving him a sad smile before leaving the room.

"Could you please close the door on your way out?" Jack asked.

He leaned back into the depths of his childhood, stared around and remembered his mother bringing him here in his youth. He loved the dusty smell, the shelves of books reaching to the ceiling.

There was a special shelf down low that his mother kept stocked with fairy tales and adventure stories. When he was young, he had been allowed to pick any one he wanted. However, his father demanded that books be returned later to exactly the right place. He was scared to disobey. The old man had a temper. Nevertheless, his mother had brought love and sunshine into his days. Now, with her gone and the windows covered, long streams of gloom seemed to ooze from every corner of the room. Worn piles of papers covered his father's desk. *Why does he bother reading all that old stuff?* thought Jack. *He's embedded in the past.* No longer frightened by his father, he waited patiently for a full hour before he heard footsteps approach. The door slammed open and his father entered.

"Betty told me you barged your way in. Who do you think you are arriving unannounced like this?"

"I'm your son, Jack. Remember?"

"A queer is no son of mine."

"Look, I'm sorry God made me this way... take it up with him. But I'm here today to plea for your soon-to-be-born grandchild. Rosaline's parents died long ago. You're the only grandparent the child will ever know. Please find it in your heart to be there for the baby."

"To think of all I've done for you and this is all the thanks I get. A sniveling request to play the soppy grandpa. Out! Out! I want nothing to do with you or your brother."

"Alright, I'm going then. One last thing, though. Betty doesn't look well. Do take care of her. She's been good to you and Mother."

"Don't tell me what to do! For God's sake, leave me in peace and leave now!"

Jack, realizing that further talk would only inflame his father more, stood up and without another word, walked out.

Whenever Norman was in a rage, he turned to playing solitaire. But, before he dealt out the cards, he jumped up and locked the den door. *Best if Betty doesn't see what I'm doing. Might think me frivolous. Might not treat me with the proper respect. The world turns on respect.*

The following morning, Betty arrived at the house right after breakfast. Norman was still fuming.

"Can I make you a second cup of coffee? I think you deserve to relax a little longer after all the troubles you've had."

"Thank you, Betty. At least you understand."

"Oh yes, if they were my children, I'd throw them out of the house as well. They don't deserve your generosity. After all you've done for them, you'd think they would show a little more respect."

"More? They don't show me any at all. If it weren't for you, Betty, I'd be completely abandoned... just wither away to nothing... brings tears to my eyes."

"Oh Judge, I would never let that happen to you. You can count on my loyalty."

"By the way, you're looking quite pale. Are you alright?"

"I'll manage, though it's hard, what with my husband in constant pain sitting all day in an unheated apartment without a TV, and my heart giving me trouble all the time," she replied, as she grabbed at the wrong side of her chest. "But I'm not complaining. Buck up and smile, that's my philosophy."

A week later, angry about his sons and moved by the plight of Betty, Norman had an inspiration. Calling his lawyer, he announced, "I want the will changed. I'm leaving everything to the housekeeper Betty Abel. That's right. I'm finished with Nathan and Jack... cutting them out."

"I'll change it for you, but are you sure? That's a pretty drastic measure."

"Drastic conditions, drastic measures. If you're tossed an apple, toss it back."

"Norman, I think you mean a grenade?"

"You know very well what I mean. Change the will!"

Betty, ear to the door, broke into a big smile. She even did a jig right there in the hall.

A few days later, on a Tuesday afternoon, Flack arrived at the Whitney house. Betty was out shopping so Norman himself answered the door.

"Good morning, Joe," said Norman. "Come on into the den."

His lawyer found a seat across the desk from his client, pulled papers out of his briefcase and laid them before him. "I rewrote the will, as you wanted. Best read it over, make sure it's in order. Then sign it. I'll give you a couple of hours and be back around three to pick it up. That should be time enough to review everything. But, once again, I urge you to think this over carefully. Those boys of yours aren't so bad. Why do this to them?"

"Because they have destroyed this family's fine reputation. They hardly deserve an inheritance!"

Flack was gone by the time Betty returned. "I'll take my lunch in the den today," Norman told her. "I have things to do."

I've waited long enough. I'm not getting any younger. Time to make my move, Betty said to herself. *He's in his den poring over those boring old papers he's always reading. Now. I'll do it now.* An hour later, she brought him a large bowl of his favorite thick pea soup swirling with small bits of ham. "Just set it over by the window," Norman said from his seat behind the desk. He proceeded to read. It didn't take him long to finish. Nor did he linger over his decision but picked up a pen and signed with an angry flourish. Then he stood up, retrieved his soup, and brought it back to the desk where he wolfed it down.

A half-hour passed. Betty returned to find the judge slumped over his desk, face down in the bowl, pea soup slopped everywhere.

"Oh Lord!" Hands shaking, she felt for his pulse. There was none. Dead. Dead as roadkill. And what a mess! *Dear God. I must clean this up quickly so no one gets suspicious.* She used her apron and, lifting his head, wiped great globs of thick mushy stuff off his face. Next, she picked ham fragments out of his mustache. With considerable effort, she managed to push Norman upright and leaned him back in his chair. Rushing into the kitchen, she found a dustpan and brush and returned to sweep the disgusting soup covered 'old' papers off his desk. Then she grabbed a cloth and furniture polish, wiped down the surface until it shined. *Nobody will question this clean room. I'm known to be a good housekeeper.* She was patting Norman's gray hair into place, when she realized his cotton sweater had taken on a pea green patina. *Evidence!* With great effort, she managed to pull off one sleeve, then the other. Into the laundry it went. The shirt underneath was clean. "Dignity," she said out loud. "I left him with his dignity." Before she had time to do more, Flack rang the doorbell.

"Oh, mercy," she muttered as she took one more look around the room and headed for the door.

"Help, help!" she cried when she saw the lawyer. "I just found Judge Norman slumped over his desk!"

Flack dialed 911. An emergency medical team arrived 15 minutes later. It was immediately apparent that the judge was beyond help.

Betty stood to the side, mumbling, "His poor heart. It must have been his heart." She wept loudly into her apron.

Flack, looking at his expired client, said, "Guess the old ticker finally gave out." Then, puzzled, he surveyed the desk, clean as a whistle. His gaze roamed about the room until falling on a wastepaper basket in the far corner. He ambled over to take a closer look. There, in a heap at the bottom, he spotted green soggy papers. Grimacing, he leaned down to take a closer look, then suddenly checked himself, stood up, and walked away.

An hour later, after the body had been removed and everyone had left, Betty stayed on to set the house in order. *No-one will fault me for cleaning up. After all, that's my job,* she reflected. The dishes were washed, the floors cleaned, the furniture dusted, and the trash set out for pick-up in the morning.

A week later, the funeral over, a somber Nathan, Rosaline, Jack, and Russ sat stiffly in straight-backed chairs at the lawyer's office. Betty was there, too, dressed in black, legs crossed, foot bobbing up and down.

Flack addressed the sons. "Let me say again how sorry I am at the loss of the old... I mean to say, at the loss of your father. It's now time to move on to the will. First, to Betty." She leaned forward with the slightest flicker of excitement. "The judge left a month's salary to tide you over until you find another job, as well as the gold-rimmed porcelain you like so much." Like a deflated balloon, her face went slack and her mouth drooped. She sank back into her chair. "Nathan and Jack, the rest has been left to the two of you." The brothers stared at one another in amazement.

After everyone had been duly escorted out of the office, Flack closed the door, settled back in his chair and with the slightest glimmer of a smile murmured, "Fate works in peculiar ways. Sometimes, though, it gets a little help."

Dropping the Ball

He runs for glory, gasping, breath steaming in the frigid air. "I've got it, I've got it," roars through his head... or is it the roaring crowds? The sliding, the sideways glide snaps him to attention. Panic grips the wheel... the snow-covered road... thud... the whir of tires... engine cut... quiet.

He's going nowhere.

Waldo, a hulk of a man, opens the door, steps out, shiny black shoes crunching the snow. "Damn it to hell!" Lodged in a drift. Nobody around. He reaches for his cell... help when he wants it. Not this time. No bars.

Late, he's late. Annoyed. Annoyed at the inconvenience. Angry. Angry the road was not in better shape.

Waldo, a football hero, spiffy in his suit, is careless in his haste.

A back road. Might be, nobody will come along for hours. Could freeze to death.

Out of nowhere, a man appears: blue jeans, torn thin jacket, older, gaunt, and smiling. "Need help?"

"Damn straight! Friggin' road! Stupid plows! Idiot phone!"

"Mebbe we can push her out."

"I'm not dressed to go messing around in the cold!"

"Tell ya what then. You drive, I'll do the pushing."

Tucked back in the warmth, hands on the wheel, foot to the pedal.

Older man outside, shivering, leaning into the push.

Nothing.

Again.

Nothing.

Window down, leaning out, "This is stupid, it's not working at all."

"Tell ya what. My truck's down the road a piece. Rope on board. I'll pull ya out of your trouble."

Battered truck pulls up to the BMW. Waldo snickers.

Older man lying on ice under the car... numb hands struggling to attach a rope. Finished. Out he crawls.

"Ready? Hop in your car there, I'm gonna pull ya."

Waldo, unused to taking orders, scowls... scowls but gets in. Truck revs up, car lurches forward, slides back, lurches forward, slides back.

"Turn ya wheel more, ease up on the gas. One more time, buddy," calls the good Samaritan to the irritable driver. Car creeps forward... four wheels on the road again.

"Thanks, dude. Gotta go now. Late to my meeting." Waldo hightails it down the road, learning nothing from the event, not of speed, patience, or gratitude.

The good Samaritan gets back in his truck, heads for Walmart... pulls into the parking lot, far side... engine off. Neon lights haze down on the rusty pickup, duct-taped fender, cracked window. Opening the tailgate, he slides into his truck bed. Crouching under the low cap, he wriggles into his sleeping bag, turns several times like a dog settling down and curls into a fitful sleep. He dreams of a hot meal, shower and soft bed.

"Hey big boy, what took ya?" says a slim woman decked out in black lace. She sits on a bar stool, knees crossed, swinging one high-heeled sparkly boot back and forth.

"Not my fault! Blasted county… poor roads… dangerous trip… slid into a snowbank," barks Waldo.

"Ah, too bad, tootsie pie. How'd you get out?"

"Some old dude pulled me with his rattle trap of a truck. What a junk heap! Amazed it even worked. Guess God was looking out for me."

"God? Sounds more like the 'old dude' was looking out for you."

"Yeah, well, God provided him. Though I must say, he could have provided a little better. Didn't think his truck up to the job… barely made it out of there."

"You thank the guy?"

"What are you, my mother? Of course I thanked him."

"With what?"

"With a thank you, smart ass."

"That's all? Just thank you? You, the hero rolling in dough? NFL star? All you offered was a word of thanks? Awesome… so thoughtful."

"Hey. Hold on. I barely know you and you're lecturing me already?"

"I'm just saying… is all. Fate's a crap shoot… doesn't touch everyone the same. Some get the ugly version; you got the lucky one."

"It wasn't luck. I worked hard to get where I am. Folks don't know how rough it is… train, train, train, then out on the field. Spectators ripping you to shreds when you don't perform."

"You're paid for it. Handsomely," she says, hiking up her skirt a bit.

"I deserve it," he says, laying his paw on her thigh.

"Hey, Waldo, you're a hero. Fans love you. You've worked hard, but you were born lucky. Got some natural talent in those genes. Wonder how much luck that other guy's ever had?"

"Okay, I got it. Get off the subject. Good looking woman like you should know her place," he says, his hand starting to travel. "I'll get you another drink, then dinner, then…"

Late that night, exhausted from romping, lying beside his date, staring at the ceiling. "By the way, I've been thinking. You might be right. Maybe I should've done something for the guy. The thing is, I don't know who he is. Can't fix it now."

"Why not? With Facebook, Twitter, you think you can't find him?"

"Got no time. Got training to worry about, keeping in shape."

"Ah, but I do have time. If I find him, would you reward him? Poor guy… sounds like he's hard up."

"Sure. I'll do that."

Two days later, Facebook coughs up the man: living out of his truck… downsized from his job… aged out of the market… weary.

"Waldo, I found him. His situation's tough. Can you help him out?" Waldo listens.

"That's terrible. Sure. Free ticket to a game and a tee shirt. He should love it. How do I get it to him?"

"Free ticket? That's it? Wow, your generosity is staggering," she says. "Alright then. He lives out of his truck. It's at Walmart. You can find him there."

"Are you kidding? Slink around the parking lot looking for his old jalopy? I wouldn't be caught dead doing that. I'll hire someone to deliver it," he declares in a classic football hand-off.

Weeks later, the old guy attends the playoffs, having parked his truck on a street 2 miles away (no fee charged) and walked to the stadium, sandwich in his pocket (vendor food too expensive).

Game over, he slides back into his trouble. In a Walmart parking lot, neon lights haze down on the rusty paneled pickup, duct-taped fender, cracked window. Crouching under the low cap, he wriggles into his sleeping bag, turns several times like a dog settling down and curls into a fitful sleep. He dreams of a hot meal, shower and soft bed.

The Wedding Dress

Drapes pulled aside, light cascades into the den, spotlighting weeks of dust. Sarah sits at an antique desk above which hangs a carved wooden cross. She is studying a sealed envelope postmarked 1951. Return address: George Barrett, addressee: Lucy Blau.

"Good heavens!" she exclaims to no one but herself, for she is quite alone in the home of her father-in-law who had recently passed away.

Lucy and I were such good friends back in our school days, but I never knew anything about this! What could they have been writing about? I haven't thought of Lucy for years. I wonder what ever happened to her.

More unopened envelopes lie stacked in a box, most from George to Lucy, one or two from Lucy to George.

Sarah feels a stir of air as temptation leans over and whispers in her ear, "Aren't you curious?"

She sits on a wooden chair, knees spread. Her cotton dress stretched between her legs makes a pocket into which she drops the letters, one after another.

Recognized for her efficiency, Sarah had been asked to sort through Bertha's (recently deceased) papers. Having little else to do, home life holding as much excitement as a rag mop, she had agreed. The tatters of Bertha's years consist of gourmet recipes, letters, two small blue feathers (peacock's?), an invitation to a party at the governor's estate, another from a senator, a lock of hair held together with a faded lavender ribbon, a brown corsage pressed between two sheets of paper, and part of a poem by Emily Dickinson. She reads the lines.

"Hope" is the thing with feathers –
That perches in the soul –
And sings the tune without the words –
And never stops – at all –

What a surprise to find this poem, as out of place as those feathers tucked into the detritus of Bertha's life. To think, maybe this proper wife was not as content as she appeared. How many others, perhaps like her, put on a good face but suffer behind the mask?

Astonished at finding the unopened letters, she picks them up with care as if they were breakable. Clearly these letters had never been delivered. Not without a sense of guilt, she lifts Bertha's aged ivory letter opener and slices open the first envelope to spy on the penned sentiments of two lovers longing for each other.

My Dearest Lucy,

How I miss you, my love. When will you return from your summer in Maine? My impatience grows as I wait to hear from you. How long will it be? When we next meet, let us seal the union with marriage and never leave each other again. I grow anxious as the days pass without word from you. My sweetest flower, could it be that you are ill? Or perhaps my last letter never reached you? Please assure me that all is well so I can rest in the knowledge that we will be reunited soon. Like the bee and flower, we are meant for

41

one another. Please, send a quick reply, that I may know all is well.

Your affectionate and devoted lover,
George

Such an undelivered plea might well bring tears to the reader, but not to Sarah who leans back in the chair, her dark hair slipping from a tightly coiled bun. She sits a minute, her slender weight leaning against the back, as if resting from a long journey. In fact, it feels like that. Marriage has not been kind. Its rough edges show in her prematurely-lined face. Her thoughts drift about the room before settling on a resolution.

I will read a few more letters to be sure I understand. If things are as they appear, maybe I can then right this wrong done years ago. Is it not said that bringing joy to another will bring happiness to the giver? That will certainly be true in this case, reflects Sarah, *and I could use some joy right now.*

She speculates on why the letters were intercepted. Lucy not classy enough? Not wealthy enough? Not Catholic?

Two days later, her dark-suited husband, briefcase in one hand, umbrella in the other, departs for his law office. Sarah has a second cup of tea, then settles herself in a chair at the kitchen table, drags the black phone from its nook in the wall, lifts the receiver, and dials the operator.

"Could you please find the number for Miss Mabel School in Georgia and connect me?" She and Lucy had been students and friends there from 1945 to 1949.

So begins her search. Do they have an address for Lucy Blau? They do, but it is old, dating back to her first job as a secretary after graduating. *That will do. It is a start.*

The next two weeks follow a similar pattern. Every day, as soon as her husband stalks stiffly out the door, Sarah primes herself with a second cup of tea, then grabs the phone and continues her search. It feels like she is circling her quarry, not unlike a spider moving around the outside of a web as it works toward the center. Sarah and Lucy have not been in touch since graduation. The threads connecting them have unraveled but Sarah is not deterred. So much at stake.

As the search progresses, she writes each new phone number on lined paper. Before her husband comes home, this record of activity is carefully stashed inside her bible. *He mustn't find out what I'm doing. Disdaining religion as he does, he will never look there.*

At last, success! A telephone call to the University of Massachusetts and she is connected to the library where Lucy works. She waits while a clerk is sent scurrying to hunt up Sarah's prey. The suspense intolerable, Sarah nervously wiggles her toes in her sensible black shoes and waits.

A scrabbling on the other end of the line and suddenly Lucy is there.

"Sarah! What a surprise! It's been what, fifteen years? How wonderful to hear your voice again… Yes, I'd love to get together. Where are you? How did you find me? Do you live near here?… Oh, that's not so far away. When can we see each other?"

Saturday, a week hence, is decided upon. They will meet at the Village Coffee House in Amherst. Sarah plans to visit, spending the night at the Lord Jeff. Her only obstacle? Her husband's reluctance to let her go. Or perhaps, reluctance is too gracious a word, call it rather refusal. Sarah explains to him that she wants to visit the Emily Dickinson House in Amherst.

Why can't this wife of mine do something more frivolous? She's always so serious, her husband thinks. *Drive all that way to visit a historic house? I wish she wanted to do something more fun. It gets boring at home with her cleaning house all the time and chasing after history like she does.*

While Sarah is thinking, *How to work around his objection?*

"But dear, I just want to visit the Dickinson home because I was impressed with that poem I found while going through Bertha's papers. Imagine being able to write like that, especially the line: 'Hope' is the thing with feathers – ...'"

"Hogwash, Sarah. It's not hope that brings success, it's hard work and brains. How do you think I got where I am today? It wasn't hope that did it! Indeed not."

"Yes, dear, I realize that. But not all of us can be so clever. Surely you won't mind if I take a little overnight trip to Amherst? I will call as soon as I get there and let you know I'm alright. It's only a two-hour drive."

"So, this home I work so hard to provide isn't good enough for you? Why can't you just stick around and be content with all you have? You're rather ungrateful, it seems to me."

Sarah continues to badger him for his consent until, finally relenting, he says, "Here's a thought. If you're really so determined, I have a distant widowed aunt who lives in that town. I might ask if you could stay there. It would be a safe place. Maybe I'll talk to her and see what she says."

Oh no, thinks Sarah, *safe from what? Can I never get away?* She wiggles her toes some more and smooths her skirt down to discreetly cover her knees. *I will be patient and wait him out, but I will find a way,* she promises herself.

A week later her husband announces, "I contacted Aunt Meryl. She lives in Amherst. You can stay with her. She will go with you to the Emily Dickinson home. That way I won't have to worry about your safety."

Sarah expresses gratitude though she is much annoyed. She doesn't want an elderly chaperone treading her heels. *He's always so suspicious, never letting me get away except for my one morning at the kindergarten.* But she realizes her only chance is to accept. She will figure it out when she gets there.

Two days later she drives herself, with an excessive number of instructions from her husband, to the home of his Aunt Meryl. She is welcomed by a buxom, well-rounded woman wearing a red shawl over a bright yellow dress, plump feet overflowing flat shoes, gray hair in two long braids falling to her waist.

"Marvelous! Great balls of fire! You're here! Never thought the old badger would let you out of his sight. Why, look at you," exclaims Aunt Meryl. "So lovely and slender. Wish I could go back to the days of being lithe."

Oh, my goodness, thinks Sarah, *another holdover from ancient days.* But out loud she murmurs, "Aunt Meryl, good to see you. I hope this is not too much of an imposition. I do so want to visit the Dickinson house and staying here gives me a chance to see you as well."

"Imposition? Of course not. Come, I'll show you to your room. While you unpack, I'll put on the pot for tea. Then you can fill me in on everything." *This is going to be awkward,* thinks Sarah.

In the bedroom, she looks around with some dismay. A pile of rumpled clothes occupies the one chair and cushions are stacked on the floor. The bed is made up with a beautiful lavender and green quilt, but one side is starting to unravel. *I can't imagine leaving things in such disarray,* Sarah thinks as she unpacks and tries to make the best of it.

Descending the once grand but now worn staircase, she settles herself in a faded, upholstered chair and looks out the wide glass window at a grassy area filled with unrestrained flowers running wild in all directions. Aunt Meryl comes in with a tray, pours tea in lovely but chipped porcelain cups and begins to talk, "So, tell me about yourself. How are you two? What are you doing with yourself? Why do you want to visit the Dickinson house?"

"Well, we're doing fine. The law business is going well. I am a part-time assistant kindergarten teacher. I long to get my license so I can be a full-time teacher."

"So why not do it?"

"Too busy with our home. I could never do that and keep up my end of the marriage. I do my best... though it never seems to be quite enough."

"For whom, you or him?"

"Oh, for him."

"And is that what he wants?" Aunt Meryl says before looking at the clock and suddenly leaping up from her sagging armchair. "Good heavens. It's late! I'm supposed to meet my friends in 15 minutes. We're going out for dinner together and to see a show. Would you like to come? There will just be three of us: Mary, she's a musician from Jamaica; Julia, my British actress friend; and myself. Join us. It will be fun!"

"Thank you so much, but I fear I'd be intruding. I'm perfectly content to stay here. I have my bible to read. I won't be bored." *What an odd assortment of people she goes to meet*, thinks Sarah, *I'm not sure I'd fit in.*

"Your bible? I have much better things to read than that." Aunt Meryl circles the sun-filled room and collects journals from off the floor, the windowsills, and the chairs. She casually tosses *Hollywood Star Galaxy, Adventures in the Jungle, Sailing Around the World, Alpine Expeditions,* and *Tennis* in a pile by Sarah. "Take a look through those for some good reading."

Aunt Meryl crosses the room, opens a closet door and pulls out a red felt hat. She snugs it down on her head, takes a quick glance in the mirror and starts for the door. "If you prefer to stay here, I'll not stand in your way. After all, I believe in respecting a person's wishes. Tomorrow the Dickinson House opens at 10. Shall I wake you at 8? Will that be time enough to get ready? I'd love to go with you. I'm so looking forward to seeing the place again. Even though it's close by, I've not been there in several years. It should be such fun. Have you read a lot of her work? She's one of my favorite poets. We can talk more about her tomorrow."

Oh dear. Come with me? And how can I talk with her about Dickinson? I don't know anything about her poetry. And how ever will I get away to meet with Lucy at 4 p.m.?

The next morning finds both women ready at 10 a.m. Breakfast conversation about Dickinson has gone better than expected. In Aunt Meryl's absence the evening before, Sarah had perused the extensive book collection and found a large volume of Dickinson poetry. She had spent a couple of hours reading and was pleasantly surprised at how the words, penned years ago, still had appeal. Unfortunately for her, she never did get to reading Aunt Meryl's magazines.

Having perused her poetry, the tour of the Dickinson house is more moving than Sarah had anticipated. But now, she is challenged by how to escape to meet Lucy. The problem is unexpectedly solved. Aunt Meryl announces that she has a meeting at four. Would Sarah be all right by herself for the afternoon? They could meet again later at home for a delicious meal of wild mushrooms that she has prepared.

"I'll be fine," replies Sarah, greatly relieved but a little worried about the supper. "I'll go for a walk around this lovely village." And so, 4 p.m. finds her waiting at a table in the shadows of the rather spacious interior of the Tudor-style Village Coffee House. Lucy, dressed in a flowered dress and large straw hat, comes bouncing in the door, a smile spread across her elfin face, her eyes squinting with delight.

"What a treat! I can't believe we're together again after so many years! What have you been doing with yourself? Are you married? Have children? Tell me all," Lucy gushes.

"Oh yes, I'm married. No children. I help with kindergarten one morning a week. The children are cute, but in great need of discipline, so it's a challenging job."

"Discipline? Those adorable little ones? I like to see them run free to do as they please. Children are so creative and fun on their own. But I'm sure you don't overdo it. You have always been so correct in everything. Anyway, tell me about your marriage. Are you happy? What is your husband like?"

"I'll tell you everything, but first let's order tea."

Lucy is ready for a glass of wine but decides to go with the tea in a gesture of solidarity.

Once they have been served, Sarah begins. "My husband is a very fine lawyer, greatly respected by the community. He provides well. I want for nothing. But now tell me about yourself. Are you married?"

"No, I'm not. Came close years ago but was left high and dry. I've never found anyone since who matched the man. Funny thing... he was also studying to be a lawyer. But I have a full life. I'm not about to let that ruin the good times. I work at the library...

sometimes meet interesting people there. But the days can be long. I try to go out after work as often as possible to make up for my job. I love to go dancing, hear music, attend parties. My evenings are quite happy."

"Who was the man who left you high and dry? What a cruel thing to do."

"There must have been a good reason, though I can scarcely guess what it was. He was the most brilliant man I've ever met. Handsome, too. He seemed so in love with me at the time. His name was George Barrett."

Sarah breaks into a grin, something rarely seen on her somber face. "I have exciting news for you, Lucy." And with that, she tells the story of how she found the letters addressed to Lucy but never delivered.

Now Lucy's face expresses something *she* rarely shows: shock! After a moment's silence, the questions come flying.

"Who asked you to clear out that house? What is your connection? Tell me more."

"I will tell you everything, but all in good time. For now, I'm happy to hear you're not yet married and that I'm the deliverer of good news. You don't know what great joy it brings me. Look, I brought the letters along. I must admit, I peeked at a couple." With that, Sarah, pushes away their cups, wipes down the table with her napkin, then lifts the leather case lying at her feet. Out of it she pulls two folded letters and a pile of sealed envelopes. She lays them out in front of her friend.

Lucy leans forward, eyes wide with surprise, picks up a letter and eagerly begins to read. Happiness lights up her almond shaped eyes. Sarah leans back, watching in silence, as her beautiful companion breathes in the sentiments dancing across the page. Lucy sets the first letter down and eagerly reaches for the next.

Suddenly Aunt Meryl appears at the table.

Sarah looks up in dismay, "Why Aunt Meryl! What are you doing here?"

"I should ask the same thing. I'm here because our Top Act Theater committee just finished its meeting in the back room. So, tell me, who is your lovely friend?"

Sarah is at a loss for words, but Lucy stands up, puts out her hand and says, "Hello. I'm Lucy Blau, an old school mate of Sarah's. So nice to meet you. Sarah has brought old letters from a past flame of mine. This is the first time I've ever seen them. They were never delivered. She hasn't told me yet how she came by them."

Aunt Meryl looks down, sees the return name on one of the envelopes: George Barrett. She manages to stifle a gasp of surprise, then lifts an eyebrow while turning to Sarah. Sarah looks stricken but stays silent.

I'll say nothing now, thinks Aunt Meryl, *but Sarah has clearly been keeping secrets.*

"Why, how lovely! This must be quite a surprise for you! Did you know him for long?" she manages to ask.

"Oh, yes. In fact, I had thought we would be married, but he suddenly broke off the romance. I never understood why. I'm hoping to find a clue in these letters that Sarah so thoughtfully delivered to me."

"Well, isn't that amazing! It must be upsetting for you to read them now, so I'll leave you two to your affairs. Come home when you're ready, Sarah. I'll have the mushrooms prepared." Aunt Meryl silently leaves, footsteps muffled by her bright red sneakers.

Sarah gags, then quickly recovers. She despises mushrooms. *Like eating mold, and plucked from God knows where.*

Picking up the conversation again, she continues, "My dear Lucy, I just thought by reading these letters you'd realize you were not betrayed in love. That George really did mean to see you again. I hope this makes you feel better."

"In a way it does, but in a way I'm so sad. My mother once told me that if I married a successful man and treated him like the emperor he thinks he is, I would not have to work and could have a fun life. I thought George was that man."

At 6:30, Sarah returns, head drooping. She says nothing. Aunt Meryl jumps up from her chair, runs over and embraces Sarah. "Why, aren't you just the old fox!" she says with a grin on her face, "Who is Lucy? Where did those letters come from? Why didn't you tell me what you were up to? What's going on? Sit down and tell all."

After Aunt Meryl releases her, Sarah remains standing, her head still down. "I guess I should have said something, but I was afraid you'd disapprove because he's your nephew." Following a pause, she goes on, "It's like this. After his father died, George asked me to go over to the house and sort through his late mother's papers. Of course, he never expected there to be anything worth seeing or he would not have asked."

So much for what George Barrett thinks of women, observes Aunt Meryl.

"That's where I found those undelivered letters. Years ago, his mother must have opposed his relationship with Lucy and intercepted their letters."

"Interesting. Not surprised. Bertha was a tough one. Not the most joyful flower in the garden. Lousy thing to do. Probably, she guessed from her name that Lucy was Jewish. But how do you know Lucy? And why show her the letters now?"

"Lucy and I went to school together years ago. I just thought she'd feel better if she knew she had not been stood up, that George's letters had never reached her."

Aunt Meryl sits quietly, listening. Sarah finally walks over to the nearest chair and sits down on the edge of the seat, hands folded in her lap. At first, Aunt Meryl says nothing, then she gets up, crosses the room and, to Sarah's surprise, leans over and gives her another big hug.

"Let's hear it, girl. Your story rings hollow. You can tell me everything. It will go no further. You look as miserable as a hangdog in a rainstorm."

"Oh, Aunt Meryl. I didn't want you to know. You're right. I'm so unhappy married to George. He wants me to stay home and wait on him all the time. He hates me going out to work. I've tried to be a dutiful wife, keep a clean, upright home, but he seems to resent everything I do, complains that our lives are just boring. In fact, I can't seem to do anything right. I'm so depressed." Sarah begins to cry.

Aunt Meryl hugs Sarah a little tighter, passes her a handkerchief, then walks toward the kitchen, calling back over her shoulder, "I think, my dear, before we go on, you could use a little restorative." She returns a few minutes later with a glass full of rum. "Here child, drink up. This will settle you down"

"Oh, I couldn't."

"Ah, but you can and you must. You need to quiet down... stop with all the tears. Nothing to cry about. In fact, I'm very proud of you. I always wondered how you could put up with George. He's so arrogant!"

Sarah obediently takes a swallow, then quickly takes another before leaning back in her chair.

"Oh, my goodness! Is that what you think of him?" And the tears flow even harder.

"I guess I'd cry, too, if I lived with that man. He's handsome and smart, I can see why you fell for him. He's also very stuffy. But, enough. Cat's out of the bag now. So, tell me the rest. Why were you really showing those letters to Lucy?"

Sarah dabs at her eyes with the tattered handkerchief, dries her tears, sniffles a few times, then takes a few more sips of rum. "Aunt Meryl! He's your nephew. How can you say such things about him?"

"He is and I love him, but I'm not a blind bat. So, tell me, what's going on?"

"The truth is, our marriage is not a happy one. George is often angry with me. After trying hard to improve things, I asked for a divorce, but he refused. Said Catholics couldn't divorce and it would look bad for his family and colleagues if we parted ways. When I found these papers, I thought maybe I could reunite those two lovers and then he'd let me go."

"Why, Sarah, what a marvelous scheme! I didn't think you had it in you. A great plan!" And Aunt Meryl begins to chuckle. Sarah downs another gulp of rum. The glimmer of a smile breaks out on her face and soon she is chuckling, too. The chuckles grow louder and next thing the two are laughing uproariously.

When they finally calm down, Sarah reflects that maybe Aunt Meryl isn't so bad after all. However, she remains conflicted. "But I'm being so deceitful... absolutely wicked. I'll have a lot to confess in church next week. I shouldn't really feel so good about all this."

"Why not, my dear? You're showing more spunk than a rabbit in love!"

"Yes, but completely immoral. How can I ever forgive myself for such deceit?"

"Oh pollywogs! Who gives a damn? Misery is misery."

"And if I get the divorce, I'm not sure I can support myself."

"Of course you can. You are a smart, capable woman. Besides, haven't you ever heard of alimony? You won't be left high and dry. Especially if *he* asks for the divorce."

"I never thought of that. Maybe then I could finish my schooling and work full-time as a teacher."

"So, how do you plan to get around his scruples about divorce?"

"Well, when I read those letters, I realized how very in love Lucy and George were. George will have no problem breaking church law if it suits *his* purposes. Besides, with his parents gone, he won't feel as restricted."

"And how will you handle all this?"

"I don't know. Maybe there's a more useful life out there for me... teaching and doing charity work. It might atone for the sin of divorce."

"You could indeed do those things. Not as atonement, but because you want to. Step one in your liberation! Let me tell you, my dear, there's a lot of fine living awaiting those who break social and religious codes."

"But that's so blasphemous."

"Perhaps it is, but who wrote those codes and who are they to decide what's best for everyone else?"

This aunt is a little crazy. Should I be listening to her at all? "I don't know. I never thought of it quite that way. Oh dear, it's all so confusing. Here I'm dying to get a divorce, and yet it's against church law. Now, I'm not sure I should really go through with this plan."

Aunt Meryl sighs deeply. "Listen, my dear, if you want to get Lucy and George together, I have an idea how we can do it. But you need to make up your mind. No waffling around. Decide now or forget the whole thing. Remember, 'hope' is the thing with feathers. Let's fly with this!"

She's right. Maybe that's why that line touched me. No more game playing. Lucy will be pleased, I will be pleased, Aunt Meryl is clearly ready to help, and George? Who knows? I think it will work as long as he thinks it's his own idea. "You're right. If you can help me, I guess I'm ready for the next step."

And with that, they hatch a plot. *How devious I've become. I'm not sure this eccentric aunt is such a healthy influence, though, I must say, she's certainly charming.*

"Super! Now that we've got it all figured out, let's dig into the mushroom stroganoff."

Aunt Meryl clears books and papers off one end of the dining table, then serves supper. Out of politeness, Sarah smiles and takes a bite. Halfway through eating, it is no longer politeness, but enjoyment that causes her to finish every last morsel. "Aunt Meryl, how did you learn about wild mushrooms? I never would have dreamed of trying something so odd."

"Odd? Odd things bring zest to life. They are the topping on dessert, the spice in our days. Never pass up the odd if you want to live life to its fullest. An old witch let me in on that secret."

A couple of weeks later, George arrives at Aunt Meryl's home alone. "I do apologize for Sarah's absence. I did think she could at least pull herself together and try to make the trip, but she said she was feeling too ill. However, I'm most delighted to see you again.

Thank you once more for hosting Sarah on her visit to Amherst, and thank you for inviting us to visit."

"The pleasure is mine. Sarah's so lovely. What a lucky man you are to be married to such a knock-out wife.

That's hardly the way I would describe her, thought George.

"By the way," continues Aunt Meryl, "thinking that Sarah would be here, I ran into an old classmate of hers and had already invited her to join us before I heard that Sarah wasn't coming. I couldn't very well un-invite her, so she will be joining us for supper."

"I'm sure that will be fine. Who is she and how did you meet her?"

"Her name is Lucy. She works at the U. Mass. library here. I was over there searching for books on the history of the magpie when I ran into her. We started talking and discovered we had a mutual friend in Sarah."

Good grief, I wonder if it's Lucy Blau? She stood me up years ago... don't know that I want to run into her again, thought George.

"And what's Lucy's last name?"

Oh Lord... don't want him to know, he'll think it's a setup and flee, thought Aunt Meryl.

"Ah, come to think of it, I never asked."

"Never mind then. I'm sure it will be a pleasant evening.

At 6 p.m., the doorbell rings. Aunt Meryl answers, chuckling to herself. *Can't wait to see how this goes down. What fun it's going to be tonight!* "Hi Lucy, good to see you again. Welcome. Unfortunately, at the last minute, Sarah fell ill and couldn't make it. I'm truly sorry. However, her husband is here. Come on in."

"I'm so sorry, but thank you for having me anyway, Mrs. Wiser."

"Not Mrs. Wiser. Just call me Aunt Meryl. Everyone else does, related or not."

With that, she leads Lucy into the living room where George, in a dark suit, is waiting. He stands up immediately and gives Lucy a long stare, his handsome face betraying nothing. Lucy, dressed in a low-cut blouse and high-cut skirt, looks over at George. Her eyebrows shoot up, her jaw drops in surprise. She stands stock still, not thinking to lift a hand to the trembling one that George extends.

"Oh, my goodness! Do you know each other?" Aunt Meryl's question is met by silence.

Finally, George finds his voice. "Yes, we do," he replies with a catch in his voice. "At least we did. Knew each other back some years ago."

"Why, how lovely! I had no idea," says the sly Aunt Meryl. "I'll just go pour wine and bring out some appetizers. You two will have to entertain each other until I get back."

After she leaves the room, George, still standing, continues to stare at Lucy and says, "Hmm, you certainly act surprised to see me. Surely you knew I was married to Sarah?"

"George, I had no idea who she married! I'm as shocked as you."

"So, you didn't know? After you broke off our affair years back, I married her. A wife is good for business. So, who did you finally marry?"

"I never married anyone! In fact, I never broke off the affair. I wrote but I never heard anything from you. In fact, I wrote you a couple of times, but not hearing back, I gave up. Oh George, you broke my heart. I never could understand it."

"Now, that's strange. I wrote you several letters, but also not hearing back, gave up. Sarah was not my first choice, but she *is* a good Catholic. The family approved. I'm afraid your being Jewish was unacceptable to them. Let's sit down, Lucy. We can talk about this later when we have more time alone. This is beyond belief. Are you free tomorrow? I could meet you wherever you suggest."

"It just happens I'm off tomorrow. How about The Village Coffee House on Main?"

"Fine. Ten o'clock?"

"Yes. I'll be seated in the back."

Aunt Meryl returns carrying a tray of glasses, a bottle of white wine, crackers, and guacamole. "Help yourselves and then let's all get to know each other better," the host, face bathed in innocence, proposes.

The evening, despite all, proves to be relaxed. Lucy fills them in on her passion for Irish dancing and the Celtic performance troupe she has joined. She chatters away, full of laughter. George begins to relax. He even joins in the talk as Aunt Meryl chuckles along, keeps filling their glasses, and eventually produces a supper of broiled fish and arugula salad.

George can't take his eyes off Lucy, who babbles about one thing and another, occasionally showing a little leg and a hint of cleavage.

"Working in a library earns me a living, but can be monotonous. Music, on the other hand, brings such joy to life," she remarks.

Dinner finished, George begins to unwind, his tie loosened, his jacket removed. Under the influence of Lucy and the wine, he leans back in his chair, uncrosses his legs, stretches them out before him, and watches his old flame, a smile on his usually somber, mustached face. He is clearly enthralled.

If I had married her, she would have brought joy to our home...
would have cheered me up after a long day at the office. She's so
happy and light-hearted!

Thanks to Aunt Meryl's stories about African villages, Arabian camel rides, and the time she was shipwrecked on the Great Barrier Reef, the evening passes less awkwardly than might have been expected. Lucy loves the stories. "What a wonderful life you've had! I envy you all those adventures!"

At 11 o'clock, Lucy jumps up and declares it's past time she left. When George learns that she lives on the next block and had walked over, he offers to escort her home.

No sooner are they out of the house than Aunt Meryl rushes to the phone. "Hello, my sweet. It's working! A wonderful evening here and George is walking Lucy home as we speak! I think we're on our way to solving your problem."

"Aunt Meryl. I can't thank you enough for your understanding. I do hope we're doing the right thing. Tell me we are."

Aunt Meryl, rolling her eyes, replies, "Damned right, we are! Now, be happy and get some sleep. Fate's mighty river is on a roll."

Two months later, George, instead of striding off to work, remains at the breakfast table. "Sarah, there's something we need to discuss. I think it's time for a divorce. You've never appreciated the good life I've given you. I've decided to set you free."

Sarah, still in dressing gown, hair pulled back in a bun, sits quietly for a moment, her solemn face even more serious than usual. *Finally! How benevolent the cad behaves, as if he's doing this for me. Yes, my plan is clearly working. I did it! I've pulled this off! If I can do this, then I can do anything. I'll be okay...*

make a better life for myself. "All right, then. I believe it would be best for us both. Let's proceed."

George maintains a stony face, but thoughts churn in his head. *I'll be free at last to marry Lucy. She's so breezy and cheerful. She'll bring fun into my life. I think with her I'll be able to leave worries at the office. Sarah brings me down, Lucy raises me up. And with my parents gone, I can break with the church and marry who I want, offending no one."*

No sooner is the divorce finalized and the two parted ways than Sarah hears the gossip: Lucy and George are engaged. *Perfect!* As soon as she hears, she calls Aunt Meryl. "It's happening. They're engaged!"

"Dandy candy!" replies Aunt Meryl. "You did it! How very clever." *There's more to Sarah than I first suspected. She'll do just fine.*

"I amazed myself. However, nothing is final until its final. I want to make sure Lucy goes through with this, so I'm not quite done. Here's the idea." She lays out the final step of her plan. "What do you think?" Aunt Meryl's response is a long hardy laugh. *This girl is A-okay.*

A few days later, Sarah calls Lucy. They had not spoken since meeting in Amherst. "Hi Lucy, this is Sarah. I just wanted to call and congratulate you on your engagement."

A momentary silence follows, then, "Sarah! You set this whole thing up, didn't you? I'm shocked. At first, I had no idea that George, such a successful man, was your very own husband! Why did you do it?"

"Because you two are made for each other. George and I were never a good match. The desire for a divorce was mutual. You aren't mad at me, are you?"

Lucy listened, then burst into giggles. "Of course not! How could I be? I'm so happy, like a schoolgirl in love. Oh, Sarah!"

Now, Sarah lets out a little giggle as the two old friends discover the humor of it all. "When are you getting married?"

"In three months.'

"Wonderful! Listen, Lucy, this may sound a little odd, but I would love to go with you to pick out your wedding dress."

"Are you serious? That *is* odd! I'd love it."

In just six months: the wedding. Lucy, a lively bride dressed in a rather low-cut white satin dress, dances away the evening with her new husband. At times, she kicks her heels high, in most unladylike moves, to reveal legs sheathed in bright pink stockings. Sometimes, when she leans over, a tiny rose tattoo is spotted just above her left breast. He, in formal tuxedo and unused to such frivolity is, nevertheless, grinning like a mischievous kid.

Aunt Meryl is there, decked out in a cream and chartreuse Moroccan qaftan borrowed from the Top Act Theater. "A special outfit for a special wedding!" she declars as sedate folks gaze on in amazement.

And Sarah? She is now far away, free to pursue a teaching degree. She looks forward to a future without the encumbrance of a husband and plans to devote her time to charity work, atoning for the one great deceit she ever committed in her virtuous, duty-bound life.

Lucy, on the other hand, is delighted to quit her job and serve George's needs while sparking up the marriage with adventure and merriment. And George? He is ecstatic with his lively, carefree partner. The bee has finally found his flower.

THE TICKET

by

Bonnie Harlan-Stankus

and

Caperton Tissot

Maddie makes a lazy swipe at the pile of dishes left from last evening, then pauses to gaze out the window. The view? ... a brick wall on the other side of an air shaft. The kitchen, little more than a closet, is off an equally tiny living room. That does not bother the starry-eyed Maddie. She thinks with joy about her life and her love, Rich. Standing barefoot in a long, flowered skirt, beads cascading over her blouse, she would seem more at home in a meadow of long grass and daisies than in this hot, steamy apartment.

Suddenly, the door bursts open and a young sweaty man dressed in torn jeans and a ragged shirt bounces into the room.

"Maddie my love,
You are a perfect darling.
In my dreams,
You're always starring.
It is with you, my dearest,
I intend on unifying."

"Oh Rich! My impoverished poet! My one and only. How magnificent!" Maddie replies, falling into his widespread arms. After a minute, Maddie pulls back. "When can we marry? I feel like a cactus waiting for rain... not able to bloom until we're truly united."

"Soon, but your ma called, said she'd have no problem with our marrying as long as we first get pre-marriage counseling. It's a nutty idea but to keep her happy, I invited this dude named Reverend Hooke to come over and talk to us today. After that, it's a go. We can tie the knot at the town hall."

"She *said* that? I thought she was against our marrying at all... considered you too poor for me, even though I've explained you would always be Rich, no matter what!" The couple wrap their arms around each other again, stagger over to a sagging sofa and fall into its clutches.

"Right, so what if my father cut me off for not joining his Wall Street scoundrels. One day soon, he'll see. The world will know me as a great and talented poet." Pulling away from Maddie, he suddenly stands up and walks over to the TV, which has been running at low volume. "Hey, Dr Phil is on. What's he talkin' about?" Maddie stands up and looks over at the screen.

"He was giving advice to newlyweds, but now he's breaking for the lottery numbers."

Rich turns slightly and shielding his action from Maddie's eyes, reaches into his pocket and pulls out a ticket. Holding it closely, he glances down and follows the numbers as they are read out. But not closely enough. Maddie doesn't miss what he's doing.

"You bought a lottery ticket? I can't believe it! Why in the world? I thought you didn't believe in throwing your money away. Besides, you always said you wanted to earn your own way in life, not take handouts!" she bursts out.

Suddenly Rich leans forward, ignoring her completely. His eyes grow big. He checks his ticket again, then leaps into the air. "Maddie! I won, I won! Oh my God! I just won two million dollars! Oh my God! Oh my God! I can't believe it. Maddie! Maddie! Now, I'm doubly rich! And it's all for us! I can't believe this! Look, just look at that!" he says, turning and waving it before her eyes.

But Maddie, a stricken look on her pale face, backs away without saying a word.

"Fantastic isn't it? A dream come true! Hot dog! Hot Cat! If I owned one, I'd eat my hat!" he continues, ignoring her reaction.

Maddie is less than enthused. "Wait a minute, my love. Let's think on this. Will that ticket really bring joy? Not! It will only corrupt, as money does. Why in the world did you buy it? I thought you were a struggling, idealistic poet, yet before my very eyes you're transforming into a freakin' capitalist! The lure of wealth… it's like a magic wand waving before you. You're changing into a materialistic toad! That is not who I wanted to marry!" Maddie begins to walk away into the kitchen, then stares again out the dusty window at the brick wall. Rich skips in behind her and throws his arms around Maddie.

"Hey! What's the matter? We should be celebrating!"

"Sorry, Rich, but that ticket? It reeks of gambling, injustice, privilege. Better out of my sight. It might taint my aura. No, it isn't good. I didn't think you'd grovel before money like this. What happened to our ideals? To see the underside… live in poverty… starve a bit … suffer evictions, shiver in ragged clothes… shunned by the elite. So wonderful! Now, give all that up? You've deserted our crusade."

"No, I haven't. I just think life is a dance, we should go with the flow, be open to chance. My love, you always talk of change, now when it comes, you won't rearrange. The road ahead is paved in gold and yet you're there acting so strange."

"Maybe for you, but it's not gold I want. Nor am I so sure I want you, either. Maybe better not go through with the wedding quite yet." After a pause, Maddie turns to him, "Wait, I have an idea how to solve this. Give me the ticket." He nervously hands it over. Like a sprite, Maddie flies out of the kitchen into the living room and tosses the ticket out the open window. The wind catches and hurls it away. Rich, running up behind her, grabs at her arms, but too late.

"My God! You didn't! Oh my God! You did! How could you do that to me! My big chance, gone with the wind."

"Frankly, my dear, I don't give a damn."

"Oh why, why, why... good life, good-bye! What a bummer. Sigh."

"Good life good-bye? Nonsense. Oh, my money-corrupted poet, not really. With that threat gone, I'm ready to marry you again."

Backing away, Rich says, "Yah, but me? I'm not so sure I want to marry *you* anymore. You're not the flexible girl I thought you were... too afraid of change. I've got to think about this. Huh, roses are red, violets blue, I've got to admit though, you know how to screw."

"You mean, after all my sacrifices for you, you're backing out on me?" she replied.

"Wait, you were going to back out on me first. What's the diff?" he asks.

"The diff is, I didn't *want* to back out… just wanted to be true to my ideals. I still love you. But you suddenly act like you don't love me anymore."

"Maddie, Maddie. I really do, but you're too stuck in your ways, not open to new adventures, whatever they may be. One day, I'll be a rich and famous poet. Life will change, it surely will, like it or not, like rum in a still."

"Like rum? Life isn't like rum… even if it does rhyme."

"Oh yes, it is. Too much rum, the sadder you become. Except for me. The more I drink, the better I think. I plan to imbibe fully before we all sink."

Fortunately, a knock at the door interrupts the unstoppable poet. Rich opens it to his neighbor, a long-haired man in canvas overalls. "Hey Luke, how the hell are you? Long time, no see," says Rich as he high-fives his friend.

"I'm great, old buddy. Listen. This may be my lucky day," Luke says. "I just parked my truck out front, opened the door, looked down and found this lottery ticket lying on the street. There must be a reason it was lying there waiting for me. Who knows? Maybe it's a winner! Thought I'd drop in, say hello and share the moment with you guys. Wonder what it was doing there?"

"A lottery ticket?" says Rich as he strokes his chin and contemplates his friend.

Maddie, who has been standing quietly in the corner, slightly annoyed at being interrupted, pulls herself together to say, "Hi Luke. I'll tell you what it was doing there. It's a winner, alright. But if you turn it in, you might as well turn yourself in at the same time, turn yourself into a capitalist pig! Greed and fraud will fill your withered soul. We were just discussing that when it went out the window."

"It's a winning ticket? Wow! But I don't want it for myself. No, I want it for others. This is a dream come true. I'll use every penny to help those in need. Awesome! Now I can donate to the Soup Kitchen, the Children's Education Fund, and the Goat Farmers of America. This is fantastic!"

Maddie and Rich stand stock still, staring at one another. Then Maddie whispers in an aside to Rich "Why didn't *we* think of that? We could claim it and donate it all ourselves. This will never do!" Suddenly she turns back to Luke. "That ticket is actually ours. It blew out the window. We were just on our way outside to find it. If you'll please hand it over, we'll take care of it."

Luke tucks the ticket deep in his pocket, then stands there looking at the floor, quietly thinking. Finally, he lifts his head and says, "Excuse me, my friends, but I think you just explained why you didn't want it. As they say, finders, keepers."

Maddie and Rich glance at each other. As disputes often are, this one was forgotten in the face of a much greater crisis. Rich thinks he sees a way to retrieve the ticket. He can persuade Maddie later that it's okay to spend it on themselves, at least some of it. She wants it back to give away to charities. The couple exchange looks. Then, like practiced warriors, all at once they pounce on Luke, trying to wrestle the ticket from his pocket. While so engaged, the sound of a motorcycle comes through the open window, growing louder and louder until it stops right outside the building. A few minutes later, knocks at the door go unanswered as the three one-time friends continue to struggle for possession of the ticket.

The door opens and a man enters dressed in a black leather jacket, white collar turned backwards. Around his neck is a gold chain. Hanging from it is a cross emblazoned with the words:

Reverend on a Harley. "I believe you were expecting me? I am Reverend Hooke. Dear Lord. What the hell is going on? I command you, with the power vested in me by God Almighty, break it up!" With that, he pulls a gun from his holster. This gets the attention of Rich, Maddie, and Luke, who slowly back away from each other, eyes wide, hands in the air.

Rich, his mouth open in astonishment, struggles to say something. "You–you, a re-re-reverend, carry a gun?"

"I do indeed. Calms things down, helps with dispute resolution. Like now. By the way, remember the words of the Lord, 'Speak softly and carry a big stick'."

"Wrong guy," counters Maddie quietly, "that was Roosevelt."

"Whatever. It's close enough," Hooke responds.

Maddie, Rich and Luke stand stiffly apart until the good reverend lowers his gun.

"Now, let's hear it. What's this about?"

The three relax a bit. All start to speak at once. Reverend Hooke raises his hand. "Wait! For God's sake! I only have two ears and one of 'em's deaf, so please, one person at a time, here on my left side," he says, turning his paunchy face to the right.

Luke beats out the others. "So, I found this ticket on the sidewalk, told these dudes and they tried to steal it from me! Some friends they are and… "

Rich interrupts, "It's not quite that way. It was our ticket… blew out the window… we were going out to look for it when Luke here came by and picked it up. Now, he won't give it back."

Luke walks back and forth listening, his hands clenched. Suddenly, he stops, pounds his fist into the palm of his hand. "That's a lie, Reverend. In fact, these two had argued over the ticket before I even came along. I'm thinking that Maddie here might have thrown it out the window."

Reverend Hooke reaches behind him and pulls up a stool, lowers his bulgy buttocks onto it and speaks. "First, let's all sit down."

Rich grabs a straight-backed chair, offers it to Maddie, then finds one for himself. Sitting next to her, he lays his arm across the back of her chair. At first, she leans forward, but with a sigh, changes her mind and sinks backward as Rich's arm slips down around her shoulders.

Luke, unwilling to take orders from a stranger, remains standing.

"Now, I was asked to come by and offer a little pre-wedding counseling. I think this is as good a time to start as any," says the reverend.

"Then I'm outta here. Never catch me getting hooked up to some broad, especially now that I see what happens. Besides, your cross says you're a reverend on a Harley. Way I see it, when you're not on your Harley, you're not a Reverend."

Reverend Hooke, gun still in hand, casually raises and waves it at Luke. "Not so fast my good friend. I work with bikers and truckers, on *or off* wheels. I think you need to hear this, too. What I have to say applies to everyone, getting hitched or not, so stay where you are. Now, first of all, hand that ticket over to me. I will hold on to it while we work this out. After that, I have a few things to say." Luke looks at the others, raises an eyebrow. Rich shrugs his shoulders.

"He's a Reverend. We can probably trust him," says Maddie. Somewhat reluctantly, Luke walks across the room and slams the ticket into Reverend Hooke's hand. He pockets it.

Standing up, the reverend says, "Now, as you have just witnessed, money and gambling make for bad juju. Let me think on this a moment. Let's see. What to do?" Putting his hand to his chin, he turns his back on the three, walks a short distance away and appears to be thinking. However, he is not. What he is doing is sliding his handkerchief out of his pocket as if to cover a sneeze. In the process, he conceals the ticket inside the handkerchief and returns it to his pocket. He then puts his other hand to his mouth, starts chewing and follows that with a swig from a flask hanging from his belt. Turning back to the threesome, he proclaims, "Praise Jesus! Problem solved. In order to bring peace, one must destroy the source of despair. I have done that. I ate the ticket. It will no longer cause bad blood between neighbors and couples. You'll continue as before in friendship, love, and poverty. Order is restored. Always remember, destroy the root of evil and all will be well. Now, go about your ways and peace be with you."

Maddie, Rich, and Luke sit bolt upright in shock. They stare at the reverend in disbelief until Rich leaps up, crying out, "You ate our ticket? No, don't tell me! You carry a gun and eat tickets? I'll be damned!"

"Oh my God! You didn't! Oh no! What kind of a reverend are you?" asks Maddie.

"Ah, my good friends, I'm the kind who solves problems. And now I suggest you all go out and have a drink, or three or four. It will help you understand the wisdom of my action. Celebrate your renewed friendship. Now, if I may, I would like to linger here a moment and pray for you all."

"Celebrate? Celebrate?" moans Luke. "It's hardly an occasion for that!"

"Oh, but it is, "responds Reverend Hooke, "No longer will that ticket come between you. Love conquers all."

Maddie sits back in her chair, thinking. After all, this is pretty much what she believes as well. A moment later, she stands up, sidles up to Rich and says, "Okay, he's right and he's real. Only a reverend could have solved our problem. Now we can all be friends again. Evil banished. We should celebrate, just as he says. Reverend Hooke, you may stay to pray for us. Just don't let the cat out when you leave."

The three of them slowly gather their coats, look once more at the Reverend, then get ready to depart.

"Maybe you have a point. I had forgotten how money can ruin lives. Here's to love and gratitude," says Rich. "Maddie, I do love you. Luke, can we be friends again?"

Luke grunts out something that sounds like, "I'll take my truck. Where you going for drinks?"

"We'll meet you down at *The Thistle and Heather* to toast the reverend who pulled us together." Maddie, Rich, and Luke head for the door. The reverend rolls his eyes.

No sooner are they gone than Reverend Hooke reaches in his pocket, pulls out the ticket, and holds it up in admiration.

"Suckers! They actually believed I would eat this? No way! This is my ticket to the good life. I've waited so long. Pathetic, those losers going for God talk. Good luck to them! There is only one God. Money! And I will have it at last." He tucks the ticket back in his pocket, pats it, grins, and continues talking to himself. Or so he thought. "So many things I can finally own: horses, sports cars, casinos, a mega yacht, and women! Life is good if you know how to play it."

He does a little jig around the floor, then suddenly clutches his chest, lets out a groan and collapses. The last thing he hears as his eyes roll up in the back of his head is a deep voice thundering: "The Lord giveth... *and*... the Lord taketh away. Especially from scoundrels!"

Rose Hall

1935

Clara lifted a silver spoon, pinkie held to the side, and like a baby bird waiting to be fed, opened her mouth, closed her eyes and let the tiny bite of an oh-so-sweet biscuit slide into her delicate mouth. Pleasantly surprised, she smiled across the table at Millie May, saying, "Cook got it just right this morning, don't you think?" Millie May not responding, Clara went on, "If she were more attentive to her work, we would be blessed with a breakfast like this every day. Such an imposition to put up with the likes of Tilly, sloppy servant that she is. I've often wished to let her go, but she was a favorite of Papa's and he would never have approved."

She gazed at Millie May, appreciating her lovely complexion, rosy cheeks, clear blue eyes and the golden locks flowing over the shoulders of her lacy dressing gown. Sitting in a beam of sunshine, was ever a being so lovely? Not a wrinkle in her skin, not a hint of age. Clara finished eating, walked around behind Millie May's chair and, leaning over her shoulder, wrapped her arms around her waist. Then, with a ferocity of expression, she suddenly lifted up her companion and flung her across the room where the victim of this abuse slid down the wall and lay in a heap in the corner. As Clara stared down at Millie May, her face grew red and twisted. She suddenly burst into a flood of angry tears.

1945

"Good morning ladies and gentlemen. I am Clara Beaufort, Mistress of Rose Hall." In a full-length frilly, yellow dress and holding a parasol over her head, the elegant Southern matron beams a welcome to her guests. The sun, breaking through clouds, spotlights the large handsome white brick mansion behind her: black shutters frame three stories of windows. Steps lead up from a circular drive to large double doors crowned by a half-moon window. The imposing estate springs out of wall-clinging greenery which overflows with roses.

"Welcome to my home. Please join me inside. Though it *is* July, I hope you all will partake of some mulled cider. My home is decorated for Christmas. You see, Christmas-time is when the house looks best, so I've decided to keep it this way year-round."

1905

"I want to see your face, just once?" asked 5-year-old Clara as she reached to lift her mother's veil. Mary Lee grabbed the tiny hand and pulled it away.

"Oh no, child. I've been scarred with smallpox. It's not a face to see." And for the rest of her mother's life, Clara never saw her face. The veil hung between them like a dark curtain. As the days went by, Clara became ever more distant from her mother, but increasingly close to her father, William Beaufort. He, a wealthy engineer, owner of a 200-acre estate, loved not only his house and lands, but especially Clara. He would take this favorite child on carriage rides around his property, pointing out the beautifully manicured gardens, the split-rail bound fields where he liked to hunt turkeys, and the well-stocked ponds maintained for fishing.

Clara was a shy child savoring a silvered life. When young, she liked to play with a Victorian dollhouse set up in the nursery. Some of the dolls were imported from Europe, some her father found on business trips and brought back to her. She would place them around an exquisitely carved small table on which sat a tiny porcelain tea set. Velvet curtains locked out the intrusive sun. Deep carpets softened every step.

Alas, she played there alone. Her sister, Emma Joy, three years older, preferred to be outside where she could climb trees, chase butterflies and splash in the mud. Rejecting the nursery heirlooms, this tomboy sister remained indoors only on the stormiest of days.

Tilly, who served as both cook and maid, was assigned to stay outside with Emma Joy, keeping an eye on the whimsical child. While a host of employees cared for the estate, only Tilly and her husband were trusted enough to work in close proximity to the family. Thus, they often did double duty. Tilly, a tanned stick of a woman with a head of dull, copper curly hair, looked a bit like a pole topped by an orange flag. Surely a strong breeze would have blown her clean away. Perhaps for this reason, she preferred staying indoors out of the wind and sun where calm and order prevailed. But duty was duty, so she remained in the garden until her charge was ready to go inside.

When the sisters were older, their mother introduced them to the art of needlepoint. Clara took to it right away, loving how tiny stitches and many-colored threads could be transformed into beautiful pictures of flowers and birds. Emma Joy did not take to it at all. Her stitches were sloppy and angry. She preferred real flowers and birds.

A governess was brought in to teach the girls how to read, speak French, and play the piano. The older sister resisted sitting still or learning. Not so Clara. She was the perfect obedient pupil.

And so, the girls' teen years passed until Emma Joy turned a boisterous nineteen. In December, she met a Westerner at a Christmas ball held by nearby neighbors. After a quick courtship, she shockingly eloped with this rancher, a man considered beneath her social station. Emma Joy knew that. Perhaps that is why she did it. She moved west where the wild winds blew, tumbleweeds tumbled, jagged mountains thrust high into blue skies and folks played guitars, stomped their feet, and didn't give a damn where you came from. The West changed her, and she changed her name... from Emma Joy to just Joy. Visits back to Rose Hall were rare. But when she did come some years later, she entered the shadowy, high-ceilinged house like a gust of fresh air, playful, full of zest, and trailing two unruly sun-browned kids. It was a trial for the refined, Southern family.

Many evenings during those visits, unable to cope with the turmoil, Clara would feign a headache and retire early. But, later, unable to sleep, she would creep out in her nightdress to crouch like a lost waif at the head of the grand staircase, listening to family laughter rising in the warm night air. She felt so alone. *When have I ever been as free and happy as my sister? Why does she have all the fun?* Then she would admonish herself for thinking such irreverent thoughts. Returning to her bedside, many the night she knelt and prayed, "Dear Lord forgive my wayward thoughts. I am happy with all I have and grateful for my distinguished family, especially for my papa."

Clara was sixteen when her sister moved out. One lonely year followed another, the days spent embroidering hankies and napkins and pillow covers. When not occupied with such duties, she read her bible, planned meals, made shopping lists, and on beautiful days had the chauffeur, Tilly's husband Noah, drive her around the countryside. The only time she appeared in public was to go to church with her father and mother.

Every morning, the newspaper was laid by her father's place at the breakfast table. He would read it from beginning to end, then pass it on to his daughter. She devoured every picture and read every word. When she did not understand a term or reference, she asked her father. He would pull his chair up next to her, one hand resting on her shoulders, the other stroking her leg. As gently as possible, he would try to answer questions about such things as gambling, prostitutes, and corrupt politicians. There were often accompanying photos of those unseemly characters and Clara would study them with a sense of horror. *The world is such a terrible place*, she reflected, *Rose Hall is so peaceful. I never want to leave here.* She was frightened of all the wickedness she read about. Except for the newspaper, she was carefully cushioned against things hard and ugly outside the gates of Rose Hall.

Clara was not yet twenty when her mother took sick and died. Nobody discussed what she died of; that was considered improper. When Clara knelt at their mother's death bed, she was finally able to lift the veil that had concealed her all these years. To her shock she discovered a face that was not scarred, but very beautiful. She leapt back in horror as she realized that her mother was the famous gorgeous Madam Mary she had seen pictured in a photo in the newspaper. "Oh Mummy, you lied to me!" she shrieked. "I am the daughter of a prostitute! How can I go on? Who else knows? I am ruined!"

Clara never told her father that she had learned her mother's true identity, nor did she ask her father anything about it. She was afraid of what he might say. She so adored him. She wanted nothing to come between them.

After his wife died, William, anxious to remove the temptation of his daughter, and with an eye to marrying her off, continued entertaining. Handsome men in black and white formal dress, and women in a rainbow of colored gowns attended these occasions. They dined on quails' eggs, roast pheasant, and an abundance of Southern delicacies served by Tilly. Noah did duty as the butler, refilling wine glasses and providing cigars in the smoking room. This was followed by dancing to a string quartet in the high-domed ballroom. Hoping to find a suitor, her father introduced Clara to his guests, expecting her to curtsy, smile, make light conversation and dance when asked. None of this came easily. Though beautiful in her frilly evening gown, she was sure she was the laughingstock of Virginia. How could she think anything else after learning the identify of her mother? *I wonder who else knows about my background?* she asked herself. Still, she held out hope that someone would ask to marry her. Visitors found there was something ethereal about Clara. She seemed to float rather than walk. Her slanted eyes, soft mouth and tiny nose appeared slightly out of focus, as if she were in a cloud.

One day, it happened. Reginald Kenworthy, an engineer from England, came to consult with William. He was invited to join the dinner party taking place that evening. After that, he returned again and again. Eventually, unaware of the family history, he asked William if he might propose to Clara. The answer was an enthusiastic 'yes'. Reginald was delighted and William relieved, glad to see his daughter attach herself to someone outside the family. Things did not go as planned.

The evening finally came when Reginald, dropping to one knee, asked for Clara's hand. "Oh Reginald, what a surprise! But I know so little about you... where you come from, your family, your role in society. We should talk about that first."

"No, I think I'd rather not. Love me for who I am. You'll not regret it."

Clara was silent while thinking. *This handsome Englishman would make quite an impression on Virginian society, regardless of his background.* Who would ever know if he wasn't up to their standards? *In fact, her father was aging and needed a male successor. Reginald would do. But what would it be like to have another man in the house? How would her father deal with it?* So much to ponder. *Perhaps, however, I should accept while I have the chance.*

"Oh, yes! I've loved you from the first moment we met. I would be charmed to be your wife. It will bring such joy to Rose Hall to have you as part of the family. I accept. I do, I do."

"Nothing could make me happier." He leaned over, his tall frame towering above, and kissed her upturned face. She gazed upon this handsome man, silently thanking God for such an unexpected blessing.

"After the wedding, we'll leave at once for your new home in England. You'll love it there and fit in easily," announced Reginald.

"Leave Rose Hall? But I couldn't do that. What would happen to Papa if I'm not here for him, and who would look after our estate when he's gone? It's not as if this is just any home. No, this is Rose Hall, finest house in all Virginia. It takes a raft of workers to care for this estate. I must remain here to run the place and maintain its splendor. You can work for Papa. He's constantly busy with engineering projects and needs assistance. I know he'll be thrilled to have someone in the family to work with."

"I greatly appreciate your sentiment, beloved, but I need you to come with me. I do not plan to remain in America beyond this trip. I've business in England to attend to. Your family has been most kind, including me in the lovely evenings at Rose Hall, but it's time to return. I wish to bring you, my darling, to my home. You can always come back for visits."

Clara pulled out of his arms, stepped back, looked lovingly at Reginald as tears sprung into her eyes. "The very thought of leaving is too much. It will never do," she declared. "My home, my people, my world is here. I wouldn't dream of moving away. Papa likes you a lot. He'd be delighted to have you work for him."

Reginald Kenworthy had other ideas and soon departed, never to visit again. That was the one and only offer she ever received.

After that, she was not seen at church for many months. There were rumors. She became more and more reclusive after Reginald departed, no longer going downstairs to meet the guests that her father bravely continued to invite for dinners and dances.

The invitations that used to arrive at Rose Hall eventually dried up. As the years passed, William entertained less and less. He spent much of his time glued to the desk in his bedroom, designing bridges, his specialty. Occasionally he made trips to consult on building projects. Tilly served suppers, no longer in the dining room, unless there was company, but in her employer's bedroom where Clara joined him for the evening meal. Those were long evenings, after which Papa's daughter would reappear, somewhat disheveled, her clothes askew, her hair slipped out of its bun and hanging loose around her shoulders. Tilly, fearing the worse, was tempted to remonstrate but dreading potential rages of her mercurial mistress, refrained from saying anything. Clara, on the other hand, often berated Tilly about the quality of meals, her style of dusting and her sometimes slightly wrinkled uniform. Nevertheless, out of loyalty to the family, Tilly stayed on.

Clara was 30 years old when her father was killed in a riding accident while out on a fox hunt. Neighbors from near and far arrived for the funeral at Rose Hall. Clara, with the help of the undertaker, made the arrangements. Her sister arrived for the day of the funeral but had to immediately return home. Tilly and Noah did all the work: setting up chairs in the ballroom for the guests, arranging a place for the minister to deliver the eulogy, and providing food and drink for everyone afterwards.

Clara appeared wearing a veil. "How spooky," the guests muttered behind cupped hands, "just like her mother." She spoke little except to murmur a thank you when condolences were extended.

There was just enough inheritance to keep Rose Hall running. Tilly and Noah stayed on to look after Clara. Some workers had to be let go. Clara went out rarely after that, except to attend church, now always wearing a black veil. Nights she slept in her father's bedroom.

One evening, while going through papers in his desk, she found an old yellowed envelope addressed to her father. It had been carefully pressed between tobacco leaves, a common means of preserving documents. Curious, she opened it to discover a letter dated 1920 from her one and only suitor. What a shock!

Upon reading it, she learned that he was a nobleman of high position with an estate of hundreds of acres. "Please do not share this with your daughter," she read, "I want her to marry me for who I am, not for my position."

Clara dropped the letter in her lap. She sat there staring out the window, agonizing. *Did I make a mistake? Why did Papa never tell me this? If I had known, I might have followed him to England instead of staying here. I think maybe Papa loved me too much.*

Most days found Clara in the nursery where she whiled away the best days of her thirties in an old rocking chair. The nursery, unchanged since she and her sister had been children, still featured the same toys, same drapes on the windows, same carpet on the floor. There was but one addition: a cross-stitched sampler hung on the wall proclaiming: "I slept and dreamed that life was beauty, I woke and found that life is duty." There she would embroider, read the bible and play the piano. Her governess had taught her music many years earlier. The only songs she had learned were nursery rhymes, and she now played these over and over. On a warm summer day, the notes would float out the window and the occasional driver, making a delivery to the house, would wonder if a child was concealed inside somewhere.

One day, on the rare occasion when Clara sat outside under the shade of a great spreading oak, a little puppy appeared, running up to her. "Are you lost, little one?" asked Clara. "It's not fun to be lost. You must be lonely. That's no fun, either." She swooped the puppy into her arms, settling him in her lap.

A few minutes later, she heard a child's voice calling "Goldie! Here Goldie. Where are you?" A young blonde girl with braids, rosy cheeks, and wearing a blue-checked gingham dress came running into the yard. She suddenly stopped and stared in alarm when she saw her puppy in Clara's lap. Clara stared back in surprise. *Is this her? How lovely she's become! She did not turn out badly after all. She has Papa's eyes. Oh, my heart!*

"If you can't take better care of your puppy, you don't deserve to get him back," she snapped, as a plan tumbled into her head.

"Oh please, Miss Clara, he just ran away, I do take good care of him. And he's mine!" But Clara had other ideas, thinking to herself, *If I keep this puppy, she will come back to visit often. How wonderful she is. Oh, my child!*

Noah happened to be working in the garden nearby. He overheard the exchange. Taking matters in hand, despite the danger of repercussions, he emerged from the flowerbed where he had been weeding.

"Good morning, Ida Pearl," he said. "I saw your puppy jump out of your arms and run into the yard here. How fortunate, Miss Clara, that you were able to catch him."

"She should learn to know a good thing when she has it," declared Clara.

Noah gave Clara a long stare and said, "I'm sure she has learned that now. By the way, you are very lucky, Ida Pearl, that Miss Clara caught your dog because she is a generous woman and would never *really* think of not returning him." With that, Clara grimaced and reluctantly tossed the puppy to the ground. The puppy wagged his tail, then made a beeline for Ida Pearl.

"Thank you, Miss Clara," she said. "I do love him so." The child disappeared through a hole in the boxwood hedge. Clara was left in a pool of solitude and remorse. Then another idea came to her. Christmas was coming. In the spirit of days gone by, and to see the child again, it would not seem unusual if she were to invite neighborhood children to a party. She would casually include Ida Pearl.

December arrived and she sent Tilly around to the neighbors with invitations for their children to visit Rose Hall for a holiday gathering. The families accepted, sending their reluctant but obedient children to attend. Clara was considered a strange, boring spinster. However, urged on by their mothers, the children arrived, dressed up for the occasion. Clara toured them through the nursery, admonishing them not to touch the, by now, antique toys. She gave special attention to Ida Pearl, inviting her to stop by next spring and bring her puppy anytime she saw Clara outside in the garden. Then Tilly served hot chocolate and cinnamon toast, after which each child was given an orange and chocolate bar. Unaware that such things were hardly special anymore, Clara made a great ceremony of handing out the gifts. The children thanked her politely, but on leaving, all but Ida Pearl, who was too kind to join in, heaved the gifts into the neglected yard of Rose Hall.

When spring came, Clara was found sitting outside more often than in former days. Her color began to improve, her appetite picked up. Eventually, to her delight, Ida Pearl and her now-grown dog showed up one day. They stood nervously at some distance. To Ida Pearl's surprise, Clara announced she had two cookies in her pocket. Like an animal trainer, she enticed the child and dog to come near by offering each a treat. After giving them the cookies and while leaning over to pat the dog, she began telling a fairy tale to Ida Pearl. During the next several months, the little girl returned often. Gradually a bond grew between the lonely spinster and the shy wide-eyed child.

The inheritance left to maintain the estate eventually proved to be insufficient for proper upkeep. Rose Hall's great front door began to warp. Paint peeled off the bricks in strips, like bark from a dead tree. Moss sprouted from the roof, and vines obscured the windows, as if the garden itself was absorbing the house.

After several years, Joy, alerted by the family solicitor, arrived from out West to assess the situation. She first went directly to the kitchen.

"Tilly!" she exclaimed, opening her arms to embrace her, "I've missed you all these years. You haven't changed a bit. Are you and Noah alright? I know you do your best to take care of my sister. I appreciate that, thank you so much."

Tilly was slightly taken aback by Joy's informality, but couldn't hold out long against her exuberance.

"I don't like what's happening to your sister," she said. "She just doesn't seem right."

Joy went upstairs and found Clara sitting in the nursery. After a warm embrace and a bit of small talk, Joy got right down to business. "Sis, there's clearly not enough money to maintain the estate. We need to sell some of the land."

"Break it up?" shrieked Clara. "The estate our father loved and cared for all these years! Never, never!" she cried, stamping her dainty foot. "What do you care, you with your uncouth cowboy living in the Wild West? You have no loyalty to family tradition… never had!" And tears of rage began to flow.

Joy stared at her sister for a long moment, then without a word, left the room, descending to the kitchen.

"Tilly, we do indeed have a problem. She isn't right in her head, is she? Does my sister ever see other people?"

"On occasion," replied Tilly. "She goes to church on Sundays, and for the past few years, has developed a close friendship with little Ida Pearl who lives next door. They have been meeting each other in the garden. But now, Ida Pearl is growing up and losing interest and visits only rarely. Clara sees the reverend who visits here occasionally, but no one else. Her behavior *has* become a bit odd, if you'll forgive me for saying so."

Joy gave Tilly a long stare before asking, "Is there something I'm not understanding here?"

Tilly lowered her eyes, murmuring, "I can say no more."

Joy stayed but a couple of days, finding the condition of the old homestead, as well as that of her sister, soul stifling. *Sometimes,* she decided, *there are no answers.* Tilly and Noah, ever faithful to the family, promised to stay on and cope as best they could. Joy returned to the West, where tradition hindered no one.

The years dragged on at Rose Hall. Eventually, even the roses stopped blooming, despite Noah's best efforts. Clara no longer attended church and was seen only by the visiting reverend. He reported she was frail and slowly withering away.

A wracking cough was heard throughout the house, a macabre echo of the guttural calls of ominous crows gathered in nearby trees. Noah and Tilly could not remember just when Clara first started coughing, but they noticed it was slowly growing worse. Tilly suggested to Clara that the doctor come check on her.

"No, no, no," screamed Clara. "I won't have a man pawing over my body. I'm perfectly fine! It's not your place to suggest such a thing to me!" Tilly talked to the reverend on his next visit to the house, but even he was unable to persuade this member of his flock to seek help.

As Clara began to wither, Tilly, taking on more and more of the decision making, seemed to bloom. Her once gaunt figure filled out, her wrinkles faded, her curly hair took on a brighter hue. She even appeared taller. Noah noticed, wondered, and was pleased. He himself, however, aged rapidly, his lanky frame becoming bent, his gray hair thinning, his eyes sinking deeper in his skull.

"I don't know what's happening to Clara," declared Tilly to Noah one morning. "Today, when I went to the nursery to pick up her breakfast dishes, I found her favorite doll, Millie May, thrown into a corner. Clara was in her bedroom and would not answer when I knocked. After picking up her breakfast tray and leaving the nursery, I paused outside the door and heard her sobbing.

"She's becoming stranger and stranger," commented Noah, "and Rose Hall is becoming stranger as well. It's no longer the estate it once was. I can't keep up with all the work this place requires, and the cost of repairs is beyond the budget. So sad to remember what a beautiful home it used to be, how much the town admired and respected Mr. Beaufort. I wish we could bring those days back."

"But I still love this place," said Tilly. "The high-ceilinged rooms, the carved woodwork, the elegant furniture, the paintings. If I was mistress, I'd be ashamed to let it fall into such disrepair. I would share its beauty with everyone. This is a place to treasure."

When Clara was 40 years old, Tilly went into the nursery one morning with the breakfast tray, only to find her mistress in her white nightdress collapsed on the floor like a wilted lily. From her mouth issued a puddle of blood. An ambulance was called and Clara was taken to the hospital, but it was too late for help. She died before sunset that same day. Tuberculosis had taken its toll.

Her funeral, arranged by the reverend and the family lawyer, was attended by Tilly, Noah, and Joy. Ida Pearl was spotted in a back pew, silently weeping. Nobody else was there. Long ago, a trust had been set up by William Beaufort to care for Tilly and Noah in their retirement. Joy inherited as well, but to village folk's bewilderment, Ida Pearl was also included in the will and bequeathed a small life stipend. Joy offered to let Tilly pick something from the house for a keepsake. She knew immediately what she wanted: one of Clara's floor-length ruffled dresses.

The house, fully-furnished, was put up for sale, but in its dilapidated state, there were no takers. It didn't help that stories about the estate were whispered throughout the region: how Mr. Beaufort was said to have married the infamous "Madam Mary" who had mysteriously disappeared off the streets years ago, how Clara had gone mad, and how the ghost of a child wandered the halls late at night.

Noah and Tilly moved from their quarters on the estate to a leased cottage in the village. He devoted his time to working in a small garden; she volunteered at the church.

After sitting abandoned for two years, the house was auctioned off for unpaid taxes. The local and well-funded historical association was delighted to pick it up. With Noah's intimate knowledge of the estate, he was asked to help plan the restoration. Eventually, workers were hired to start bringing Rose Hall back to its original glory.

Noah came home one evening, after spending time at the historical association, and said to Tilly, "They're planning to open the house for visitors next year. They'll need a volunteer to lead the tours."

"Oh, Noah, I would love to do that! To be back at Rose Hall… a wish come true. I wonder if I should apply."

"Of course you should. Who knows the place better than you?"

And so, Tilly was hired, becoming the new "Mistress of Rose Hall." Dressed as Clara, she guided tourists through the elegant estate. She had become the grand Southern lady she had always believed was her due.

Beauty and the Frog

His passion? Poison dart frogs. Leopold Wheeler, a 30-year-old herpetologist, living in the jungles of South America, had been studying them for the last ten years. A stocky man with a long beard and sideburns, he had recently returned to the States to collaborate with his 40-year-old brother Alphonse, a professor and medical researcher.

Back only two days, he set out on a mission far more challenging to him than any vine-filled, snake-crawling jungle. Now, in an unfamiliar place, he was afraid heads would roll, and they did. One hit the floor with a sickening hollow thud, bounced twice and lay still. Leopold stared down in despair. This wasn't supposed to happen. He looked around for witnesses. He had forgotten about the cameras. Suddenly, someone came walking toward him, a small badge discernible on his dark green shirt. Security guard.

"You're in trouble," he said.

"Yes," answered Leopold.

"I thought this was going to happen," said the guard. "They stack those icebergs way too high. It's not your fault." The guard got on his phone, calling someone to come clean up the floor and re-stack the lettuce. Then he leaned over, picked one up and handed it to Leopold. "This what you were trying to reach?" asked the guard. By this time, other shoppers were gathering around and, for lack of anything more exciting, gawked at Leopold. He, in heavy duty sandals, khaki shorts, bulging muscular calves and wild unkempt hair, looked down at the floor, avoiding the stares of others. He was deeply embarrassed at causing such a ruckus.

He finished shopping, checked out quickly, never looking up until he was outdoors again. After throwing the bags in the trunk, he slid in behind the wheel of his brother's Ford, sat back and breathed a sigh of relief. No longer used to American grocery stores, he had nevertheless offered to shop for his brother's wife, Coco, in appreciation for letting him stay with them. Now, leaning against the headrest, he ran his fingers through his hair and gazed out at the sunny sky. *Same sun, different world,* he thought. *Too many people here, too many products, too much noise. How do folks do this every day? It crowds my brain; I can't think straight. Maybe those folks don't worry about that... or anything else, for that matter. Like frogs, rain forests, and medical research. Like extinction.* After a moment, Leopold sat up, turned the key and drove out of the parking lot headed for his brother's house. *Even the traffic is overwhelming. Can't wait to get back to the jungle.*

Alphonse had insisted Leopold stay with him while he was in the States. "You won't have to worry about cooking and commuting. You can devote all your time to our research project. Besides, Coco wouldn't hear of your staying anywhere else," he had said. Now, as Leopold drove towards his older brother's home, he wondered about all the houses he passed along the way, surrounded by miles of bleak grass. *Such a contrast to the lively jungle. Amazing, how the lawn industry has managed to make sterile, lifeless ground a status symbol. They've surely made millions selling mowers and weed poison. Why don't people question this?*

When he spotted a meadow with a colorful profusion of daisies, black-eyed Susans and chicory, he smiled. This was Coco's doing: an island of wildflowers in defiance of neighborhood custom. He pulled up to the house which sat in the midst of this meadow, unloaded and put away the groceries, then walked into the living room where Coco was stretched out on the couch. Despite a headache, she immediately sat up and gave her brother-in-law a big smile. She was a buxom woman with a round face and a braid of golden hair wrapped around her head. To Leopold, she seemed like Mother Earth herself. He imagined lovely green vines twining through her hair and a scarlet macaw sitting on her shoulder. She seemed, to him, woefully out of place in such a suburban setting.

"And how did the shopping go?" she asked.

"Okay, I guess. I put the groceries away as best I could." Though he found Coco less intimidating than most women, he was, nevertheless, shy in her presence, especially when his brother was not home. "I'll be in my room for a while," he continued, "I still have some unpacking to do." Coco thought that unlikely as he had already had a couple of days to get settled in. She wisely did not question him.

That evening, Alphonse, Coco, and Leopold sat around a wooden kitchen table. Bunches of dried herbs hung from ceiling rafters. Stainless steel appliances were polished until they gleamed. After Coco scooped stew into handmade clay bowls, they commenced eating in silence. Once finished, Alphonse leaned his chair back and asked his brother if he was rested up from travel and ready to join him at the lab. Leopold said he was ready but did find all the noise of urban life quite exhausting.

"Come on," responded Alphonse, a tall thin man sporting close cropped dark hair and wire- rimmed glasses, "it's not like the jungle's any quieter. The times I've been down there, nights were filled with a steady cacophony of hoots, shrieks, and roars. It's not exactly silent in your part of the world either." Leopold put down his spoon, wiped his mouth on his sleeve, and took a moment to think about that. As a scientist, he believed in keeping an open mind to argument... if it was built on fact.

"I guess you're right, but for me, jungle sounds stir the soul, touch something primal in our beings; urban sounds drown all that out. I mean, didn't you feel a kind of call of the wild when you heard the night voices in the jungle?"

"Interesting way to look at it," responded Alphonse, as he reached up to straighten his bow tie. "You make a good point. Those sounds did stir something up... but mostly fright."

"Huh. Well, that makes us even. Only, it's urban life that frightens me."

Coco pushed back her chair, stood up and began to leisurely clear the table. "You all want some coffee?" she asked.

"Now, that's what stirs my primal need," responded her husband. "Yes. You too?" he asked looking at his brother. And there the discussion ended.

Later that night, Coco pulled on her flannel nightshirt, undid her braid and climbed in bed to snuggle up to Alphonse. "I worry about your brother," she whispered so as not to be heard in the next room. "He's a kind man, but so awkward around other people, even me. I can imagine how the jungle suits him better," she said.

"But he's around people there, too, you know, living in a small remote village as he does. The natives greatly admire him. I saw it firsthand when I visited. The respect is mutual."

"Good. That makes me feel better. But why do you think he has such a hard time when he's back in this country?"

Alphonse rolled over to look at his wife and murmured, "Maybe it's the rigid code of behavior expected here in Philadelphia. Jungle dwellers don't know what to expect from a solitary white man. They probably assume that whatever he does is the white man's normal. As long as he does no harm, they take him as he is."

"That makes sense. We could learn something from that," she said. "Let's not talk anymore, I'm in need of something else, like you." With that, she threw one leg over him and, wrapped in each other's arms, they left the talking behind for other diversions.

The next morning, Leopold accompanied Alphonse to the Medical Laboratory at the University. The brothers were the beneficiaries of a substantial inheritance as their grandfather had made a killing building railroads. Or rather, as the brothers often remarked, a lot of workers were killed in the process of building their grandfather's fortune. To counter this sorry circumstance, they opted to gift the University with a medical research lab where Alphonse now worked.

The previous year, Alphonse had visited his younger brother in a remote jungle of Brazil and brought back several poison dart frogs to be used in research. This time, Leopold brought more frogs with him. Getting them through customs was a challenge. He had the appropriate paperwork, but still had to do some explaining. "It says the contents of this box are highly poisonous. Paperwork or not, that constitutes weapons of mass destruction," insisted the customs official.

"Yes sir, I understand your concern," replied Leopold, "but if you look through that little glass window, you'll see that these are just frogs."

The official looked, scratched his head and announced, "There's something fishy, or maybe I should say, froggy about all this. You'll have to step over here and wait while we investigate further." Getting back into a paranoid country was a lot harder than Leopold had anticipated. His wild appearance didn't help much either.

Alphonse, waiting for him at the luggage carousel was baffled at the delay. Hours of phone calls passed before things were straightened out. Leopold and his frogs were released to his brother who, before driving home, delivered the menagerie to the lab where the frogs were decanted into specially prepared terrariums.

Now, a couple of days later, Leopold was ready to start work in the lab.

"Let me introduce you to my top assistant, Lizette. She's a post doc and doing amazing research on how poison compounds in these frogs cause toxicity. Based on her findings, we've got some good data on which to base our research. She is well aware that if we can find a link leading our results to a more efficient use of pain killers, we'll have made a major contribution to the medical world."

Leopold stared at Lizette, grunted a hello, then stared some more. She was an eyeful.

Her dark blue eyes slanting up at the corners and her carefully waxed eyebrows making a lovely delicate arch. Elegant high cheekbones and a tiny pip of a mouth completed a perfect face. It was topped off by a gathering of luxurious red curls piled on top of her head. To many, those curls might have been gorgeous. To Leopold, they looked like flames erupting from a volcano. *She's beautiful but dangerous, just like my frogs,* he concluded.

For the next couple of weeks, the brothers worked well together, making good progress. While Lizette's work provided a starting point, their own research moved well beyond that. As she played less and less of a role in their work, she became more and more disagreeable to Leopold. "How's the jungle boy?" she would ask, then laugh and add, "Just joking." Leopold suspected she was unhappy about his presence in the lab. Alphonse and she had worked pretty closely up until then.

Just when things were going really nicely with the brothers' research, their collaboration began to break down. To Alphonse's despair, every experiment Leopold carried out seemed to go astray, either because of a mistake in the setup or missing notes or clumsy handling of the frogs which lived in a variety of terrariums, all carefully locked down to prevent escape.

Because of her interest in the frogs, Alphonse had brought his wife to the lab several times. She couldn't get enough of them.

"Absolutely gorgeous!" Coco exclaimed as she asked about each kind. Some were electric blue, some golden, some bright red, others displayed loops of green and black or were tri-colored with orange, black, and camouflage patterns. "How I would love to see them in their native habitat. It must be wonderful!"

"You're better off here watching them behind glass," her husband remarked. "The jungle is too dangerous for a suburban housewife." Coco bristled at being so described, sort of like a hedgehog on guard.

"Try me sometime. Take me along on your next trip."

"Not likely," responded Alphonse. "I would never submit my wife to such hardship."

Coco leaned close to the terrariums, continuing to stare though the glass, spellbound. "How do you handle them without getting poisoned?" she asked.

"Carefully," was the answer. "Though, some of them are no longer dangerous, like those in that terrarium you're looking at. They've been bred in captivity away from the toxic ants they feed on in the jungle. They're no longer poisonous. We use them as a control group. The poisonous ones are okay to handle quickly as long as you don't have a cut on your hands. Better yet, we use gloves."

"And how's the research coming?" she asked. There was no answer.

Later that night, lying in bed, Coco brought up the topic again now that they were out of hearing of her brother-in-law.

"It's not going well. I don't understand it. Last time Leopold was here, we got on swimmingly; this time, everything he touches seems to go astray. Lizette and I were making such good progress before he arrived."

Ah, Lizette, why plaster on the heavy makeup just to work in a lab? It's a wonder her skin doesn't sag, thought Coco who wore no makeup at all, preferring the natural look. It was unclear whether her husband also preferred the natural look. Coco had her suspicions.

Things had grown tense between the brothers. Stresses built up under the surface. An explosion was inevitable. One day, Alphonse suggested that he and his brother go out for lunch instead of eating sandwiches in the cafeteria.

"Doesn't matter to me where we eat, but if you want a good restaurant meal, that's fine with me," responded Leopold.

Alphonse took them to a small half-empty, poorly-patronized bar. It hardly looked like a source of good food. They took a table well in the back, ordered their meal and sat waiting.

"Why did you pick this place?" asked Leopold.

"Because it's off the beaten track. University folks with over-sized ears never frequent this trough," Alphonse responded, revealing that he didn't think much of it either. "I wanted to talk in private. I don't quite know how to bring this up. It's difficult, but time we take the bull by the balls."

"Don't you mean by the horns," Leopold replied with a rare grin on his face. His brother had always had a hard time with aphorisms, leading to many laughs. This time, though, there was no laughter.

"Listen, we have to get serious. It seems to me that something is off. Your experiments are crashing pretty often, your research has flaws. I'm wondering if you haven't just lived too long in the jungle. I'm wondering if it is even possible to continue this partnership."

"I'm glad you've finally said something. We do need to talk. I've got to tell you, I'm beginning to suspect Lizette of sabotaging my research. Do you think that's possible?"

"Absolutely not! What a preposterous idea. She's been the star of this lab. I trust her implicitly."

"Well, I apologize for suggesting it. But what's going on these days doesn't make much sense to me either. I've never been a forgetful person, always been careful about documenting everything. How can you be so sure she's not messing with my work?"

"Because she's been an excellent researcher ever since she started with me. Loyal and smart."

"Okay, if you say so. But could we give this a little more time so I can figure out for myself why everything is going amiss? Something just doesn't add up."

At this point, the waitress brought their food. There was silence as they devoured greasy hamburgers and an absurdly over-sized pile of fries which spilled onto to the plasticized wooden table. The waitress brought the bill. Alphonse paid. She thanked him, smiled, and asked, "Where's your wife today? She sure is a looker."

Leopold stared at his brother. *A looker? That hardly described Coco.*

"So…" Alphonse said, "maybe we should stay for one more cup of coffee. I can explain." The brothers took off the jackets they had just pulled on and ordered more coffee. Then, Alphonse began, "It's hard being locked up all day in the lab with a gorgeous woman. I tried to keep it professional. She's a star assistant, the best I've ever had. Her experiments in the lab are impressive. She was increasingly excited as we learned more about the mechanism that lets these frogs become toxic. Many evenings she found it hard to put an end to the day and stayed late to work with me. I don't know exactly how it happened, but I soon found myself taking her home after work, then stopping for a drink at her apartment. From there, it wasn't far to her bedroom. Please don't say anything. It would be devastating for Coco if she found out. I don't want to hurt her. It's just one of those things that happens."

Leopold listened without interrupting. When his brother finished he said, "Just happens? Those things don't just happen, you have to make them happen. I would never let your wife know, it would break her heart. She doesn't deserve that."

"Leopold, you've got to understand, working next to a beauty like Lizette would test any man's resistance."

Wouldn't test mine, thought Leopold, *A star? Yes, a cold and distant one.*

"It sounds to me that, as a science professor, you've lost your edge. You're no longer objective about your post doc. I don't share your sense of trust, even less so now that I know the facts. I'd like to stay on a little longer and see if I can figure out what's going on."

"Okay, but I don't think your accusation holds any salt."

Leopold smiled inwardly. *There he goes again.*

That evening, Alphonse had a faculty meeting. Leopold and Coco were at home alone with each other. After supper, they took their wine into the living room. Within the bow of a bay window was a padded bench providing a perfect sitting nook where Coco ensconced herself. Leopold opted instead for a basket chair. It reminded him a bit of the jungle. Still, he mused on what a cozy room it was. He wondered, *How long must I politely stay here before retiring to my room?* It turned out not to be a problem. Coco put him at ease immediately by asking about his life in the jungle.

"I love to read," she said. "I sit by this window where I can look out on the flowers from time to time. Since you moved to Brazil, I have spent a lot of time poring through books about it. But I don't believe any of the writers know as much about life there as you do."

Leopold was launched. Nobody had ever expressed such interest before. To his amazement, he talked for almost an hour. Coco listened from the window seat, leaning her head back and gazing at him as he rambled on. The lovely hour ended with a phone call from her husband. He would be late, the meeting was running over. "Don't stay up for me." Coco hung up. She turned to Leopold.

"By the way, just what do you think of Lizette? I haven't heard you mention her, but Alphonse tells me she's a topnotch researcher. Funny, her name makes me think of a lizard. Do lizards eat frogs?" she asked.

"Sometimes," he responded, "but if they messed with a dart frog they would die instantly."

"Interesting," replied Coco. "Tell me, what is it about these poison frogs that got you so hooked on studying them?"

"It's hard to say. I think the fact they are so tiny yet so powerful, so beautiful."

"Yes, I can see that. Small certainly doesn't have to mean weak," she answered.

"And, the loss of their habitat to logging puts them in danger of extinction. It makes it important to learn all we can about them before they disappear entirely."

"Mm-hm. I'd say the same description would fit a lot of scenarios," was Coco's cryptic reply.

And there the discussion ended. After saying goodnight, each retreated to the safety of their own habitats.

Three days later, Leopold was even more convinced that corruption had entered the lab. *That lizard, oops,* he thought, *that Lizette is tampering with my work. Could she be jealous of my research?* He shared his thoughts with his brother. Alphonse thought Leopold had probably overheard Lizette's comment. She had described Leopold as looking a bit like a frog with his bulging eyes. *That's probably why my brother is so paranoid about her.*

The result, Alphonse became increasingly distant, spending more time now with Lizette than with Leopold. Sometimes Leopold would take the bus home while his brother stayed late working. That meant more time with Coco, to whom Leopold was becoming increasingly attached.

"Do you think a white woman could survive jungle life?" she asked.

"I don't know," replied Leopold. "It's not very luxurious but it *is* rewarding... and peaceful. Native people are warm and friendly. The jungle is fascinating and full of wonderful strange wildlife."

"I think I'd like that," she responded.

"Would you like to hear a recording of the native people playing drums and pipes?

"Oh, yes, please."

Leopold retrieved his laptop, found the file and turned it on. The audio was soft but audible. Coco listened to the odd pipe notes. They were not very melodic but with the drum rhythm, oddly stirring. First, she started tapping her foot, then she rose from the chintz flowered sofa and began to slowly sway her hips and her arms. She made Leopold think of wind blowing through the branches of a willow tree. She smiled and beckoned him to join her.

"I don't know how to dance," he objected and remained sitting, but his foot was also tapping with the rhythm. *Though I surely wish I did. How can my brother ignore his wife for that hussy in the lab? If Coco were mine, I'd never let her go. But how does one approach such a Goddess?*

Leopold heard his brother come home around 11 p.m., but he had long since gone to bed... alone. Alphonse climbed into bed with his wife. He was asleep in seconds, unaware of what lay ahead.

It was just 8 a.m. the next day when Alphonse and Leopold arrived at the lab. On unlocking the door and walking in, they were welcomed by a brilliant golden frog sitting on the counter. It looked like it was grinning at the success of its escape.

"I'll be damned!" shouted his brother. "How'd he get loose? What a disaster!" They looked around and began spotting others.

A bright red frog clung to one of the desk lamp shades, a green and yellow one was sitting on the end of a pencil stuck in a holder, a tri-colored one stared at them from his perch atop a test tube. Everywhere, there was a flurry of small creatures hopping, a virtual frog circus.

"My God, which frogs are they? I hope not the poisonous ones!" The brothers dashed through the lab to the back room where the labeled terrariums were lined up on wire shelves. There, they stopped in horror at a ghastly sight. Lizette was lying on her back on the floor, red curls cascading around her deathly still face, raincoat tied at her waist, feet flopped at strange angles, her long fingers with blood red nails gripping her throat. A flashlight, shining a weak beam, had rolled out of her hand and come to rest against the leg of a stool. Lizette's eyes were open and staring, her lips as blue as the brilliant frog sitting on her nose.

Alphonse turned pale and began to shake. Leopold, a jungle man used to crisis, was steadier than his brother. He grabbed his phone and dialed 911. But they both knew, help was clearly too late.

"We've got to capture the frogs before the medics arrive," Leopold told his brother as he put his arms around his shoulders and led him away from the body. Alphonse, still dazed, followed his younger brother's instructions. "First we need to find which terrarium they escaped from," he continued. It didn't take long to see the top of the non-poisonous frog habitat had been carefully removed and was leaning against the wall behind it.

"So, the frogs that are loose are safe to handle, so..." said Alphonse.

"Not the blue," interrupted Leopold. "As one of my experiments, I put a poisonous blue in with this batch of non-poisonous frogs last evening. I documented it at the time but was going to put a warning label on the terrarium this morning."

"Looks like you're too late!" exploded his brother. Leopold said nothing. It was clear now that Lizette had been rudely interrupted in the act of tampering with his research. *Why torture his brother with so obvious a truth?*

A week later, after the funeral, the brothers returned to their research. They hardly mentioned Lizette again. A police investigation revealed that she had entered the lab after hours by the light of a flashlight and had opened what she probably thought was a terrarium control group of non-dangerous frogs. What nefarious plan she had in mind was not clear to the investigators. However, one of the frogs, unbeknownst to her, *was* poisonous. She still might have been okay except that she had a cut on the palm of her hand. The poison had entered her system and done its work with expediency.

Strange to tell, the brothers began to get along better. After a month, their research was back on track. There were no more late nights at the lab. Alphonse was home with Coco every evening. But he often wondered: *The label warning that the blue frog was poisonous, did Leopold leave it off on purpose?* He wasn't sure he wanted to know.

Four months later, their research was published and recognized by the medical community as a major contribution toward the use of pain killers.

Leopold had booked his flight back to Brazil, happy in the knowledge that if he couldn't have her himself, at least Coco would now be treated better by his brother.

He was packing up his equipment when Alphonse entered the lab and interrupted him. "I'd like to introduce you to the new post doc. She will be working with me."

His brother looked up. There, standing before him was a beautiful young woman. But, unlike what Alphonse saw, Leopold saw only... more trouble.

BEST BUDDIES

Rosy untangled herself from the strangling hold of her husband's arms. He had her trapped deep in the heart of a squishy orange sofa until he remembered... football.

"Hey, turn on the game, babe." Glad to escape his clutches, she stood up. Walking across the room, she swore under her breath as she kicked at the empty cans littering the floor. The TV was propped on a wooden chair. She leaned over to angle the screen in his direction.

"Can you see it from there?"

"Nah, but I can see your sexy butt, and I'm liking it." Her husband Karl was a skinny guy with a thin face, his eyes in dark hollows set too close together. Sitting up, he leaned forward better to see. "You're almost better than football. Almost," he added.

"You're horny. This isn't the time. Our friends will be here any minute. We need to get ready." Rosy, a plump blond wearing a sparkly blouse half-tucked into her short shorts, walked off to the kitchen, returning a few minutes later with a bowl of chips and a jar of salsa. "Where are Walt and Dawn? I thought they'd be here by now."

"He's always late. Guy can't read, not even his watch. Got one that sings out the time every half-hour. Good buddy, but a real moron!"

"You ought to be glad," she said with a smirk on her face. "Makes it easier to cheat him out of his savings."

"Good point, Rosy. Not bad for a dumb chick." Karl suddenly held up his beer and stared at the label. "Wait, this isn't the beer Walt drinks. What the hell have you gone and done! He hates this beer!"

"Come on, Karl, I tried to buy the right brand but seeing as how you guys go to Red's to watch football, how could I know what Walt likes? What am I, some kind of witch with magic powers?"

"Witch, yes. Magic powers, no. You could have asked. That's a woman for ya. You're all the same... lame." When the doorbell rang, Karl mumbled, "You better answer it, this being your idea of a fun evening."

As she headed for the door, she looked back over her shoulder, "Well, why not? Why should we always stay at home while the men go out to watch the game? Wives like football, too, you know."

"Give me a break. You bimbos are too squeamish for football. It's a game of strategy and power... way beyond your butterfly brains," answered her insufferable husband.

Rosy opened the door. "Hi Walt, hi Dawn. You're just in time. The game hasn't started yet. Come on in."

"Huh," grunted Walt, who was dressed in Levi's, a bulging leather jacket, and black boots. He stood with his arm around his long-legged, mini-skirted wife.

"Well, don't just stand there, come on in," Rosy repeated.

"Hi everyone," said Dawn. Then looking at Rosy, she murmured in an aside, "What a night this will be." The two women exchanged grins. Karl was busy hanging up their guests' jackets.

"Hey, dude. What's up?" asked Walt as he walked in and high-fived Karl.

"Not much, buddy. Wife bought the wrong beer. Not your brand. Hope it won't bloat you too bad. Your gastric explosions could blow us out of these digs."

"What the hell. I'll try it. Women! Never get a damned thing right. Well… one thing."

"Grab a can. Have a seat."

Walt dropped his beer-bloated body onto the sofa. The springs protested, sagging badly under his weight. Dawn plopped herself down next to him, her high heels and long frame causing her tiny skirt to pretty much disappear into her lap. She tossed a pink plastic purse by her feet where it popped open, spilling its contents.

"So, this should be a kicker," said Walt, "Watching the game with our chicks peeping away, like bein' in a barnyard. Think you skirts can shut up for a while?"

"You'd be surprised what we keep quiet about, stud," answered Dawn as she settled back into the cushions.

Rosy smiled from the bean bag chair where she was snugly ensconced. Karl had grabbed a wooden chair, spun it around to straddle the seat. His shiny pant legs hiked up to reveal black nylon socks and pointy shoes. He sat, arms resting on the high back, one hand nursing a beer. Then he noticed the purse.

"Hey, Dawn, your purse is spillin' its guts all over the floor," said Karl.

Walt looked down and spied a small photo in the jumble of keys, lipsticks, and bills scattered at her feet. Leaning over, he reached for it just as Dawn did the same.

"Uh-uh," he said, as he grabbed the photo, holding it high out of her reach. "Well, look what we have here, if it isn't a photo of you, Karl! Great balls of fire! Now just what is that doing in your purse, Dawn?"

"Oh, that. Rosy gave it to me when we were comparing how you guys dress," replied Dawn. "See, doesn't Karl just look the part for his profession: a slick loan shark ready to cheat the little guy out of his savings? Just kidding, Karl! And you, Walt, you look like one of Hell's Angels on Jell-o. I mean, look at that bouncy bulge under your jacket. Ha, ha, ha. All good fun!"

"Hold on, Dawn. I don't remember giving you a photo. Are you messing with my man?" demanded Rosy. "Okay, big boy," she continued, as she looked over at her husband, "what's this all about?"

"What? I don't know a damn thing about it! No idea where Dawn got that picture!" he said.

Turning to face his wife, Walt exploded at her. "You're a liar! Messin' around with Karl, are you?"

"But Rosy did give it to me," Dawn whined, "She just forgot. Rosy, don't you remember how we were making fun about the silly clothes these guys wear?"

At this, both men sat up straight. Karl tucked his rayon shirt in a little tighter, Walt slicked his black hair back off his beefy forehead. They scowled at one another.

"I sure as hell don't remember that and *I* also want to know what you're doing with a photo of my husband! You've got some explaining to do. You too, Karl!" said Rosy.

"I swear to God I have no idea what this is about. You'd hardly find me touching Dawn, she doesn't turn me on!" said Karl.

That was too much for Dawn who burst out with, "Karl, you're a low-down snake... a rattle snake! It's too late now. Why don't you tell the truth? Too scared? You, the big boss of your slimy operation. Afraid of what Walt might do?"

"I'm not afraid of anybody. Walt, surely you don't believe this crap?"

107

"Actually, I think I do," said Walt. "Some pal you are, Karl. Screwing my wife! I have an urge to blow your head off. Maybe you get away with this with other suckers, but *I* sure won't put up with that crap. Why'd you do it, Dawn?"

"Oh God. I didn't want it to come to this," she said. "I didn't want to sleep with that snake, but he threatened to expose you if I didn't. I was just trying to protect you. He said he'd go to the cops… tell them about your counterfeiting. You know I love you. How could you possibly think I would go for such a lowlife?"

"What a bastard! You slept with her? I'll see you in your grave before you touch me again!" exploded Rosy.

"Hey, wait a minute everyone. This is crazy! It's all a blasted lie. Why would I want to screw your pitiful excuse of a wife anyway?" responded Karl.

"That's it, Karl," exploded Walt. "You're history. You don't get away with insulting and banging my wife!" With that, Walt jumped up, fists raised and made a dive for Karl. Karl scrambled to his feet, retreating into a corner of the room, arms up to protect his face. Then the women leapt up, trying to interfere as they futilely pawed at Walt's back.

"Cut it out, cut it out *now!*" screamed Rosy, "before you bust up the furniture and bleed all over the rugs. I won't have it!"

Walt paused, momentarily distracted by the surprise attack of the 'barn chicks' as he called them. In that moment, Karl, like a crazed fox, bolted for the door.

Walt, reaching under his jacket, pulled out a gun and exited in pursuit. The hunt was on.

Dawn and Rosy, left standing in the silence, made their way to the sofa, collapsing onto it. Shortly after, they heard a shot. The women jumped up again, hands over their mouths, and stood waiting.

All at once, the door flung open, hitting the wall with a loud crash and Walt barreled in. "Nailed the bastard out in the driveway. Deader than roadkill. You squaws happy now? Thank me for getting rid of that lowdown no-good husband, Rosy."

"You killed the scumbag? I can't believe it! Now what?"

"Right," chimed in Dawn, "How're you gonna get rid of the body?

"No problem. I'll carry him to the car... always was a lightweight... drive him out of the city and find me a nice river somewhere. You all just sit tight till I get back. I'll figure the alibis. Not the first time I've dealt with this kinda thing."

The women, pale and nervous, sat back down. Dawn's fingers drummed the wooden arm of the sofa. Rosy twisted her hands around and around. They sat staring at one another. With their open mouths framed by bright red lips, they looked a bit like fish gasping for air, or maybe gasping for something else. Suddenly, the door opened again and Walt came crashing back into the room.

"The goddamned car keys! Where'd I put them?" he shouted. In a panic, he began rummaging through the pockets of his jacket hanging on the coat rack. Not finding them, he patted down his pants pockets once more, then yelled at Dawn. "You got the fucking keys, Dawn?"

"No, for God's sake, why would I have them?"

"'Cuz they're not here!" He returned to the coat rack, running his fingers deep into each pocket until suddenly, "Right! Got 'em!" Walt dashed out of the room, slamming the door behind him.

"Typical," declared Dawn, throwing her hands up in exasperation. Rosy shook her head slowly side to side before grabbing the cell from her pocket.

"Wait," said Dawn, "a little longer."

The two women stood up and began pacing the floor, Dawn's heels clattering with every step.

"Hey!" Rosy burst out, "We forgot the game. We're missing the first quarter!"

"Damn, you're right. Quick, turn it on."

"Wow! Three zero, Giants! We're winning!" exclaimed Rosy. They both sat down on the sofa, leaning forward with excitement.

A couple of minutes later, Rosy grabbed the phone again, "Now?"

Dawn nodded, eyes still fixed on the screen. Rosy dialed 911, yelling into the phone. "Help! There's been a murder. The killer escaped in a white car with a body inside. The plate?" She put her hand over the phone and turned to Dawn, "Quick, what's the plate number?"

Dawn's mouth dropped open, her eyes grew big, "Damn, I never thought of that! Wait, I think I know. It begins with G-A-G and then some numbers."

Uncovering the receiver again, Rosy reported, "It's G-A-G, gag, and then some numbers. No, this is *not* a joke. Please, please hurry, he just drove away on Avenue C heading toward the freeway. Help!" Rosy hung up. "Done, my darling, one dead, one going to prison. Mission accomplished!"

The women rushed into each other's arms. Their kiss was long and passionate, their hands all over one another. Finally, pulling away, Rosy announced, "By the way, I saved champagne for this moment. I'll get it." She disappeared into the kitchen. Dawn heard the pop of a cork. Her lover returned holding an overflowing bottle and two glasses. Not knowing much about champagne, she poured the bubbly to the rims of the tall Giant-emblazoned beer glasses. "That should do it," she said, as they toasted one another and settled back on the sofa. But, they failed to hear the snake rattle.

In the middle of the 4th quarter, the abused door was slammed open again. The impact shook the windows, sending shock waves through the house as it hit the dented wall. Rosy and Dawn jumped up, clutching one another, fear contorted their lovely faces. Into the room strode the very alive duo: Karl and Walt.

"I'll be damned. Look at the two lovers cuddling in their nest! Not so clever anymore!" Karl proclaimed. "You forgot, never step on a snake. We were on to you before you half began. What da ya think? We'd turn on each other? Never, we're best buddies, remember?"

Truth at Play

"Why does he have to live with us? He's a grump."

"Now, Billy, don't ever say that again. It's not nice. You just don't know him well because he's been so far away. He's coming to live with us because he needs help," replied his mother, who had just picked up her 5-year-old son from after-school care.

"He never talked to me. I don't like him," declared Billy, kicking his feet against the back of the driver's seat.

Janet, a weary mom who had just put in a long day at the office, responded, "Now, now. Let's try to be kind. Remember, the poor man has been unable to speak since he had a stroke. You're going to have to accept him the way he is."

"He never talked to me anyway, so I don't really care," said the incorrigible child.

Granddad, a WWII veteran, moved in the following week, sleeping in a spare bedroom of the old Victorian house. It was a hard adjustment for Billy's mother, Janet. After all, it was her husband's father and he was a stern, taciturn man. She also hadn't found him easy to talk to, even when he could converse. *How are we going to get along now?* she wondered.

With time, Janet, a slender woman, her heart shaped face showing signs of strain, slowly became used to his silent presence. He seemed to understand what was going on and would step up to help wash dishes or clear the table. He did not help with cooking, that was something his recently deceased wife had always done. Since her passing, he had primarily sustained himself on peanut butter sandwiches and wine. That was one of the reasons Janet and her husband Gerry had brought him to live with them. On arrival, he was gaunt and pale, his eyes droopy. Good nutrition was slowly restoring his health. Maybe being with family played a role as well.

But, when it came to his grandson, he only watched from a distance. That worked for Billy, who rarely stayed in the same vicinity as his granddad any longer than it took to eat a meal or help with the cleanup. Soon afterwards, he would escape to his room and his toys.

Billy's rug was covered with tiny dark green plastic soldiers. He grouped and regrouped them, sometimes set them up to attack each other, but often had them work as a team. His parents, busy with their jobs, cooking, and housework, had little time for their son. They would have preferred to see his room vacuumed and kept in good order. However, they realized that demanding he pick his toys up off the rug was maybe asking too much. They left him to play as he wanted.

Billy was not an easy child. He had trouble getting along with other children. He lagged behind in kindergarten. This cute little boy with blond hair falling in his eyes, a round face, and a slightly chubby build, preferred home life to school life.

Every day, after Billy had gone to kindergarten and Gerry and Janet had left for work, Granddad roamed the house. He always ended up in Billy's room, where he would sit on the bed and stare at the soldiers. One day, he reached out, picked one up and placed it on top of the toy box.

When Billy came home and saw it, he mumbled to the stranded soldier, "I don't remember putting you there. How'd that happen?" And then, a minute later said, "Hey, you can be the lookout." He left the soldier where he was.

113

The next day, when he got home, he had a snack, went to his room and discovered four soldiers were lying down side-by-side. *I bet the cat got in and knocked them over*, he thought. Another day he found one of the soldiers standing on his bedside table. "Wait, how'd you get up here?" he asked.

Each day after that, on returning home from school, Billy rushed to his room to see if anything was different. It usually was. "Mom, I think my toy soldiers come alive when I'm not home, just like in Toy Story! Do you think they do?"

"I don't know. Why do you think that?" she replied.

"'Cause they're all kinda lined up when I go to school and when I come home, they're in different places."

"Maybe you just forgot where you left them."

"No, I didn't. They're all different," said Billy throwing his arms wide for emphasis.

After a pause, his mother asked, "Is that a problem?"

"Not really," Billy replied while looking down at the floor.

"In that case," said his mother as she put her arm around his shoulders, "why not just wait and see what happens next?"

"Hey, I just thought of something. Do you think Granddad could be moving them?"

"Why don't you ask him?" she replied.

"But he can't talk. How can he tell me?"

"He can't talk but he can nod his head."

That evening, the family was seated for supper. Gerry, a handsome, dark-haired carpenter, still in his work clothes, sat at one end of the table; Janet at the other. After she served the Mac n' cheese to everyone, she ventured, "Billy, I think you wanted to ask Granddad something." Billy shrank down in his seat, lowered his head and said nothing.

"Well, go ahead," his father prompted, "spit it out."

"Umm, did you move my soldiers?" he softly mumbled, not daring to look up.

"Look at your granddad when you speak to him," Gerry said in a kindly voice.

Granddad looked across the table at his grandson. His face angular, his beard and mustache a tangle of wiry hair, his eyes wide and staring. Billy looked up just in time to see him shake his head.

"Well," said Janet, "I guess that's that. Now, can I serve you all some nice fresh salad?"

Later that night, after Billy and Granddad had gone to bed, Janet and Gerry were snuggling quietly on the couch trying to unwind from the day.

Suddenly, Janet spoke up, "He was lying, of course. What do we do about that?"

"Lying? What are you talking about?"

Janet filled him in on the story of the toy soldiers.

"Look, he probably is, but what's the harm? My poor Dad is trying to have a little fun with his grandson. In fact, I'm surprised. It's the first time he's shown any interest in him," responded Gerry.

"But it's not right to lie to Billy. He'll grow up thinking it's okay," she said, getting up to pour herself a glass of wine.

"This from the mom who reads him stories about Santa Claus and the Easter Bunny?"

"That's different," she replied, settling back down next to her husband.

"Seems the same to me," he said. "I think fairy tales are an easier way for kids to learn about the world, the good and the bad.

So, what if he thinks his soldiers come alive. Let him have some fun. He'll learn the truth soon enough."

"But when he finds out he's been fooled, he'll be traumatized," Janet persisted.

"Oh, come on. How traumatized were you when you found out about Santa Claus?"

Janet leaned forward, took a sip of wine from the glass on the coffee table, then leaned back before answering, "I don't remember."

"Point made. It didn't mess you up, at least not too badly," he said laughing as he roughed up her carefully combed hair. "Look, he's a sweet child but awkward and lonely. If thinking his soldiers come alive makes him happier, all the better. So, let's not dwell on this anymore. I've got something else I want to do," he said, wrapping his arms around her.

"I hope," said Janet to her husband the next morning as they enjoyed their coffee before the others were up, "now that Granddad had been confronted, he will stop tricking Billy with this nonsense."

"And I hope," replied Gerry, "that you won't mention it. Let's see what happens. Billy seems happy enough. Why ruin a good thing?"

Janet agreed not to interfere, but she wasn't happy about it. *On the other hand*, she thought, *Gerry did have a point about Santa Claus. Sometimes it's hard to know what's right and what's wrong.*

The drive home from after-school care gave Janet and Billy rare moments for just the two of them to be together. "I wonder what my soldiers have done today?" he often pondered as soon as he got in the car. Janet would quickly change the subject so as not to encourage his fantasy. *It will only make the fall harder when he finds out the truth,* she reflected.

On returning home each day, Billy would rush to his room before eating his snack. Some days, the soldiers were right where he left them. When that happened, he would go downstairs to sit quietly and have his milk and cookies. But other days, he would find the soldiers had been busy in his absence. Then he would forget about his snack and call his mother. "Mom, Mom!" he would shout, "Come see what my soldiers have done now!"

And what had they done? One time he found a small piece of cardboard folded to make a tent. Two soldiers were lying inside. Another time, he found a small paper airplane with dragons drawn on the wings. And most curious, was a kind of contraption he discovered consisting of a wooden sewing spool with a long stick attached by an elastic. "What is it Mom?"

Mom didn't know. "Maybe ask your dad when he gets home."

Gerry was delighted to share his son's excitement over the latest activities in his room. When he saw the new contraption sitting on the floor, he broke into a wide grin. "Ah," he said, picking the thing up, "it's a tank. See how the edges of the spool are cut jagged? Those are its tracks." Watch what happens when I wind up the elastic with the stick." After giving the stick several turns until the rubber band was completely twisted in knots, Gerry set it down on the floor. To Billy's amazement, the tank took off on its own, driving across the rug, up and over a dirty sock lying in its path.

That evening at supper, Billy couldn't stop talking about the tank. "It's really cool! It goes all by itself. I don't even have to push it or anything." Across the table, the old man sat expressionless as usual, but closer observation would have revealed a shine in his eyes as he watched his grandson talk.

"Are you sure you didn't make that tank?" Billy asked him.

Once more, Granddad shook his head, denying all knowledge of it.

That evening, still sitting at the supper table after Billy had gone to his room and Grandpa had retired to fall asleep watching a Netflix program, Janet opened the discussion again. "I just can't stand this lying any longer, Gerry. It has to stop."

"Okay. How about we make a pact. You tell him about Granddad, but you also have to tell him that Santa Claus and the Easter Bunny are lies as well."

"Unfair!" his wife snapped back as she jumped up from her chair and began pacing.

"Why?"

"Because it will break his heart."

"And this won't?"

There seemed to be no resolution to their conflict until one day when the nurse at school called Janet. "Billy's got a tummy ache and doesn't feel well. Could you come pick him up?"

"I'll need some time to wrap up at work, but I'll be there as soon as I can." An hour later, Janet stopped at the nurse's office where Billie was waiting. She drove him home. "You go up and lie down. I'm going to fix you a ginger ale and bring it up," This time he didn't run up the stairs, but dragged himself quietly to his room where a surprise was waiting. There, on his knees on the floor, was his granddad.

"Granddad!" the boy exclaimed, "What's the matter?"

Granddad slowly turned, looked at his grandson and winked. In one hand he held a tiny ladder made of sewing thread. Billy watched in awe as his granddad tied it to the back of the chair where the lookout soldier was positioned. Then, awkwardly and with much effort, the old man got to his feet, put his finger to his lips, signaling him not to tell, and padded quietly out of the room. Billy, forgetting about his tummy ache, went closer to take a look. He dropped down on the rug, grabbed the lookout soldier and was making him descend the ladder when he heard his mother coming up the stairs. In a flash, he jumped into bed and lay there curled in a ball.

"Oh, you poor child," she said. "Here, try a sip of soda." Billy obliged but as soon as his mother left the room, he was out of bed again to admire the amazing ladder. Suddenly, he felt better.

Later, Billie heard his mother coming upstairs and dove under his covers just in time. She leaned down and kissed him, and offered to read a story. To her surprise, he refused, saying he just wanted to sleep.

"Maybe you'd like a little supper?" she asked.

"Okay," he replied in a weak voice.

"We'll bring it up to you," she replied. "You must be feeling a little better."

An hour later, hearing footsteps, he stopped playing, made another quick retreat and pretended to be asleep as the door opened.

But, this time, it was Granddad who entered the room, carrying a tray. He set it down next to the bed, then stepped over to the chair, untied the thread ladder and moved it to the bedside table. Taking a role of tape out of his pocket, he attached the ladder to the table edge. Then he made three soldiers break rank and march over to the ladder which they climbed to reach the table.

Billy, eyes crinkled in delight, began to giggle. Then he grabbed one of the green men and sent him for a swim in his soup. Granddad grabbed the other two and tossed them in as well.

Suddenly, in no time, all the soldiers began to sink in the watery chicken soup. Granddad to the rescue. He floated a piece of toast into the soup to save the swimmers and bring them to shore. Billy, kicking his heels high like a young colt, rolled about the bed and couldn't stop laughing.

Granddad returned downstairs to eat. Gerry had just that minute come in from work. When the meal was over, he went up to see his son.

"Mom says you were sick today. You feeling better?"

Billy allowed how he was. After talking and hugging his son, Gerry picked up the tray and took it downstairs.

"What a mess!" his mother exclaimed. "There's soup everywhere. Whatever is the matter with that boy!"

Billy went back to school the next day, suddenly feeling better. That afternoon, after he returned home and had his snack, his mother told him she had to do laundry and vacuum the house, and she would be busy until supper.

Billy ran upstairs, but this time, he stopped off at Granddad's room and knocked softly. The door swung open. Billy, stumbling over his words, said, "Umm, Granddad, you... you... want to come pl-play?"

For the first time in many weeks, the old haggard face broke into a grin and he followed Billy down the hall to his room where the two of them maneuvered soldiers around the floor until it was time to eat.

Things began to change for both grandson and granddad. Billy was happier at school. Granddad perked up, sometimes a smile even flickered across his old face.

The afternoon rendezvouses went on for several days until Billy could contain himself no longer. One night, after his mother

120

read him a story and had leaned down to kiss him goodnight, he whispered in her ear, "I have a secret."

"You do?"

"Yes, but I shouldn't tell."

"Well then, don't."

"But I can tell you. You want to know what it is?"

"If you want to tell me."

"I know how my soldiers moved around and got all that equipment."

"You do? How?" With alarm, she waited to hear what he would say.

"Granddad!" he burst out, "Granddad did all that! Isn't that cool? I thought he didn't like me, but he does!"

Janet sat up in astonishment.

Two months later, death came to call. Grandpa was briefly hospitalized before closing his eyes for the last time. Billy was inconsolable. His soldiers lay scattered about the rug where he kicked them about in anger. His parents were deeply pained, not only by the loss of Gerry's father, but at the loss of Billy's happy childhood. He was distraught and moody. He barely touched his food. They read him stories, let him watch movies, and bought him a bike with training wheels. Nothing helped.

"He left me. I thought he liked me," Billie sobbed. "He was my bestest friend ever."

"You know what?" asked his Dad. "I think he didn't really leave. He's probably watching down from heaven. He's probably very unhappy seeing you feeling so bad. You don't want him unhappy, do you?"

"Then he shouldn't have gone away like that."

It was a couple of weeks later when, after his snack, Billy dragged up to his room. There, to his amazement, stood his soldiers, all lined up in neat ranks. The tank was sitting on a bump in the carpet, ready to go. The ladder up to the chair was in place. The tent was back with soldiers sleeping inside.

Billy ran downstairs. "Mom, Mom! Come look at my soldiers!"

She followed him back to his room, smiling. "Why look at that!" she exclaimed.

"Did Dad do that?" Billy asked as he dropped to his knees.

"No, he couldn't. He's been at work all day"

"Did you do it?"

"No, sweetheart, I've been at work, too.'

"Then who did?" he asked.

"I have no idea," she said.

Billy started to giggle. He reached for the tank and began winding up the elastic. Then he paused to look up at his mother, his eyes shining.

"I do," he said, "but it's a secret. I'm not telling."

Slip-Sliding Away

He stared down from atop a Manhattan skyscraper. Far below, traffic on the streets seemed like nothing more than colonies of ants on the march. He stood before the glass wall of his hushed, carpeted office, high above the scurry of humanity. Interior decorators had designed his world of mahogany furniture, marble walls, and strategically placed plants. He wondered if the plants were real or synthetic. If real, somebody, he didn't know who, must have been watering them; if fake, well, he didn't really care one way or the other. He had made it to the top: top of the building, top of society, one of the wealthiest people in the country. Investment banking had paid off in a big way for Albert, or so he thought.

The phone on his desk rang. He walked over and pushed a button lighting a line to Annette, his personal stiletto-heeled secretary.

"Your wife is on the phone. Do you want me to connect you?"

"Tell her I'm in a conference, but that I'll meet her and the Bryans at the club at six. That should give us time to eat before the opera."

"Yes sir, I'll do that. Is there anything else?" she asked.

"No, not at the moment."

Albert hung up, but continued to stare at the phone, thinking about Annette: efficient, discreet, and beautiful in a New Yorker kind of way... which meant tall, glamorous, perfectly made up, but cold and remote. He gave an involuntary shiver before turning to stare out the window again.

He was a tall 50-year-old man, gray hair neatly combed, face clean shaven, his frame trim from daily gym workouts. In truth, there wasn't much about Albert to distinguish him from the other Wall Street suits whose butts were settled in comfy desk chairs throughout the building.

It was hard to gauge the outside temperature. Sealed offices locked out weather extremes. Climate change meant nothing to those buffered from its effects. *I should be grateful for such privilege. I guess I am,* he thought, before turning away to reconnect with the three computer screens on his polished desk.

At 5 o'clock, Annette rang up to say she was leaving. Albert remained. There were emails waiting for a response, more stock news to read, more meetings to set up. He was a bit bored with it all, found it hard to concentrate. One hour to kill until time to meet his wife Nettie, and Fred and his wife Sue. Albert stood up again, stretched, wandered to the glass wall and stared out at the endless landscape of cement high rises, paved streets and dots of yellow lights. *What are all those people in all those rooms in all those towers doing?* he wondered. *Are they ever bored like I am?*

Dinner at the club was predictable. Albert was greeted at the front desk by a familiar face. "Good evening, Mr. Hackney. Your wife and the Bryans have arrived. You'll find them seated in the corner by the fireplace."

"Thank you, Benson. Think I'll stop at the bar before heading to the table. Hope you are well this evening."

"Yes sir, very well, sir," said the clerk, bowing his balding head.

As he approached the white-clad dinner table, drink in hand, he realized once more what a good-looking wife he had. Nettie was striking in a style similar to all the other women he knew. Personal trainers, manicurists, pedicurists, massage therapists, and cosmetic surgeons insured their good looks. Hair dyed to deceive, wrinkles erased to mimic youth, jewelry worn to impress. Nettie was almost as tall as he was, her blonde hair swept back in a glamorous wave, her tight silk blouse and skirt leaving no doubt to what lay underneath. As he approached, he saw that she was talking. She was always talking. *What did she have left to say?* he wondered.

"It was a frustrating day," she recounted, "first the salon manager, she always does my hair herself, you know, so first she kept me waiting, complained her husband was ill and she had to run home to care for him... hardly know what that was all about. Then I stopped at Julie's for a latte and salad but they were all out of spinach so I had to eat Romaine instead, of all things... Oh, hello darling, I didn't see you come in," she said, giving Albert a flashy smile of large white teeth. Somehow, those teeth reminded him of a shark.

The Bryans looked up, seeming relieved at the interruption. "Good to see you, Albert," said Fred as he stood up to greet him.

"Darling, it's been so long," Sue said from where she was sitting. She offered him a long, languorous hand.

"Please, Nettie, don't let me interrupt the fascinating account you were giving the Bryans of your day."

Eventually, conversation moved on to a discussion of the upcoming opera.

"The *New York Times* gave it a rave review."

"Then it must be excellent, if the *Times* says so. I'm sure we'll love it," Sue responded.

Talk dragged on through dinner. The opera was a welcome change. Once the lights went down and the curtain went up, Albert relaxed, knowing he no longer had to respond to anyone.

Afterwards, the others gushed over the fabulous performance. Albert, on the other hand, thought it rather dreadful, but was careful not to say something that might displease anyone. The next morning, to his delight, the paper printed a scathing commentary on the previous night's production.

Yes, Albert reminded himself a few days later as he settled into an armchair on his private jet, *Yes, I have it all.* The jet revved up, flew down the runway and zoomed into the sky. *Just like my career,* reflected Albert. *A fast rise.*

At last totally alone, he dug into his briefcase and pulled out Robert Louis Stevenson's *A Child's Garden of Verses.* With no one looking over his shoulder, he was free to indulge in his secret love of the verse. The poems took him back to childhood, to a time when life was wondrous and exciting, when Nanny's love and homemade cookies filled his days. *Where had it all gone? When had he last felt such joy?* he asked himself.

A couple of hours later, the co-pilot walked back to announce they would have to land short of Las Vegas. "Bad weather up ahead." Not long after, they came down at a small airport somewhere in the middle of nowhere. It looked like a moonscape to Albert, who was more familiar with photos of the moon's surface than he was of western America.

"I can drive you from here," the pilot announced.

"Thanks, but I'll drive myself, if they even have anything like a car rental service in this God-forsaken place," Albert answered. "I'd rather you both stay with the plane and make sure nobody

126

tampers with it. You never know what outlaws might populate a place like this."

Headlights hit a wall of white. He drove straight into the blasting wind. Leaning forward, hands gripping the wheel, eyes fixed ahead, Albert struggled to stay on the road. *Where the Hell is the center line?* he wondered just as the car began to slide. Frantic, he steered in the direction of the skid, but to no avail. The car slid off the edge. He heard a loud crack, the sound of steel ripping. The car rolled over onto the driver's side, then stopped with a soft thud. He checked his cell phone – no bars. Alone, totally alone. *What to do? Hours from the next town, no coat packed.* Instinctively, Albert reached for the ignition and turned the key. The engine shut down, the headlights went out. Dark silence enveloped him, as well as cold air. He was on a business trip; he never expected to set foot outdoors the whole time. His private jet was to have delivered him to the airport, a limousine taken him to his hotel, enclosed walkway given him access to the convention center. Bad weather had upended his plans.

Albert opened his eyes. *Where am I? Did I pass out?* Suddenly, it all came back. He tried to loosen his seat belt, but it was wedged fast. He felt something on his face and reached up: sticky blood running down his forehead. It slowly dawned on him that his chance of rescue was nil. He had seen nobody else on the road. Even if someone should come along, they would not be able to see his car over the embankment. He wasn't expected at the convention center until tomorrow. He'd made reservations, but if he didn't show up, the hotel would hardly notice until the next day. Nettie wouldn't miss him as he rarely called her when he was away on business trips. They never had much to say to each other, anyway.

He tried to rest against the car door, wiped his sleeve across his bleeding face, then leaned his head back and closed his eyes. His feet, clad in street shoes and thin socks, began to chill. Shortly after, his legs started to shake. *Was it the cold or nerves? And damn it, why didn't I think to bring a winter jacket with me? So, this is it,* he thought. *It all ends here.* He began to imagine what would be said about him after he died. *'Albert Hackney, highly successful investment banker, owner of three palatial homes in California, New York, and London, left behind his wife Nettie of twenty years. There were no children.'*

How did I ever get talked into that? All because Nettie didn't want to spoil her figure with pregnancy and her social life with the care of kids. I should have objected. I was too caught up with work. So, what will I be remembered for? My wealth? What else? Nothing. Nothing! All those years working so hard, what did it get me? I don't know. I'm not sure. Nettie will be fine. She won't miss me for long.

Suddenly, in a moment of clarity, it occurred to Albert he should leave the headlights on. Should, by a miracle, someone were to come along, they might notice them. He leaned forward, turned the ignition key part way, switched on the lights, then settled back. He was tired, so tired, and cold. His mind grew fuzzy. He began to think back to his youth, to the rope swing that carried him high into the sky. No height ever thrilled him again as much as the one when he would stretch his legs out and tried to touch the clouds. And, when the training wheels came off his bike, that was real excitement. And his wonderful Nanny. *Nanny. Nanny would miss me, if she was still alive, just as I have always missed her.* His head fell forward as he slid into a light slumber. He was aware of a buzzing, bees in the garden, more buzzing, then a knocking, a light shining in his eyes. He opened them wide.

"Hey there, you okay?" shouted a man as he banged his glove against the windshield.

"Oh my God. I don't know. I'm stuck. Can't get out."

"Hang on. I'm coming in the passenger door to cut you loose." Albert heard the door open and a man armed with a flashlight and knife climbed in above him. In no time, he had slit the seat belt free.

"Okay, try to hoist yourself up to the passenger door. I'll help." It was a struggle, the stranger giving him a hand, he trying to find a foothold. He made it, but once outside, began to shiver violently in the howling snowstorm.

"Got a coat in there somewhere?" asked the man.

"Got a suit jacket, in my bag."

The Good Samaritan, flashlight in hand, dove back inside the car, fished around for a while and came out with a briefcase.

"Can't get your bag. It's wedged under the crushed side of the car." His rescuer then slipped off his own padded jacket and helped Albert to put it on. The men were of a similar size, so it fit pretty well. The stranger grabbed Albert's hand again and helped him up the embankment to the road. There, motor running, sat a snowmobile.

Albert's rescuer turned the flashlight on his own face and said, "I'm Jack. What's your name?" The beam of light shone on a face with a long, dark beard, mustache, and sideburns topped with a red wool ear-flap hat.

"Albert Hackney," he replied.

"Well, Albert, I see you haven't got gloves either. Hop on the back, put your arms around me and stick your hands in my pockets so they don't freeze."

It was an awkward thing to do for this overly civilized man. *I don't think I've ever been this close to another body, except for Nettie. Strange, but I have little choice.*

In twenty minutes, they arrived at Jack's house. Light poured from windows; the door opened as they drove up and a woman's voice shouted, "Did you find him?"

"Nope," answered Jack, "but I found someone else."

Albert was so cold and stiff he could hardly get off the snowmobile. Jack put his arm over his shoulders and led him inside to a pine planked kitchen, wood stove blazing in the corner, table and chairs in the middle.

"Have a seat." He turned to a dark-skinned, broad-faced woman with a long black braid hanging down her back. "Maria, this is Albert. I found him while out looking for Nestor. Albert, meet Maria. She'll clean up that gash on your head. Looks like it needs a little glue to close it up."

"Glue? Isn't there a doctor around who could stitch it?"

Crow's feet wrinkled around Maria's smiling eyes as she patted Albert on the back and said, "A doctor? Hardly. The nearest one is fifty miles away and in a storm like this, nobody goes anywhere. But not to worry. I'll take care of you. Krazy glue is part of our first aid kit. We use it on wounds all the time. Works wonders."

"Thanks. You are awfully kind, but I think I better call my wife first and let her know I'm okay. Do cells work here?"

"No, but you can borrow my sat phone and call."

Albert called his wife and told her what had happened. She listened before replying. "Well, sounds like you're safe now. You really got yourself into a mess! Call me when you're headed home again." She hung up.

Maria began working on Albert's cut. Her touch gentle. He was fixed up in no time.

Just then, 6-year-old Rose, a small replica of her mother, came running in from another room. "Dad, did you find him?" the little girl cried.

"No, sweetie, I did not. But don't worry too much. Nestor is probably curled up under a log somewhere and sleeping until the storm passes. Wait, you'll see. He'll come bounding back tomorrow." Turning to Albert, he explained that he had been out looking for their dog who had disappeared in the storm. That's when he saw the car's headlights shining in the trees.

"Nestor?" asked Albert. "Interesting name for a dog. Where'd that come from?"

"In a school play about the Odyssey. Nestor was the king of Pylos. I liked the name," Rose said and began to sob. "Poor Nestor, he must be so cold."

"I never heard of a school teaching kids about Homer. What kind of a school does she go to?"

"It's a Waldorf school, but it's a long way from here. The kids have to ride the bus for an hour to get there. We think it's worth it."

"You have other children?"

"Yes, Spring. Where is she, Maria?"

"She's working on the wheel. Rose, run get her, would you?"

The wheel? wondered Albert. *What in the world does that mean?* It soon became apparent when Spring, an 11-year-old, entered covered with wet clay. She was tall for her years, blonde-haired and lighter-skinned than her sister, but shared the same broad face and sparkling brown eyes. She was introduced.

"Where's Nestor? Did you find him?" she asked.

"No, sweet," answered Maria, "but Dad thinks he'll be okay for one night out there."

"I sure hope so," she said before begging to go back and finish the pot she was turning.

"The school has a pottery wheel and the kids loved it so much, we set one up one at home so they could work on it whenever they want. We also built a kiln outside to fire their handiwork. We won't be able to use it until the snow melts. Until then, their pots sit on shelves in the back room."

"Well, that's wonderful." Then turning to Jack, Albert continued, "I really appreciate your rescuing me, but I do need that car towed so I can get back on the road. Who do I call for that?"

"I'm afraid you won't be going anywhere just yet. This is a major blizzard, expected to last through tomorrow. Nobody will be coming out until it's over. We have plenty of space for a visitor and we're glad to have you. You can sleep in Rose's room." Jack smiled at Rose, "Why don't you find the hammock and we'll hang it up so you can sleep here in the kitchen."

"Oh goodie! Finally. I've been begging to hang it inside. This will be fun." And the child went running off to retrieve the hammock.

"I hate to put you out like this. Also, I don't have any clothes with me."

"It's not putting us out at all. Listen, you and I are about the same size, you can borrow from me for the time being. Meanwhile, you must be hungry. We're about to eat and there's plenty for everyone."

Maria served up an onion and beef pie. Albert couldn't remember having tasted anything so delicious. "Wonderful meal. How did you do that?"

"I didn't. The meat comes from healthy cattle. The wild onions we picked last fall and stored in our root cellar. We just assemble the ingredients that the Gods provide," was her modest reply.

"Well, they certainly provide well. By the way, it looks like I won't be getting to the conference I was planning to attend. Could I borrow your phone one more time? Got to cancel my reservations and let the rental company know what happened." He didn't mention that he was also calling his pilot to update him. "I'll have to call my company in the morning."

After calling, Albert, one elbow on the table, head resting in his hand, began to doze off. Jack jumped up, "You must be exhausted. I'll change the sheets on Rose's bed and you can turn in."

The next day he woke to the sounds of somebody splitting wood, dishes clanging in the kitchen, and the piercing cries of a child throwing a tantrum. *This might be one of the reasons Nettie didn't want children,* he guessed.

A pair of Carhartt overalls, clean underwear, and a flannel shirt had been carefully laid out on the chair by his bed. *Guess those are for me,* he reckoned and put them on. It was like pulling on a new skin. He caught a glimpse of himself in the mirror. *Wow, and just who are you?* he thought, addressing his reflection.

Looking out the window, he saw the blizzard still raging. *What does one do all day when trapped in the house like this? I didn't see a TV or computer. No wonder the child is screaming.*

On entering the kitchen, he was greeted by the sight of Maria calmly washing dishes while Rose lay prone on the floor in her pink pajamas, legs kicking, fists pounding.

"Good morning!" he shouted over the racket.

Maria turned around. "Oh, I'm so sorry. Rose must have awakened you. She's a little out of sorts this morning."

133

"A little? Whatever is the matter with her?"

"Oh, she just wants to get into her room to feed her snake."

"Her snake? My God, is there a snake in there?"

"Oh, it's okay. Not to worry. He's in a terrarium. Can't hurt you anyway. He's not poisonous like some of the others around here."

"Why is she keeping a snake?"

"It's her pet."

Rose stopped crying and suddenly jumped up. "Want to watch me feed Blackie?" she asked Albert.

"Not really," he mumbled before deciding he really should be kinder. "Sure. What do you feed him?"

"Frozen mice. I'll get one now and show you."

Good God, what kind of family is this? Albert dutifully followed Rose into the bedroom where she pulled the cover off a terrarium by the bed. To his horror, he realized he had been sleeping next to an 24-inch black snake wrapped around a branch leaning against the glass. "Can he get out?" he asked.

"Only when I let him. Here, I'll show you." But that was too much for Albert who suddenly bolted from the room, declaring he was hungry and needed to eat.

"We have oatmeal or eggs," Maria announced. "What would you like?"

"Eggs sound find."

"Spring," she called, "Could you get me a couple of eggs?"

Spring came dragging in from the other room. "I'm right in the middle of the best part of my book. Do I have to?" she whined before she stopped and realized their guest was standing by the stove.

"Maybe I could get them instead," he said. "Just tell me where they are."

134

"See, Mom? He wants to go, so let him."

"You may need some help," she said, turning to Albert.

"Of course not. Just head me in the right direction."

"Okay," Maria continued, a smile on her face. "Walk down the hall, take the door at the end. That will bring you onto a covered walkway leading to several sheds. You want the second one on the right."

Albert followed her directions. He found himself outside but protected from the storm by a roof and wall on one side. The chopping got louder as he walked along. *Must be Jack in there splitting wood.*

He opened the next door assuming he would find a refrigerator. He did not. Instead he found a shed full of chickens. *So that is why Maria was smiling. Okay. I can do this, can't be that hard... just need to reach under a hen and grab an egg or two.* He proceeded to do so but Ma Hen was not happy. She flew at him, claws raking his arm while she darted a couple of pecks at his face. Albert jumped back. "Maybe I don't want eggs after all," he said aloud. "But, Hell, I can't be outdone by a chicken." And so, he moved on to the next hen, persevered despite the outraged bird's attack, and met with success. "Victory! Breakfast!"

He returned to the kitchen, trying to act like he did this kind of thing every day. Maria looked at him, saw the scratch on his face, smiled and said, "Welcome to the ranch. I'll scramble those up right away." He was glad she hadn't suggested he cook them himself as he hadn't a clue how to do it.

"Feeling rested this morning?" she asked.

"Pretty good," he responded as he took a seat and dug into a plentiful breakfast. She left him to eat in silence. She was a woman of few words.

Just as he was shoveling in the last mouthful, Jack came back into the kitchen. "It must be tough for you being stranded like this. Maybe you want to help me with chores today? It might help pass the time."

Albert thought he might as well. It was still snowing hard and he clearly wasn't going anywhere. "Could I just borrow your phone one more time to call my company?" After alerting his Eastern office that he might be stuck for a day and couldn't be easily reached, he returned to the Western reality, rather enjoying the situation.

He spent the day helping Jack. The chores, foreign to him, were nevertheless invigorating. First, they carried armfuls of firewood from the shed to a big box by the kitchen stove. Not too demanding. His years of weightlifting were paying off. Then, struggling in the raging wind and snow, he helped Jack hook a sled to the snowmobile and load on bales of hay. Following directions, he got up on the back seat, this time well bundled up in a borrowed wool jacket and hat, as well as leather gloves and rubber boots. The frigid wind burned his face and he had to squint against driving snow. It was an exciting ride as they zoomed up small slopes, then dropped over the tops, each time Albert's stomach taking a sickening plunge. It beat any thrill on a roller coaster. They rode along a fence line until a few longhorns appeared, their heads lowered, tails to the wind, waiting motionless in the driving storm.

"How many cattle do you own?" asked Albert.

"This is it. You're looking at them. We're only sustenance farmers. Just raise enough to take care of family and friends." They unloaded the hay, got back on the snowmobile, and were headed back when an animal came bounding through the snow.

"My God, is that a coyote?" asked Albert, terror lacing his words.

"No-o-o, that's Nestor! Good dog. Come on, boy. We'll get you home." And Nestor, a yellow-brown, shaggy-haired dog came leaping toward them. "We'll give him a ride. He'll never make it that far in this snow." Jack tried to coax him onto the sled they were towing, but Nestor would have none of it. He kept jumping off. "Guess you're going to have to hold him. You're not afraid of dogs, are you?" asked Jack. *I sort of am,* thought Albert. *Don't know much about the big, dirty animals. But I'm not telling Jack that.*

"No, I'm fine with them."

With that, Jack leaned over, hefted the 70-pound dog in his arms and plunked him down on Albert's lap. Albert let out a groan as he and the dog were mashed together.

"Hold him so he doesn't jump off!"

Albert, stiff with fear, tentatively wrapped his arms around the beast. *How in the world did I end up like this? What would the staff at the office think if they saw me now? Uh-oh. The office. I was supposed to give them my decision on the Trammer deal. The Hell with that, I've got more important things to worry about right now, like how am I going to survive the ride back with this elephant in my lap.*

The dog began to settle down and leaned back on Albert, who, after a few minutes, also began to relax a little. He actually began to appreciate the warm furry animal, which was keeping him warm, despite the fact that the dog drooled long trails of saliva on his gloves.

When they arrived home, the girls were ecstatic. "You found him! You found good old Nestor!"

Albert was relieved when the dog jumped down. The girls threw their arms around Nestor, who, to Albert's horror, joyfully licked the children's faces with his long slimy tongue.

Lunch was waiting: stacks of tortillas. Albert was served a generous helping. Normally, he kept his noon meal to a salad, fearful of putting on weight. Now, he wolfed down every last bite.

Afterwards, he helped Jack clean out the chicken shed, a shitty mess if ever he smelled one. Then, there was more wood to split. At first Albert just watched until Jack asked if he'd like to try his hand at it. He would and he did. He had the strength, but needed instruction on technique. Then, he really got going. "I like this," he commented to Jack. "Be happy to carry on here for a while if you have other things you need to do." *Now, this is a healthy way to get exercise,* he thought to himself, *unlike workouts in the gym that produce nothing.*

"Great. Then I'll leave you to it. Don't chop off your leg. Glue won't fix that."

In the afternoon, back in the kitchen, the only room besides the bedrooms, Spring suddenly appeared from somewhere and begged to use the cell. "It's almost 4 o'clock."

"Here it is," said Maria as she handed it over. Turning to Albert, who was sitting at the table nursing a large mug of steaming black coffee, she explained. "We give her one hour a day to text friends and surf the web, then she has to give it back. We won't allow the internet to steal our children's youth."

Maria returned to silently stirring the tomato sauce bubbling in a large pan on the wood stove. Albert sat there watching her. It was peaceful and quiet in the room with only the swish of Maria's skirt as she moved around, the wall clock ticking and the dog sleeping on the floor giving an occasional whimper and flapping his tail as he dreamed.

Shortly after, Jack appeared with a laptop. *So, they do have one.* "Weather forecast calls for an end to this storm sometime tonight. We should be able to get you out of here tomorrow after the roads are plowed," he announced.

"I didn't realize you had a computer," Albert commented.

"Yah, we're not quite the hillbillies you may think," responded Jack.

"Oh, I didn't mean that," said Albert, trying to backtrack.

"We couldn't live here without one. I need it for my work and for weather forecasts. How we spend our days is often determined by the weather. It affects everything from crops to wildfires to transportation. I guess I didn't mention it. I teach at the West Canyon Agriculture College in Wade. We're on winter break right now. I use this time to write a follow-up to the book I published on the medicinal value of high desert plants. Couldn't keep data or do the writing without a computer. Summers I collect the plants for research. I use the labs at the college, as well as help from the students. It's a pretty good set-up, though I do miss not having a clinical setting. Ever since I met Maria and learned more about the medical needs of migrants, I've focused my botany studies on the healing attributes of these amazing plants."

Just then Rose dragged into the room, complaining of boredom. "Good," replied Maria. "If you need something to do, you can start by sorting the clothes for the wash."

"That's okay. I'm not really bored. Think I'll go get Blackie out and play with him."

Oh no, thought Albert, *how can I stop her from letting that damn snake loose.* Suddenly, he remembered the book in his briefcase.

"Listen Rose, I have something I could read to you. You want to hear it?"

139

"Sure," she replied, though not really sure at all. *What could this strange man have that she would want to listen to?* Albert retrieved his briefcase, sat in a wooden rocker by the stove, and pulled out a worn book: *A Child's Garden of Verses.* He began to read. Rose, who had remained standing, slowly moved closer to Albert, then plunked herself down on the floor near his feet. It would have been hard to decide which of them was enjoying the poems the most. Rose's eyes grew large as she listened. Each time he asked if she wanted to hear more, she begged him to go on until they had to stop for supper.

They had just finished eating when they heard a roar outside followed by silence and then someone pounding on the door. They opened it to a snow-covered burly man who boomed out, "Gonna let your neighbors freeze to death standing out here in the cold?"

"Dan, welcome. Where's your wife?"

"Right here behind me, hauling the fiddle out of the side saddle. You guys up for a little music tonight?" The couple came in, stamping their feet, shaking off snow and pulling off their coats. He was short and heavyset, his red flannel shirt stretched tight over a slightly round belly. She was stocky, dark-haired and wrapped in a brightly-colored Mexican shawl. Not five minutes later the fun began. Dan pulled out his fiddle, his wife shook gourds, Spring ran and got a drum, and Jack hauled out a harmonica. The music was at times rollicking and fast. Maria tapped her foot to the music until, restraining herself no longer, she got up and danced, red skirt whipping about her legs, elbows out, hands on her waist. Rose got up and danced as well. It wasn't long before Maria was beckoning Albert to join them. He had never danced like that before, but the music, the high spirits, and

140

wine all combined to overcome his inhibitions. He was soon up stamping his feet, trying to keep up with the music and grinning ear to ear. So began the evening, a far cry from the classical works Albert was used to hearing at the Lincoln Center. Late that night, the merriment wound down, the neighbors left, and the family turned in for the night.

The next day, Albert, the last one up, looked out the window on a calm, snowy landscape rising to towering jagged white mountains covered by a deep blue cloudless sky. It was as if the violent storm had never happened.

Jack was still at the table when Albert came into the kitchen. Over a hearty breakfast of eggs, bacon, and biscuits, Jack began asking Albert about his life back home. What did he do for a living? Did he have kids? Where exactly did he live? Albert answered as best he could. He listened to himself jabber on about his investment business, his home (he didn't mention he had three), his plane grounded because of weather (he didn't mention it was his own private plane) and his wife (he didn't mention they were barely on speaking terms). Somehow, it all came out as drivel to Albert's ears, sounding hollow and detached. He got tired of talking and, to change the subject, asked about Maria who had joined them for her third cup of coffee that morning.

"When I'm not taking care of things at home, I try to help the Mexican immigrants get healthcare. West Canyon college has an infirmary for its own students, but the nearest clinic for everyone else is 50 miles away. The immigrants need an advocate and they need rides to the clinic."

"What kind of work do they do?" asked Albert. "Are they illegal?"

"Yes, they're illegal," she responded. "Some are construction workers, some work on the ranches with cattle and horses. Many of the women work as maids. Folks hiring them are glad to have their skilled labor for cheap. However, they don't give a fig about their health. When they wear out, employers fire them and hire more. I try to do what I can."

A different perspective for Albert. It cast a new light on the immigrant problem.

Jack interrupted their conversation to say, "I haven't seen a plow come through. Wonder what's keeping them? School bus can't get here if they don't clear. And we've got to get you on your way, Albert. You must be good and ready to get back." *I don't know that I am*, Albert reflected but he said nothing.

"Better call someone," suggested Maria.

He retrieved his phone and checked the messages. "Huh! Avalanche closed the road last night. Guess you'll be here a little longer, friend," he said.

Just then the children, pretty good at overhearing parent conversations, came running into the room.

"Yeah! An avalanche! No school today!" they shouted in glee.

"An avalanche? Don't folks die in avalanches?' Albert asked in astonishment.

"If they're in its path they do," Jack said with a wink. "They happen here. We try to stay out of them."

"Listen, I hate to ask again, but can I borrow your phone to make a couple of calls?"

"No problem at all. Take it to Rose's room for privacy."

Albert dialed his office, talked with one of his partners, heard news on the Trammer deal. He had blown it. Missed a good opportunity. *Somehow, I don't really care. What's happening to me?* he wondered. He explained he wouldn't be back for another couple of days at the soonest. Next, he called his pilot. Lastly, he dialed Nettie and explained the same. She didn't seem especially upset. He hung up on the New York world.

Great wealth erases debt. Until now, Albert had been beholden to no one. For the first time, that was changing. Expressing thanks is more difficult than making a gift, he discovered. Being on the receiving end was a new and humbling experience requiring grace and humility.

"So, you're stuck with me for another day. Sorry about that. I appreciate your hospitality. Can I help around here with shoveling or something?" he asked.

"Sure. There's plenty to do. It's the girls' job to shovel a path to the compost. They're putting up a fuss, but they'll have to do it, nevertheless. Our garbage is starting to reek. But I can find plenty else to work on around here." And he did.

Albert helped Jack take apart and clean the chain saw, sharpen a couple of axes on the grinding wheel, put up a wall tool rack and, most intriguing, open up flower presses to carefully remove dried plants destined to be preserved under sheets of glass for later study. Another day swept past.

In the evening, Rose begged to hear more from *A Child's Garden of Verses*. As Albert began to read, not only Rose, but the rest of the family stopped what they were doing and sat to listen. Later, they pulled out a scrabble board, teamed up and played, what to Albert's surprise, was a rousing game. There was a little cheating, a lot of laughter, and plenty of antics on the part of the kids.

The next morning, a path through the avalanche had been cleared, the road plowed, and the school bus come and gone. All this before Albert had rolled out of bed.

"Good news. You can hit the road again," announced Jack as Albert walked into the kitchen. "I'll drive you to the airport."

Albert started to protest but Jack broke in, "Don't mind at all." Albert didn't protest too hard. He could have ordered his pilot to come pick him up, but he was looking forward to spending a little more time talking with Jack on the two-hour trip. To his surprise, he missed the kids, who had departed for school. His life had never included anything as uncontrollable as children. Now, he was surprised by how much fun they were, tantrums and all.

Once on the road, Albert looked over at the younger man. "It's like I slid into another universe. Great life here, more grounded. Got my blood pumping. You planned it well."

"Didn't plan, just happened. Like you, I slid into it. I was a visiting professor at West Canyon College. Met Maria... got her pregnant... felt obliged to stay. Position came open in the biology department. I got hired."

"Well, you picked a great wife."

"She's not my wife. We never married," responded Jack as he stared ahead, focusing on the narrow-plowed track cut through high walls of snow left by the avalanche. They were both silent for a moment, Albert wondering what was to prevent those walls from suddenly collapsing on them. He found the western landscape exhilarating, keeping him constantly alert.

"Oh. But she's the mother of both girls?"

"Yes, she is."

"Illegal?"

"Yes, and afraid of deportation."

"If you marry her, wouldn't she have a better chance for a green card?"

"True." There was another long pause during which Albert reached in his jacket pocket for sunglasses. The glare off the snow was blinding. He put them on and the landscape transformed into a dreamland of rose-colored clouds and distant snow-covered peaks. He was in no rush to reach the airport.

Jack continued. "I know I should marry her. She's hinted often. I just can't bring myself to do it."

"Huh," mumbled Albert. "I get that. Me, too. Lots of things I ought to do. Status quo sucks me back every time."

"You?" asked Jack.

"Yup." Albert stretched his legs and peered at an outcropping of ledge rising on one side of the road. "Like those jagged rocks. Life's hazardous. Damned if I can figure it out. But you, look what you've got: everything, including noisy kids." His smile was lost on Jack whose focus never veered from the road.

"Rosy glasses, Albert. We've never enough money, too many chores, little time for rest. I'd love more security, fly wherever I want, go to operas, concerts."

For a while, neither of them said a word. They had brought coffee along, but had forgotten to drink it. Albert reached down, carefully picked up a black travel mug and handed it to Jack, who grabbed it in his calloused hand and took a swig.

After another 10 minutes, Albert broke the silence. "Marry her! What's keeping you?" he burst out.

Jack took his eyes off the road, glanced over at Albert. "Bullheaded. Afraid of risk."

"We have that in common. You know? I'd love to live like you do," proffered Albert.

"You're such a romantic," commented Jack. "I had you pegged the minute you pulled out those Stevenson poems. By the way, you read them well. You had us entranced."

Just then the car hit a bump, spilling Jack's coffee in his lap. "Good thing that was getting cold or there'd be no more kids for me," he laughed.

For a while, Albert brooded on his own many houses, his plane, his yacht, and the emptiness. *Back home, it was all image. Talk only of politics, sports, and money. Out here, folks seem friendlier, more practical. And Maria, helping migrants with healthcare. Impressive. What have I ever done for anyone other than myself? Yes, I guess he's right. I'm a romantic at heart. A discontented one at that.*

An idea had been simmering in his head for several hours. Suddenly, he gave it voice.

"What's the chance of West Canyon College building a medical clinic to treat the rural population?"

"None. It can barely pay its professors. Runs on a shoestring."

"What if someone donated the money for it? Would that be of interest?"

Once more, Jack's eyes had left the road to stare at his passenger as he wondered again just who this man really was.

"Do you think the college would go for something like that? Maybe include a nursing program," Albert continued.

This was too much for Jack. They were approaching a plow turn-around on the side of the road. He pulled into it, stopped the car, put it in park, and turned his head to face Albert. "Tell me more."

"Well, it's like this. I have plenty of money. I can do it. The fact is, I've never done much good for anybody but myself. I think I'm tired of the bottom line, tired of everything. I'm ready to make some changes. By the way, know anyone who could be its director?"

Jack, who was leaning forward resting his arms over the steering wheel, lowered them, leaned back in his seat and sat up.

"I do." Then he grinned at his seatmate as they high-fived one another.

Two months later, Albert, sitting in economy class, looked out the plane window as the clouds slipped by below. He remembered, as a youth, looking up at those clouds and dreaming of success, of wealth, of making it to the top.

Now, he was gazing down at the fluffy cumulus which seemed to be drifting east, even as he was slip-sliding west. In his carry-on were legal papers stashed under his wool shirts, Carhartts, and rubber boots.

Jack awaited him at the airport.

Harnessed

Rudy Jones was tall, dark, and not a bit handsome. He was, in fact, a stick of a man, topped with a nest of black hair framing a face you'd rather forget: squinty eyes, his nose sharp as a knife. Each morning, when he walked to work, neighbors peeked out from behind their blinds. He made them uneasy.

Rudy lived with his wife in a small house in a well-kept neighborhood among snow-white, pristine houses with sterile lawns and carefully-pruned pines. His wife Holly was short, wore a felt hat, and kept her head down when out shopping. That's all the neighbors knew about her. Rudy worked at the university, though precisely what he did, no one was quite sure. Some thought he was a clerk, but others said, for sure, he was the janitor. In any case, "nobody who was anybody" had ever heard of him. The truth was, he worked there in the science lab doing research, but who knew? Rudy was thought a "strange sort."

"Best keep your distance when you see him coming," warned Mrs. Vickson who lived down the street.

"He's an odd one. He doesn't fit in here at all," said Mr. Donner, the banker and head of the Neighborhood Watch. The greatest problem for this proper community, however, was that Rudy and his wife had noticeably brown-tinted skin. That added to the fodder of these well-behaved white folk when referring to their unwelcome neighbors. "How did they manage to have a house on our street anyway?" exclaimed saucy Ms. Kommet.

When Rudy came home after long workdays, he would fall into the arms of his loving wife. "Did you have a good day?" she would ask. The answer always the same: "It's slow, but I'm making progress. And what about yours?"

"I'm making progress, too." And she would tell him of the articles she had had published under a pseudonym, articles about culture and politics. She had a sharp mind and a critical eye, but cautiously kept her real name out of print.

"I'm so happy for you," her devoted husband would respond and the two of them would settle down to a modest meal, often eating in their tiny backyard where the birds serenaded them. They loved sitting under an ancient maple whose shade kept them nicely cool. Ferns grew around its trunk in unruly profusion. Interspersed through this wild garden were bright red geraniums that his wife planted each spring. The reds and greens reminded them of their favorite season: Christmas.

Rudy and his wife were rarely invited out. They had few friends. But there was one exception: Rudy had come to know the janitor, Paul, who cleaned the lab. The two of them became close, sharing similar outlooks on the academic world in which both were submerged. Paul cleaned up the detritus left behind by those of higher education. He learned a lot in the process. Rudy and Holly often invited Paul for supper. He came with pleasure. Mostly they talked of science, philosophy, and religion. Sometimes they played horseshoes.

The years passed without much change until the time Rudy came home with a new response to the usual, "How did the day go, my dear Rudolph?"

"Incredible! I have finally discovered the key to a problem I've been working on all these years. It won't be long until I publish my findings." Of course, in science, that can be quite a while. It was the case this time, as well. However, one year later, he published. The article, peer reviewed as were his earlier ones, appeared this time in the prestigious journal *International Science Research*.

The reaction was immediate. Praise poured in from the world over. Rudy, his wife, and Paul celebrated with champagne and a favorite dinner cooked by Holly: wild herb sauce over poached eggs served on cooked oats with a side of field salad greens.

Then, it was back to their daily routine. But not for long. Less than a year later, the phone rang at their home and Rudy picked it up. Holly heard her husband say, "Is this some kind of joke? Who are you?" Then silence while he listened. Then again, "How can I know you are who you say?" Another long silence, then a great wide grin cracked his angular face. His hand smacked his head as he said, "Wow and wow! Thank you, thank you. I'm overwhelmed."

He had won the Nobel Prize for discovering the key toward the development of a special type of screen. When a person stood before it, bones showed up white, healthy tissue green, and unhealthy body parts would light up in varying shades of red, depending how severe the illness. Recognition came with a tidy purse as well.

It was a joyful and lively evening. For the first time ever, supper was interrupted by continuous phone calls, some from colleagues congratulating him, others from reporters.

The newspaper blazed out headlines: *Local man wins international award*. Suddenly, the Joneses were wined and dined everywhere, but not without Paul. "By the way, who is that other man that always appears with him? Bit of an embarrassment," declared Mrs. Vickson. But Rudy knew something about prejudice. He insisted their friend come along.

Then, how the neighbors loved him, as they shouted out in glee while emerging from their doors to offer congratulations.

"Oh," said Mr. Donner, "I always knew Rudolph (for now he was suddenly called by his formal name) was brilliant." Holly was invited to coffee gatherings, given by the saucy Mrs. Kommet. Acquaintances competed with one another, trying to own a piece of him by declaring to all who would listen, "We always knew he was brilliant." Old Mrs. Vickson cooed, "Oh yes, Rudolph is a particularly good friend of ours. Such a fine, distinguished-looking gentleman."

Rudolph was promoted to director of his lab and frequently interviewed by science writers on radio and TV. Folks all tried to keep up with the Joneses.

Delighted with his new notoriety, Rudolph flourished, much like the brilliant red flowers in the garden. In fact, he more than flourished. He stood a little taller, raised his head higher, and almost pranced to work. However, his forehead became furrowed under the weight of his fame which was branching out in all directions. His face took on a slight flush and, strangest of all, his long sharp nose began to fill out. It acquired an unmistakable reddish hue.

Dealmaker

Though rent was late, taxes overdue, and his car rusting, Joe insisted on Pinot Grigio and a lobster dinner. Growing up, it was hot dogs, chips, and soda. "I'll never go back," he said.

"Back" was where shadowy streets were lined with drab high-rise tenements. There, at noon only, sunshine spilled down into the canyons when it briefly shone on children jumping rope and playing tag on crumbling sidewalks. Joe's childhood was full of gun shots, sirens, street fights, and fear. It was all cement and asphalt, unless you noticed the few strands of grass struggling to push up through pavement cracks. His parents had migrated to the U.S. to escape the violence in Bosnia, only to end up in this borough of New York. It was the only place they could afford. Poorly paid work, mounting bills, and high rent marred their lives. Stress built up. Joe's father moved out. His mother stayed. What else could she do? She raised her two sons. Meals bought with food stamps had to stretch far. Pizza was a treat which, on rare occasions, brought relief from days and days of hot dogs and beans. Her English barely passable, she found it hard to find work. "Anyway, if I get job," she would say, "what I do with kids?"

Joe (his mother had insisted both children be given American names) was 11 years old when he was hired to sweep the sidewalk in front of the local bodega. A skinny, dark-haired kid, he had felt grownup and proud of his earnings. "Close your eyes and hold out your hands," he would say to his mother. She would

152

pretend not to know why. Then he would drop into her palm the handful of change he had earned.

"Oh Joey, you no steal?" she repeated each time. He, laughing and proud, would reply, "No, Mama, I earned it all myself. It's for you." He never told her about threats from gangs which he had to endure when he walked home with his earnings. He knew his parents had come here to escape violence, unaware that America had its very own dangerous territory as well. Why worry her more? Sometimes he thought it would be a lot easier to give in, join, sell drugs, steal, and provide his family with the good life they never had. But, when he thought about doing that, he imagined his mother's heartbreak. She tried so hard to raise her boys to be good, honest citizens. "America a great place. We move here so you be safe and make it big," she frequently repeated.

His mother had struggled to keep their small flat clean, but could not keep ahead of the rats tunneling through walls, or battalions of cockroaches who swarmed the apartment at night. Days on end, she gazed out the window at a brick wall not 10 feet away. From good solid farming stock, she was a slightly plump woman with long dark hair pulled back in a bun and a lined face that still showed traces of the beauty she had once been. She dreamed that one day she could look out on trees and fields like the ones she left behind in the old country.

Such was Joe's start. When he was six, he eagerly began school. By the time he was sixteen and in high school, his enthusiasm had dried up. He, like many others, was an indifferent student. Distracted by the struggle to survive the dangers of his neighborhood, he was less than alert in class. His younger brother coped by joining the fray. He was street savvy. "You gotta learn to deal," Frank would tell Joe. "Bargain for what you want. Be a player. Don't get pushed around. That's how you survive. It's all about getting the other guy before he gets you."

The only thing that stirred Joe was sports. He loved basketball. Afternoons and weekends were spent on a nearby court, playing hard-driving games with neighborhood friends. The nets on the hoops had long ago been ripped away. It didn't slow down the kids at all.

One day, walking home from school, he stopped to watch the construction of a steel structure to support yet another high rise. One of the burly workers standing nearby noticed his interest and ambled in his direction. "Ever watched a building go up before?" he asked.

"Yeah, of course," Joe replied, trying to sound cool. The seasoned worker was not put off by his response. He began to point out details about the project. He spoke of excavation, beams, blueprints, and where he himself fitted in as a welder. "The pay is good," he told Joe. "By the way," the welder said, "I learned the trade in a program offered not far from here." Joe tried not to show it, but was, nevertheless, impressed. This was the first man who had bothered to explain anything to him in all the years since his father had moved out. *Wow. Maybe I can do that too,* he thought. *Be like this guy.*

At school the next day, he mentioned welding to a friend. One of his teachers overheard. Happy to know that something had finally sparked her student's interest, she suggested he think about transferring to a trade school and learn the skill himself.

He did. He loved the welding lessons and at 18 years old, graduated first in his class. Awarded financial aid, he continued on to a program which earned him a Master Structural Steel Welding certificate. For the second time in his life, he felt proud of his accomplishments.

Training completed, he began work as a welder and, as a result, developed more muscle. His skinny frame filled out and his clean-shaven face, framed by a crew-cut, became less angular. He wasn't especially handsome, but not ugly either. A few months later, he joined the union. Pay was good, more than he had ever dreamed of making. Finally, he could do for his mother and younger brother Frank what his father had never done: move them into a modern one-bedroom apartment away from the neighborhood where they grew up.

"That Joey, he such good boy. Take care of us so we never hungry again," exulted his mother.

Things were going well until Frank dropped out of school and began hanging around back in his old neighborhood. Drinking, then drugs, were his answer to hardship. Many the night he would stagger home at 2, waking his mother from the couch in the living room where she slept so Frank could have the bedroom. He'd demand she fix him supper.

"If Joey is such a great guy," he would slur, "why doesn't he live here? On no, he's too good for the likes of us."

"Oh Frankie, we okay. You give me money when you can. We eat, we live in safe place. I can see tree out the window. What more could I ask? Joe, he need be free. Maybe girlfriend."

Joe was swept up by the union, amazed to hear members talk about fair pay for workers, safety regulations, vacation days, and healthcare. He had never thought about those things before, much less as rights and something everyone deserved. He became fanatic about worker justice and rose in the ranks, soon becoming secretary of the local chapter. He kept the minutes and submitted articles to the chapter newsletter. Some of the guys were barely literate, rarely read so much as a newspaper. They began to look to Joe to explain union policies and issues. Some of the language was even difficult for Joe to understand.

I can do better, he thought. *Maybe I should take an English course.* A few weeks later, nervous but determined, he took himself to the local Y where it was suggested he sign up for an evening class. The other students seemed to know so much more than he did. It was humiliating. However, the instructor was encouraging. "If you want to learn more, if you want to write well... read, read, read. You have talent, you just need time." Joe began to check out books from the local library. The more he read, the more he realized how little he knew. The unthinkable slowly began to be thinkable: college!

How to go about doing that. Talking with his instructor, he learned that a local university offered night classes. "It won't be easy but well worth the effort. You can do great things with a degree."

Joe started night school. Between work and classes, he had little time for his family or dating. Frequent phoning kept him in touch with his mother. She tried, but could not understand why he wasted his time on school when he was already making good money. Joe tried to explain but his words fell on deaf ears. Frank just scoffed at the whole thing.

It took six years but at age twenty-eight, he graduated. His mother, Frank and his girlfriend Marie, attended the graduation ceremony, sitting on metal chairs in a large gymnasium converted for the occasion. His mother had given special attention to looking her very best for the occasion. She wore her Sunday outfit: green rayon dress with a wide black plastic belt. From her arm hung a large matching fake leather purse. She tried to show appreciation for Joe's accomplishment but, having managed well enough until now, she wondered why he had wasted his money on all that highbrow stuff. Frank sat slumped in the chair next to her, his hair greased and askew, his worn denims tucked into black boots. When the speeches started, he took out his cell, locking his eyes on the screen. Marie looked dazzling in black tights and a sparkling silver top. Sitting up straight, her long dark hair tossed back so she could clearly see each speaker, she listened to every word they spoke.

After celebrating at Tony's Italian Restaurant, Joe drove his mother, brother, and Marie back to their apartment in his new shiny red Ford-F150 pickup. Frank refused to be impressed, but his mother was. "You buy new?" she asked in amazement, "I never ride in new truck before. It nice!"

"So, what do you need a truck for?" grumbled his brother. "Planning to retire to the country?"

Marie spoke up, "Oh Frank, I would love it if you bought a truck. It's beautiful! And look what your brother has achieved. The first in the family to go to college. He's educated!" Frank rolled his eyes, but it did start him thinking.

The next date with Marie did not go so well. "I'm sick of hearing about Joe's success," said Frank. "So, what if he makes a bundle. Let him. He owes us all for getting where he is today."

"I don't think you should get so mad. I think you could do the same, if you really wanted. But, if you don't, then I'm out of here. I need some comfort in my life."

That ended their relationship until Frank had an awakening. *Maybe there is a way for me to make some quick money and get Marie back. I'll find a small job as a cover, but make some real dough on the streets. I've already got the contacts. Time to get in on the game.*

He found work as a night clerk in a downtown hotel. That left him free to pursue his more lucrative career. It also brought Marie back into his arms.

Meanwhile, Joe continued his welding, earning good pay. However, he was no longer satisfied with being a laborer. He began to see fellow workers and his brother as somewhat ignorant. *After all, I'm educated.* He naively believed that his learning was complete and that few others shared his level of knowledge. He started scouting around for a new kind of job. To his surprise, the world out there was not as impressed with his degree as he thought it should be. Night after night, Joe could be found sitting before his laptop filling out applications for work as editor, public relations director, college professor. When midnight rolled around, he would shut everything down, take a beer out of the fridge and sink onto his new leather sofa to watch basketball game reruns. His attempts at finding a new job were unsuccessful. Still he plowed on. *It's just a matter of time,* he told himself, *until someone discovers me.*

But time can be cruel. While months streamed by with no results, his brother's fortunes began to change. Suddenly, a lot of money was pouring into Frank's pockets. "Mama," he said one day, "how would you like to move to a two-bedroom apartment with Marie and me? I'm looking at one in the suburbs that you'll love. It includes a pool you can use whenever you want. I've already talked to Marie and she wants you to join us. She likes you a lot." Half-lie.

"Why do we have to take your mom with us? She's happy where she is. I was hoping that luxury place would be just for the two of us," Marie protested when Frank first told her his plan.

"Because I say so. She comes or the deal's off," he answered. Marie took the deal.

Of course, Mama was thrilled. She was impressed that her son was paid so well for clerking. "This wonderful America, land of opportunity. I always knew happy would be here," she said, momentarily turning off her soap opera to celebrate with another cup of coffee and a slice of the chocolate cake that Joe had dropped off for her.

"You're messing with Mama just to look good in her eyes. What happens when you go down? What happens then?" Joe asked his brother at Dino's Pizza Parlor over lunch.

"Oh," said Frank, mumbling around a pizza slice he had just stuffed in his mouth, "I'm sure you'll be the hero who saves her apartment and explains how I got caught. You always were her star!"

"I'd rather she never know where your big bucks come from," his brother returned, as he poked at a Caesar salad. "It would be the death of her. You're going to end up in major trouble."

"So, now big brother has a college degree, he's suddenly going to tell me how to live?" Frank blurted out. "No way, man. There's another world out there that you know zip about. If you think you do 'cause you have a degree, you're dead wrong," he said as he stood up, slammed cash down on the table and stalked out.

I no longer belong in this blue-collar crowd, thought Joe. *Education has lifted me to a different class of folks.* However, prospective employers didn't seem to appreciate that fact. It might have been his lingering Bronx accent, or perhaps a certain swagger that marked him as an upstart. Employers, looking for cool subservience, repeatedly turned him down. Though his frustration grew, his confidence remained high.

He moved to a better neighborhood, had a nice one-bedroom apartment, but few friends. Between welding work and looking for new employment, there was little time for socializing. What he did not realize is that most good jobs come through personal contacts. Socializing is how to find them.

One Saturday morning, when he was sitting in his neighborhood coffee shop perusing the want ads, he felt a tap on his shoulder. Turning around, he saw one of his former English professors standing there. "Joe, what a surprise. Good to see you."

"Oh, Mr. Morse, sir," said Joe, pushing back his chair and standing up to shake hands.

They shook, then stood a little awkwardly until Mr. Morse said. "Are you waiting for someone?"

"Not really."

"Mind if I sit down then?"

"Of course not," replied Joe, happy that his professor wanted to talk with him. "Go ahead."

Mr. Morse pulled out a chair, then took off a yellow nylon parka and hung it on the back before sitting down. Joe noticed his black track suit and Nikes. "Been running?" he asked.

"Yes. I took a new route through the park today, came out on Bank Street and saw this coffee shop. I've never been here before. You live in the area?"

"I have an apartment just up the street. I get my breakfast here before heading out to work," said Joe.

Mr. Morse stood up. Tall and gangling, he towered over the room. "I need some brew. Be right back," and he headed for the counter. *These runners,* thought Joe, *look like someone needs to feed them before they die of starvation.* Morse soon returned,

160

folded himself back into the chair and took a sip of coffee. "So, Joe, what have you been doing with yourself since you got your degree?"

Joe pulled himself up a little straighter, took a sip of his own coffee, stared over the rim of his mug and replied, "Don't know if you knew, Mr Morse, but I do welding work. It's paying the bills while I apply for something better. Something using my degree."

"Drop the Mr. Morse, it's Ray now. What kind of jobs are you applying for?"

"Public relations, editor, director of development."

"Any bites yet?"

"Not yet, but it takes time."

Ray sat staring across the room for a good full minute before he turned to look at his former pupil. "You want some advice?"

"Sure, I guess. Whatever."

Ray picked his words carefully. "Look, I like you, like your spunk. When you switch careers, you've got to start small and work up. Maybe you should try working as a reporter, use it as a stepping-stone. After a couple of years, try to move on from there."

"A reporter? You mean like for a newspaper? Running around taking orders and writing about petty thefts and PTA functions? You're kidding, aren't you?"

"Well, not really. Before you go for the big stuff, you have to do the grunt work."

"I've had enough of that, sir."

"I hear you but, still, think about it. You can do great things."

I like Mr. Morse, but he's obviously never spent his life struggling the way I have. What does he know about grunt work? I could teach him a thing or two, Joe reflected. Then, he tipped his chair back, ran his fingers through his hair, slammed forward again, set both fists firmly on the table and looked Ray in the eye.

"I know you mean well but I didn't study all these years to end up as someone's lackey."

After his meeting, months passed with little change in job prospects, but a big change in Joe's social life. On lunch break one day in July, he had stopped in at a neighborhood barber to get a trim. The barber was a young woman, Sophia. She and Joe had hit it off right away. They had been going out together ever since.

Sophia was a curvy, big-breasted beauty with curly, long blonde hair. Joe told friends she had the heart and face of an angel. He was madly in love with her. She was impressed with him as well, though one would be hard pressed to know if it was Joe himself she loved, or the fact that he lived in an up-and-coming neighborhood, had a modern apartment, was college-educated, and took her out for fancy meals. "This is how the upper classes eat," he told her. "Welcome to our world." It was all new to Sophia. People she knew were lucky if they managed to finish high school, and they certainly didn't eat out like that very often.

"He's really smart," she told her friends. "He's going to make it big!" And to Joe she cooed, "I've always liked educated people. You're the best."

September rolled around and Joe was back at the crowded neighborhood coffee shop having his croissant and quiche breakfast. He looked up to see his professor standing there, coffee mug in hand, this time in dark khakis, white shirt, and tie. "Good morning," said Ray "How are you doing?" He pulled out a chair and sat down.

"Great," replied Joe, his standard reply when asked that question.

Ray smiled and said, "How's the job hunt going?"

"Going great, sir," Joe replied again, sounding a bit like a parrot.

"Getting some leads?"

"Sure, it's going."

"I'm glad I found you again. I never got a phone or email address last time we met. I wanted to contact you. One of our adjunct professors was taken seriously ill just before classes were scheduled to begin. Menard College is desperate to find a replacement before next week. I remember you once wrote an excellent paper about the fun you had coaching teenagers on the basketball court. You're good with young people and a good writer as well. This job would be your chance to break into the academic world."

"What kind of classes would I teach?"

"It would be two classes three days a week in beginning English. Interested?" asked Ray.

Joe tried not to sound overly eager. "Sure. When do you need an answer?"

"Now. As head of the English Department, I can move your application along fast. But I need someone right away. If you're not interested, I need to get on with looking."

"Put that way. I guess I'll say yes. How's the pay?"

"Not great when you're an adjunct, but it's a beginning. There's a lot of potential here for you to move up."

After Ray left, Joe sat a little longer. *A professor! Awesome! Now I'm getting somewhere. I'll cut back the welding job to two days. That will still give me some extra income until I can go full time at the college.*

When he returned home that evening, he called Sophia to relate the good news. "Oh Joe, I'm so proud! You'll be a real professor. I always knew you would succeed. How's the pay?"

"Well, in the beginning, not so good, but that will change when I go full time. Until then, I'll pick up some extra with a bit of welding."

There was little time to get ready for his new job and give notice at work that he would only be available two days a week.

Ray, who stepped in to help him prepare his classes, had guessed right about this newest member of his department. Joe got off to a mostly smooth start and related well to his freshmen students. They liked him and, for the most part, seemed to enjoy his teaching. Menard was a Community College and many of the students were the first in their families to seek a degree in higher education. Joe knew what that was like. He coached and encouraged. He could relate to their dreams, even more perhaps than Ray, who had come from a privileged background.

Joe's love life was also streaming along nicely. *Maybe,* he thought, *I would appear more serious if I give up bachelorhood.* He proposed to Sophia. She was ecstatic! "Yes, oh yes," she answered. "How soon can we marry?" Joe wasn't quite that far along in his thinking. Engagements typically lasted a year in his view.

"Soon, babe. I just need to get settled in my new career. Ray likes the work I'm doing and promised to add another class next September. Then, I'll be almost full time. After that, he'll probably add one more class the following semester. Once he does, my salary will go up and I'll get benefits as well."

"Joe, I'm so excited. You're such a success. I can hardly wait till we're hitched."

It was a tough year, preparing two English classes three times a week, correcting papers, attending faculty meetings, putting in two days a week of welding, and trying to make time for Sophia.

But it would all be worth it in the end. Professor! He was on his way.

When the following August rolled around, Ray called him into his office. Joe took a seat in a wooden chair across from Ray's desk, leaning forward eagerly.

"You've done well this last year. The students are enthused. You clearly have a knack for teaching and a good deal of patience as well."

"Thank you. A lot of the students are the first in their families to go to college. That was the case for me as well. I understand their struggles."

"Good. You ready to take on a third class?" asked his mentor, as he tipped back in his chair.

"Yes sir, I can handle that. Advanced writing?"

"Glad to hear it. No, it would be another division of beginner English. It takes time to work your way up to other courses. And while we're talking, I wanted to bring up something else." Ray stood up, shoved his hands in his pockets and stared down at Joe. "Have you given thought to working on a master's degree?"

"Not really. I have a pretty heavy schedule with teaching and a part-time job. Not many hours left over for extra study."

"Well, I suggest you find a way to squeeze in the time. The college will pay for it and help you on your way."

"Thank you, sir. I'll think about it."

"I'm serious, Joe. Do more than think about it."

Joe left the office with a smile, but fuming inside. When he saw Sophia that night, he let it all hang out. "They think they're going to push me back into school again! No way! I've earned my position. I'm a good teacher and they know it."

165

"Of course they do," said Sophia as she sat in his living room and took another drag on her cigarette, stamping it out on the top of a beer can. "Say, when are you going to get a bigger apartment, this isn't good enough for a professor. You should have at least two bedrooms and a balcony, too."

"All in good time. You'll see. Next year Ray will give me a 4th class. That will make me full time with a big salary."

"He better. So, when are we getting married? You said a year but it's almost a year now. A girl can't wait forever, you know."

"Sure, babe, I know. Adjunct professors hardly get paid enough to cover their commute. Next year I'll be making the salary I'm due. Then we'll have a grand wedding and a fancy new apartment! You'll see. You won't be sorry for the delay."

Two days later, the phone rang. It was Frank. "Hey Bro, what's up?" Joe said.

"Nothing much. Just thought we could get together for a meal tonight. Haven't seen you in a bit. You up for it?'

"Sure, but I can't stay out too long, I have papers to correct."

"Hey Joe, get a life. You work too much. I'll pick you up at six."

Joe was waiting when a white BMW pulled up at the curb. *Wonder who the dude is*, he thought, when his brother stepped out of the car and beckoned him over. "Ready? Hop in." Frank, steering with one hand, sent the car hurtling down the street, horn blowing as he wove in and out of traffic.

"Like it?" Frank asked, glancing over at his passenger.

"Sure, it's nice, but what did you do to earn it?"

"Got smart. Played the streets. The dough is rolling in."

"You know Mama would be crushed if she knew what you're up to. How can you live with yourself, knowing all the lives lost to drugs?"

166

"Don't be a mama's boy. Grow up! I don't force anyone to buy the stuff. This is the real world and I live with myself just fine. You have to know how to play the game. Like I told you, it's all about the deal." They stopped for supper at Tony's. The brothers, living such different lives, had little to share with each other. Their conversation was stilted. When the food arrived, they both, with a sense of relief, focused on eating. Supper didn't last long.

Back in the car, Joe said, "Listen, Frank, take a big brother's advice. Get out of that racket while you can. It's dangerous and criminal."

"I'll think about it," said Frank as he pulled up to the curb and his brother spilled out of the BMW back into his own world again.

The following week, Joe heard that the basketball coach had had a heart attack and would be needing an assistant. *Wow, there's a sport I know like the back of my hand. Think I could help him out. It means less time with Sophia, but it'll get me points with the college. I guess Frank's right. Make an offer, get a deal. Sophia will understand.*

Joe got the coaching job. Sophia did not understand. "What do you mean we can't see each other except on Sundays. You took up coaching for that lousy extra pay? What are you, crazy?"

"Listen, I'm not crazy. I'm just playing the game. It's another step toward a full-time position. Wait a little longer. You'll see."

Joe was a good assistant coach, and he motivated the players, but his schedule was wearing him down. The year went by quickly for him, not so much for Sophia. She was getting impatient. So, one day in May, Joe stopped by Ray's office.

"Good morning, sir, do you have a minute?"

"Certainly, Joe, have a seat."

"I was just wondering about the schedule for next year. I hear that Professor White will be leaving. That means more classes to be covered. I could take on another one and would be glad to help out."

"I appreciate that, and you have done a good job. However, let me ask you again, are you ready to go for your master's?"

"As I said before, I don't really have time."

"Well, the decision on class scheduling is really not up to me. I think, at this point, you need to talk with the dean."

"Sure. I'll be glad to do that. I'll make an appointment right away." *Now we're getting somewhere,* thought Joe, as he stood up, shook hands with Ray and strode out the door.

The next week found Joe sitting in a dark-paneled office. Across from him, behind a massive oak desk, the dean leaned back in his leather chair, one hand stroking his gray goatee as he listened.

"First, I want to thank you for the privilege of working in this great college." Here the dean had trouble concealing a smirk. "And," continued Joe, "students respond well to my classes, if I do say so myself. They seem to like my teaching. Also, I've often heard them say how lucky they are to have a dean like you. In fact—"

"Excuse me Joe, but just what is it you wanted to see me about. I don't have much time."

"Yes, sir. I appreciate that. I'm short on time myself so I know how that goes…"

"Please, what is it you want?" asked the dean again as he leaned forward and began shuffling papers on his desk.

"Just this, sir. Now that Professor White will be leaving, I believe you will need someone to pick up his classes next fall. I would be happy to do that for you."

The dean raised his head to stare at Joe. "I'm glad you're bringing up the subject. It is one we need to discuss." Joe leaned forward in anticipation, arms on his knees, hands clasped together. "It has been brought to my attention that you are an excellent teacher and a good basketball coach, as well. I believe it has been suggested that you start working on your master's as a first step toward improving your position here. I don't think you clearly understand why you've been urged to do this. We at Menard have to meet certain accreditation requirements. One of those is that our full-time professors have a PhD, or are working toward one. This is not negotiable. While we appreciate your quality teaching, we cannot promote you to full-time. We're happy to keep you on as an adjunct but, under the circumstances, we can do no more than that. Should you decide to start studying for your master's and continue to a PhD, then come back and let me know. It's your only way forward."

Joe left the dean's office, head held high. He was irritated but felt far from defeated. *No way are they going to chase me back to studying again. I am as good a professor as any of them and they know it. I will find a way to a full-time job... just not quite sure how yet.*

That night he called his mother, as he did every day. He was a good and loving son.

"How are things, Mama? Life treating you okay?"

"My life good but I miss you. Come soon, Joey. Your brother good but not here much."

"Why, where is he?"

"Out working late at night. I watch a lot TV."

"And Marie? She treating you well?"

"Marie? Yeah, but she move out yesterday. Frank moody, not happy."

"What happened?"

"Don't know. I think another man. Marie friend for me. I going to miss her."

"Mama, do you see other people too?

"Yeah. I see lots people at pool when swim."

"Do you talk to them?"

"No. I just see them."

A week later, Joe called his brother. "Heard about Marie. Sorry Bro. Listen, we've got to talk about Mama. I think she's really lonely, but she'll never admit it. What can we do?"

"Huh, I've been thinking about that, too, and I've actually looked into some senior housing places. There's one not far away... upscale housing. Everyone gets their own apartment and there's a communal dining room, a pool, gardens, and lots of activities. It costs a bundle, but I can afford it."

The brothers agreed it was better for her to be in a place like that. Mama howled. "Throwing me out! Don't do this to me!" But they did. And, to her surprise she loved it. "That Frankie, he such good boy. He put me in beautiful home, lots friends here. When you going do well like him?" she asked Joe.

Her words hurt. "But Mama, I *am* doing well. I'm a college professor and spend my time with educated people." It was out of Mama's realm, beyond her comprehension.

Another year came and went, so did the extra English classes. They went to a new hire with a PhD. But even worse, Sophia went, too. "Enough," she said. "Promises, promises."

Damn! She's such a pessimist. I'll get that full-time position yet if I keep making myself useful. If I hang in, they'll give in, Joe told himself as he stared in the mirror and patted down the new mustache and goatee he now sported. But meanwhile, his welding, due to a heavy schedule, was down to one day a week. Poor pay as an adjunct had forced Joe to move from his beautiful place into

170

something he could afford. Affordable meant a cheap studio apartment distant from the campus. An hour commute was added to his daily routine. However, he insisted on shopping only at green markets and Whole Food Stores, everything organic. He was learning from colleagues that pollution and climate change were threatening the future. *Educated folks pay attention to these things,* he realized. He picked his groceries carefully. *No more hot dogs for me. Professors don't eat that stuff.* This cut even further into his budget.

Then came the hardest blow of all. He and his brother had met for a meal at Frank's latest favorite restaurant, a rather pricey one. He hoped his brother would offer to pay. But that was not the worst thing about the evening. It was the news that Frank was getting married. "Great!" said Joe, "Who's the lucky gal?"

"Sophia. Look, you gotta understand. She wants the good life I can provide. It's nothing personal."

"The Hell it isn't. How lousy! She's leaving me to marry an outlaw! Crime may buy you everything, but it doesn't buy respect. If Mama ever knew, it would kill her."

"Ah! But here's the good news. With all the money I made, I've started investing in stocks. The bucks are rolling in like never before. I've gone clean. No more drugs. I can now give major donations to worthy causes, like education, museums and research."

"Unbelievable! How do you live with yourself knowing how you did this?"

"Joe, you're a good guy but naive. Who pays for Mama to live in luxury housing? Who drives a BMW? Who's paying for dinner tonight? Who has the penthouse with a garden roof?

"Hey!" said Joe. "Did you move?"

"Yup. Last week. You'll have to come over. Like I said, it's all a game. Most of those big time CEOs who give so generously of their fortunes, how do you think they got them? By exploiting everyone else. Before they helped the needy, they were brutally greedy. But do people remember? No. First they fall on their knees worshiping the rich, then they beg for handouts. They don't care where the wealth came from. Time you face reality. Stop 'drivin' your life away, lookin' for a better way' as Eddie Rabbit used to sing."

Later, at home, Joe thought seriously about his brother's words. *No,* he concluded, *I'll do it my way. I've worked hard for my degree, never abused anyone, tried to always be honest... can hold my head high... have joined the educated of the world. I'll never go back.* But traces of his past still stuck to him like gum to his shoes. He couldn't shake them free. *A deal,* he thought, *I've just got to make that deal.*

Meanwhile, though his rent was late, taxes overdue, and his car rusting out, he insisted on Pinot Grigio and a lobster dinner. *After all,* he said to himself, *I deserve it.*

The Skier

"I'll check with you when I get down again. Please don't leave until I'm back." Words that haunted his years. Words he could not erase. Words he had shared with no one, not even his wife. How to live with those words. Robert could give classes on the subject. After all, he had survived their shadows until now. Ski bum in his early twenties, back to school in his late twenties, married in his thirties, history teacher in his forties, published writer in his fifties, washed up in his sixties.

He and Mary had a son, Mark, who had grown up and become, to Robert's dismay, a banker. "Pure materialist," commented Robert about Mark. "No concern for other folks." The two had grown apart from one another. Mark visited home infrequently.

We prop ourselves up with ideology, thought Robert, *but no matter title or position, we cannot escape the dark side of our own humanity*. He didn't think his son had discovered that yet. He would like to talk about those things with him, but hesitated. Robert's wife accused him of being too somber, too moody, too pessimistic.

"We see little enough of Mark as it is. Don't spread your gloom to him when he does visit," she said. "Don't rain on his parade."

In a way, Robert envied Mary. A slim blonde, she seemed to glide smoothly through life, her wheels well-greased with tact and diplomacy, her mind focused on how best to wash the dishes, which days to volunteer, and what to bring for potluck dinners.

He, on the other hand, cared little about such things. Sometimes he just wanted to climb a tree, carefree and mindless as when he was a child, each branch a step higher into the murmuring green leaves, beyond the reach of worry and guilt. But age pours cold water on the fires of youth. His agility diminished, he believed that was all in the past. Though still rugged looking with close-cut dark hair, a broad face, and a short, flared nose, he felt he was in the shade now, where the tree yields and the shadow takes over.

Reality is the present, he told himself. *All else is in my head.* However, that was the problem. It *was* in his head, lodged there, skiing through his conscience. He had done well in college, married, and with a modest income, managed to support his family. The early years had been busy: raising their son, caring for a home, working his job. Then, surprised at the popularity of his published book about America's expansion into the West, he had retired from the demands of teaching to focus on writing. He had looked forward to having his days to himself without others impinging on his time. He had relished the idea of doing more research, developing his creativity.

But now, Robert sat in his study. A blank computer screen stared him in the face. It was the first time in years that tasks ahead were not clearly defined. *What to write about? What will folks find as interesting as they did my last book? History or fiction? The publisher gave me two years. She thinks I can do this. It must be possible.*

Robert looked out the window. Fall leaves were drifting down, sprinkling the green grass with gold: beauty he had not noticed until then. The autumns before, he had been busy greeting students, preparing classes, attending meetings, and complaining about too much work. Now, freed of such obligations, dark clouds moved into the empty space. He had lost his way. Words would not come. He was adrift.

Mary tiptoed around the house, careful not to disturb her "famous author" in his study. She was curious to know what he was writing, but knew better than to ask. Robert was apt to flare up in anger, as he often did these days. She had made that mistake before. "What will your next book be?" she had innocently asked.

"Damn it!" he replied. "Why does everyone think it's their business to ask me that! I'll let you and the rest of the world know when I'm bloody well ready!" Later he regretted his brutal response, yet failed to tell Mary. The distance between them grew. They traveled different paths.

Days swam together. He would get up at seven, pull on sweatpants and a ragged gray sweater, then make his way downstairs to the kitchen where he would find Mary busy preparing coffee and oatmeal. They would sit down, eat breakfast and make plans; hers were to shop, to volunteer somewhere, or have lunch with a friend. His were always the same: write. He would politely kiss his wife goodbye, wish her a pleasant time with whatever endeavor she was undertaking, then shuffle off to his study, shutting the door and turning on the computer. He would progress no further. He spent a lot of time studying the design in the oriental carpet under his feet, even more time staring out the window.

One day, lifting his hands to the keyboard, he managed to tap out, "Earth is but a tiny dot in the endless universe of billions of stars in billions of galaxies. What do words matter when our entire planet teeming with life is no more than a fly speck, so inconsequential, so vulnerable? What difference one life, even Arthur's, when people die by the thousands? When war, starvation, drownings, and accidents rule the day?" Then he stopped, frozen in the past.

He could write nothing else. Not only were his days long and unproductive, his nights were as well. Unable to sleep more than a few hours, he would come wide awake, roll quietly to the edge of the bed so as not to wake his wife, swing his legs down over the side and in bare feet tiptoe out of the room to stand at the window in what was once his son's bedroom. He wore sweats and an old flannel shirt. His night attire differed little from his day one, nor did his routine. He would stare out the window. The moon and stars filled the blackness; his mind spun in circles.

One night, looking at the moon casting a pale light on the trees and yards, he caught a motion out of the corner of his eye, something down on the ground near his neighbor's house. He looked again; yes, something moving stealthily… near the bushes beside the modest white one-story house of Mike Case. He stared hard, tried to make it out when suddenly he noticed a second shadow sliding towards a nearby tree. No doubt now, he sprang into action. Running downstairs to grab the phone he had left in the kitchen, he dialed 911. It was 2:20 a.m.

"Two men sneaking toward my neighbor's house. He's at 514 Walnut Road. Come quick. Looks like they're planning a break-in."

Robert ran back to the upstairs window. Suddenly he heard sirens, though Mary, a sound sleeper, did not. The shadows bolted over a fence at the back of the property and were gone. He watched the police arrive, the lights come on next door. From where he stood, he couldn't see the front of the house but did see two officers, guns drawn, approach it. Two others circled to the back. Robert went downstairs, threw on a jacket, pulled on his sneakers and walked next door. "I was the one who called," he told the police. "I saw the men flee over the back fence."

"Thanks for reporting this. There have been several house robberies in this part of town, we came close to catching them tonight. Sooner or later we will."

Robert returned home to continue watching out the window. The officers went inside to talk to Mike, emerging a half-hour later, and leaving. *Wow*, thought Robert, *that was a close call. Can't wait to tell Mary in the morning. In fact, I think I'll follow up and pay Mike a visit tomorrow. I've never really talked to the guy except to say hello.*

The next morning, Robert arrived at breakfast wearing a pair of slacks and a long-sleeved shirt. "You're dressed to go out. How come?" asked Mary, a bit fearful of another explosive reaction.

"I am," he replied. Suddenly animated, he recounted all the details of the previous night's events. "I thought I'd pay Mike a visit, find out if he's okay. I'll give him a little time before I go. He may be sleeping late after a rough night."

"That's pretty frightening, happening right next door like that. Didn't think we had to worry about burglaries in this neighborhood. By the way, wish you'd gotten me up. Yes, you definitely should check up on Mike."

Robert paced the kitchen, walked into the living room, turned on the TV, listened to the news for a few minutes, turned it off again and resumed pacing. Finally, two hours later, he crossed the yard to his neighbor and rang his bell. Mike came to the door, a shock of gray hair hanging in his eyes, his face puffy and unshaven. "Just came over to check if you're okay," said Robert.

"Sure. Thanks for alerting the police. You want to come in for coffee?"

"Sure, if you're not too busy."

"That was a close call," said Mike. "Thanks for your help. The burglars had already broken the glass in a back window."

Robert talked with his neighbor a while before returning home. He had become rather antisocial since retiring from teaching, but after that first visit, he returned to see Mike often, looking forward to the breaks from his brooding and non-productive life. He refused to share with Mary that he was blocked, unable to write. After all, he was the successful professor, writer, family man.

Over at Mike's house, however, he was just another guy drinking coffee with a neighbor. They always sat in the bare kitchen, which displayed no curtains, no plants, no decorations, just drab green walls and old enameled appliances. A neutral place. The bond between the two men grew with conversations about politics, art, and history. Nothing personal. Robert found his neighbor unusually well-informed on a number of subjects.

Two weeks later, the police called to tell Mike that the burglars had been arrested. "That's a relief," he told Robert. "They were on drugs and desperate. It's so easy to slip over the edge when you're desperate."

Mike, a retired veterinarian, lived by himself, seemed to have no friends, and never spoke of any family. Robert came to realize there was more to this quiet neighbor than he knew. His curiosity was peaked. But, when he asked him about his past, Mike closed right down.

One day Mike asked Robert, "How's the writing going?"

"Oh no, I thought this was the one place I could escape that question," said Robert, waving his hands in frustration and accidentally spilling his coffee. He jumped up, grabbed a towel hanging by the stove and mopped up.

Mike sat where he was, undeterred. "That bad?" he quietly responded.

Robert sat very still; his jaw clenched and staring hard at his friend. "Seems there's no place in the world I can escape the prying. I thought you, at least, would leave me alone"

"Let's be honest, Robert, you've been curious about my past. What I'm asking here is no different. I have my reasons for not talking about certain things. You apparently have yours. Is it such a crime to want to know more about each other?"

This exchange was followed by a long silence. Finally, Robert pulled his outstretched legs from under the table, stood up, shook hands with Mike and said, "I'd better go."

Several weeks passed without the two seeing one another, except to politely wave in passing. Then one day, Mike showed up at his neighbor's front door. Mary answered the bell, saw her pale, stooped neighbor, thought maybe he was ill.

"Is your husband home?"

"He is, but he's in his study writing. He doesn't like to be disturbed."

"Could I ask you, this one time, to disturb him for me? I'd like to talk with him."

"Oh, I couldn't do that. He would be furious."

"Then how bout you let me disturb him myself?"

Mary stared down at her shoes, shifted her gaze back to Mike. "I wouldn't recommend it but, if you insist, go ahead." She held the door open for her neighbor, led him down a flowery, wallpapered hall to a white wooden door. She pointed to it, smiled, held up crossed fingers and tiptoed away. Mike knocked. Nothing. He knocked louder and waited.

"What do you want now?" came a roar from inside.

"It's me, Mike. I need to talk."

"Can't, I'm busy."

"Please. Just for a moment."

A long silence ensued, then Mike heard a chair scraping, footsteps, and the door opened. Robert stood there in sweats, pajama top and overrun slippers, his eyes sunk deep in his head, his jowls slack. "What do you want?"

"Robert, I'm sorry. I must have crossed a line with you. Can we talk?"

"Man, you look bad. What's the matter?" Robert said as he looked with concern at his tall neighbor leaning against the door frame, hands hanging at his side, eyes swollen: a picture of desperation. For the first time in months, Robert noticed somebody's distress other than his own. After a pause, Robert caved.

"Alright then, your house. I'll be with you in a minute. Have to close out my work." There wasn't much to close out.

And so, the two walked the short distance between their homes. Mike poured coffee, set mugs on the scarred wooden table, then slumped down in a chair opposite Robert, his lanky body seeming to collapse in on itself. Neither man spoke until after a long silence, Robert said, "Okay, I'm here. What's going on?"

Mike began to stutter. "I... I... I don't quite know... don't know what I'll do next. You're the only person who might care." Elbows on the table, he bent over, head in his hands.

Robert, in an uncharacteristic move, reached over and lightly touched Mike's shoulder. "Let's hear it."

"I killed my wife! I loved her deeply... and I killed her." Robert was stunned. "It's like this," Mike continued in a monotone, "Four years ago... I was driving her to a dentist appointment... made a left turn... never saw the ambulance... don't know how...

suddenly it was there… hit her side… killed instantly. I've tried to go on, but it's too much."

"Mike, you didn't kill her. That was an accident. You can't blame yourself."

"Accident… yes, but my fault… wasn't paying attention… careless driving… she didn't deserve it."

Robert stood up, walked over and grabbed the pot off the stove. "What do you take in your coffee?" Returning to the table, he refilled their mugs. Then, finding milk in the refrigerator, he offered it to Mike who just shook his head. Sitting down again, he noticed Mike's hands were trembling, his eyes closed. "Not an easy thing to live with," Robert finally said.

"I've tried. I retired from my practice after that, didn't trust myself with anyone, not even animals... thought if I moved away, I could escape. Leave it behind. It hasn't worked." A long silence ensued. "I just can't go on."

Silence hung over the table, a cloud blocking the light. "Do you have any friends, family you can visit? You shouldn't be alone so much. Too much time brooding doesn't help."

"No, no family. Sometimes I just don't know where to turn. Confessing like this helps, though."

The two sat for a while, Mike talking, Robert listening. After a half-hour, Mike said, "You need to get back to your writing. You've gotten me through a bad moment. Thanks for coming over. I can't impose on your time any longer"

"That's okay. I don't mind. I've got something like that in my past as well."

"You?" This got Mike's attention. "You, too?"

Robert stood up, carried his coffee to the sink, dumped the remains down the drain, then rinsed out the mug and set it upside down on the counter. He looked askance at Mike, shrugged his shoulders, let out a long sigh and began slowly walking back and forth across the kitchen floor. "It haunts me, keeps me from writing. I've never told anyone, tried to bury it, but it won't stay down."

"You going to tell me?"

"Sure. It might help you to know you're not the only one who has made a mistake. Goes way back to when I was twenty-one... had a job out in Utah loading skiers onto a chair lift. One stormy morning, weather getting worse by the hour, I was helping an old guy onto the lift... probably no older than I am now... when he said, 'I'm skiing by myself. In case they close down the mountain for bad weather, I want someone to know if I'm still up there, case I break a leg or something.' He smiled and winked at me. 'So, I'll check in when I get down again. If I don't, send someone to come look for me. I wouldn't want to freeze to death on the slopes.'

"He was bundled up in a thick parka, wool hat, goggles, and ski pants. I laughed and told him I didn't think there was much chance he'd freeze dressed like that."

"I think I know where this is going. You forgot."

"I forgot. He never came down. They found him the next day, off trail in a tree well. Dead."

"A tree well? I don't get it. What's that"

"It's the hole around a conifer that's protected from heavy snow. The snow builds up in a wall around it, sometimes as much as 10 feet high. If you ski too close, the snow collapses and pitches you into the well. If you survive the fall, there's no way out unless someone hauls you up to the top. So, there it is. It was also an accident, but I killed him through neglect. If I'd remembered his request, if I'd sent out the ski patrol, they would have found him in time. Turns out it was Arthur Stern."

"The writer Arthur Stern?"

"The very same. A star in the literary world. Folks wondered why he had not alerted anyone that he was skiing by himself. I never confessed. Later, I picked up a couple of his books. He was truly gifted."

Mike had been sitting, listening, and watching Robert pace the room. Now he, too, stood up, walked to a photo on the wall. A lovely dark-haired woman looked out at him from behind the glass. He stared back, then turned to face his neighbor.

"If ... if ... if ... our lives are full of ifs. Like the unlucky skier, there's no escape."

"Right! Damn it all!" said Robert, suddenly jumping up, "You know what? We're dragging each other down. We need to do something, like get out of here."

"Sorry, I shouldn't have bothered you. I just desperately needed to talk. Never stopped to think you might have demons too."

"Look, I'm glad I came, but I really don't know what more to say. Let's do something else other than talk. Let's go somewhere."

"Doesn't matter where we go, all this will follow," muttered Mike.

"Maybe, but we have to do something. Can't just sit brooding like this."

"Thanks, but I'm not into doing much. I'm washed up. Good for nothing."

"Don't say that! Listen, why don't we take a hike?" said Robert as he hooked a thumb toward the door.

"A hike? Nah, I don't think so."

"Not just a hike... a hike up a mountain."

"Hike a mountain? My life's mountain enough. Don't know that I can face another." Mike sat back down at the table and reached for his coffee.

"I don't know, either," said Robert, "but we can try. We could go to Mount Aery. It's not very high, only three miles round trip."

"I can't, don't have boots."

"No more ifs. Just come. Wear your flip-flops," and Robert winked at Mike.

"Right. That should do it," and the glimmer of a smile lit his neighbor's face.

"Seriously though, it's a rough trail. What size do you wear?"

"Tens."

"That's my son's size. He left a pair when he moved out. I'll go get them. We can leave right now."

"Wait, I've got dishes to wash and emails to answer. I'm still thinking about this."

"No more excuses. We just go."

Robert returned home. "Mary, do you remember where we stashed Mark's hiking boots? And where I put mine? We're going up Mount Aery. Mike doesn't have any boots."

Mary, usually in full control, was speechless. Her jaw dropped. Finally, she said, "I've been trying to get you out of here for weeks, and now you're suddenly going hiking?"

"Look, it's not for me," Robert said with some irritation, "It's for Mike. I need to help him, get him away before he goes crazy sitting in that house all by himself."

An hour later found the two men trudging up the mountain. The trail, though short, was rocky and steep. They stopped often, attention focused on trying to catch a breath. After twenty minutes,

Mike declared it was too difficult and, panting for air, sat down on a rock. "Why are we doing this anyway?"

"Because we're crazy?" Robert replied with a laugh. He stood up, reached down and grabbed Mike's hand to haul him up on his feet. "Come on, buddy, one foot in front of another. If you stay here much longer, the sun will set and then we'll really be lost." Mike sighed.

Robert pulled him up. They trudged on. The trees thinned, blue sky lay ahead. They emerged from the shade into brilliant sunshine washing over a massive granite ledge.

"Will you look at that!" exclaimed Mike. He gazed down on a patchwork of shiny blue lakes tucked in the folds of an autumn-blanket flung across the hills. Mike said nothing more, nor did Robert. They settled down on the cliff, feet dangling dangerously over the edge. Robert took a swig from his water bottle, passed it to Mike.

"It's only water. The good stuff is not advised when hiking." Mike took a long drink, passed the bottle back to Robert, leaned back on his elbows and gazed on beauty.

"I'd forgotten places like this exist. I owe you for dragging me up here."

"I'd also forgotten," responded Robert.

After sitting for an hour, basking in the sun, they turned back, hiking down to the car and home. That night, each slept as they had not in years. It was the first of several outings to the mountain.

Robert's home life began to steady itself, like a battered ship hitting calm water. Mary noticed her husband's moods leveling out. Fewer explosive reactions interrupted their talks. She had avoided questioning him about anything at all for many months.

Now, she risked it. "Why doesn't Mike buy his own boots instead of using Mark's?" To her relief, Robert responded quietly.

"Because Mark never hikes when he visits here. He doesn't use them."

"But he used to enjoy going with you when he was young. Why don't you ask him again?"

"I could, but I don't want to put him on the spot. I doubt he wants to go with an old codger anymore."

Mary, who had been clearing the breakfast table, stopped what she was doing. Still in her pink robe, blonde hair uncombed, face without makeup, circled around the table to give Robert a hearty kiss and hug. Surprised, he stood up, returned the hug, then sat back down to take a fresh look at his wife. She was indeed beautiful. Not only beautiful, but kind. He had forgotten.

The next weekend, Mark came home to visit. Through the years, in Robert's struggle to suppress the beast gnawing at his conscience, he had let slip the bond with his son. Now, an awkward space filled the gap between them. It was Saturday morning and as the family sat nursing second cups of coffee, Mary said to her son, "How's your job going?"

Now why didn't I think to ask that? thought Robert. *I'm not crazy about his going into the world of banking, but I should at least have shown some interest.*

"Job's going well. I've been promoted to a Trust Officer. Now, I'm doing what I really want: making sure folks receive the benefits and dividends they are entitled to. I work with small accounts of middle-class people. I like it. These folks often need guidance. I find I can do that and make a difference in their lives.

186

Robert sat listening. It never occurred to him that there could be a personal aspect to banking. He began to see his son in a new light.

Lunch over, Mark announced he was going to see if any of his old friends were still around.

Robert interrupted. "Any interest in taking a hike with me?"

"Wow, that sounds like fun. Sure, where to?"

"Mount Aery."

"I'll dig out my boots and get ready." Of course, his old boots weren't there. After explaining where they were and retrieving them from Mike's house, they set off.

Later that afternoon, as the sun slanted golden across the russet leaves and the lakes below turned amber, the two sat together on the ledge for the first time in years. "Fantastic!" his son exclaimed. "I get so caught up in work, I forget about such peace. I see a lot of grief in my job. It's good to get away."

"Grief? A banker sees grief?"

"I do... in the Trust Department. We try to help people avoid problems, but we can't control everything. I see families struggling without the breadwinner, folks broken up by the loss of a spouse, people betrayed in wills. There's plenty going on to fill anyone with despair. Sometimes I can help. Sometimes I can't."

"So, that gets to you?"

"Sure, it does, Dad. But life is short. I'm not about to waste it sitting around getting depressed. I do what I can to help my clients. Then I go home, move on, and try to have some fun."

Robert started to choke up. He had not been called "Dad" in years. It felt good. He reached out, laid his arm on Mark's shoulders, an awkward moment for both. Not since he was a small child had they had contact like that.

187

Suddenly his son burst out laughing. "Will you look over there! That raven," he said pointing, "riding upside down on the wind! I've heard about that, but never seen it before."

"It's crazy. I didn't know they did that." Robert grinned at the bird's antics.

Mark began visiting home more often. One day he said to his mother, "The old man seems a lot more approachable than he used to be. What's up with that?"

"I'm not sure. I've seen a change, too. He and the neighbor often hike together. Haven't seen him do that in years... says he does it to help Mike. I'm worried about him, though. I'm pretty sure he hasn't written anything for a long time and then the other day I looked out the window and saw him climbing the old linden tree in the back yard. Odd! I don't know what to make of it. Hardly dare ask."

"Yeah, that's worrisome."

Two weeks later, Mary and Robert were finishing breakfast when she leaned over and put a steadying hand on his arm. "I'm so glad you're out hiking these days, but what of your writing?" she ventured.

After a long pause, he calmly responded, "I should tell you, dear, until recently, I've been unable to write anything."

"Why is that?" she asked, her suspicion confirmed. She waited for the old burst of temper. It didn't come.

"I'm not sure, but I'm beginning to get back to it at last. I've finally managed to write a few pages the last couple of days. In fact, would you like to read them?"

Mary was thrilled. Seldom had he shared his work with her. Robert disappeared into his study and printed them out. "Arthur,

188

this one's for you," he murmured. By the time he returned, Mary had made a call to a friend to cancel her meeting.

"Something's come up. We'll talk later," she said, quickly ending the call before Robert reentered the room.

"Here it is." He casually tossed the stapled pages on the table. "I'm going to stop over at Mike's. Be back later." He grabbed his jacket from the closet, flung it around his shoulders and left. Walking across the yard, he looked up and was surprised to see a small RV parked in the driveway. *I thought he had no friends. Someone must be visiting.*

Mike opened the door before Robert had even knocked.

"See my new RV?" he asked.

"Yours?"

"Yup. I'm selling the house, hitting the road. Maybe try some of those real mountains out west. You've been a great friend, but I'm ready for a solo flight."

"You're kidding!"

"Nope. Haven't kidded in years. Let me show you the inside."

After touring the camper, Robert said, "So you're really going to do it? Desert me for the Wild West? I'll be damned!"

"Not deserting you, just finding new trails. I'll stay in touch."

Robert returned home to tell Mary. He had hardly begun to speak when she broke in. "I've just finished reading your draft. I was deeply moved by it, especially the part about the man watching the stars who forgets he's on a cliff and steps off the edge."

"Really?" He was happy to have her comment on his piece. "You think it works?"

"It more than works, it's brilliant. I'd love to talk about it, but first I think you were about to tell me something," she replied.

"Yes, I was. Guess what my buddy's doing?" And before she could, he told of Mike's plan to move on. "It worries me. I'm not sure he's ready to take off like this. It's important he have someone to talk to. He might slide into depression again."

"You may be right. You've been there for him. Now, he'll have nobody." She paused, then said, "I have a thought. What do you think about getting him a dog?"

Robert was silent, walked to the window and looked over at his neighbor's house. After a few minutes he returned to face his wife, a smile on his face. "Mary, you're amazing. That's not a bad idea. Think I'll peruse the classifieds and see what's out there."

The next day, Robert made several phone calls. All to people who had advertised puppies for adoption. He settled on a couple of possibilities and set off to see what he could find. In less than two hours, he had returned. With him came a medium-sized pup, short brown fur, big black eyes, one ear up, one down.

"What, you found one already?" said Mary.

"Just got lucky. Couldn't resist this little guy. Older folks were moving into an apartment, had to give him up. Said the pup is 3 years old. He's friendly and seemed to enjoy his ride in the car. Think I'll take him over to Mike right now."

"Boy, will he be surprised! Hope he likes him."

"We'll see."

Robert found Mike swabbing down the outside of his RV. "Hey, I found someone to travel with you."

"Come on, Robert, you should have talked to me first. I'm really not into taking anyone along. Hey, you have a dog now?"

"He's not mine. I got him for you. Traveling companion. Like him?"

Mike stopped what he was doing, dropped his rag in the bucket and squatted down to pat the wiggly pup, who immediately jumped up and licked his face.

"You got this guy for me?"

"Yup. What do you think?"

"Think? Listen, I think you were trying to be thoughtful. I don't want to seem unfriendly, but it's impossible for me to take him along, though I do appreciate the thought. Dogs are needy, require a lot of time and attention."

Exactly, thought Robert but didn't say it. Instead he responded, "Why not? He clearly likes you. He needs a friend. His owners had to give him away. Poor abandoned pup. He's really lonely, and as a vet, you're the perfect choice. You'll know exactly what he needs."

Mike, still squatting, was suddenly knocked backwards by the enthusiastic pooch.

"Hey, hold on there," he said as he fended off the dog and tried to get back on his feet. "Listen, thanks anyway. I know you meant well, but I absolutely cannot manage a dog."

"Guess what his name is," said Robert, as he leaned over to pat the little guy, ignoring Mike's decision.

"I have no idea."

"Bob."

"Bob? You're making that up!"

"I am not. It must mean something, don't you think?"

"Are you sure?" responded Mike, "You didn't just give him that tag?

"I did not. He came labeled and ready to go."

"Amazing! Is he housebroken?"

"House broken and born to travel."

"Very sneaky. Bob, huh?"

"That's him. Bob."

The two men stood side-by-side looking down at the pup. Smart dog that he was, he sat back on his haunches and with big black eyes staring mournfully up at Mike, raised a front leg and offered his paw.

Mike, squatting down to shake the paw, finally broke the silence. "Bob huh? Okay, you win. It's clearly a setup. Ready to travel, Bob?"

Out of Bounds

Oh, what a tangled web we weave,
when first we practice to deceive.

Walter Scott, 1808

She waited, alone, at the long oak bar. Her finger traced circles in water pooled at the base of her glass. Football blared from a large overhead TV: crowds cheering, players running up and down the field in what seemed a series of irrational collisions and pileups. Sports had never been her thing. Nor had drinking alone. It was odd to find herself sitting at the scruffy wooden counter in semi-darkness. She had been married a long time, some years better than others, but still, overall, pretty good. She always went out with her husband or a friend... never like this. Dressed in Levi's and a cotton sweater, she had planned to make but a brief stop, not to linger. The funny thing was, the longer she sat, the more she enjoyed being the solitary mystery woman drinking by herself.

She had come to pick up reserved tickets, which the bartender, Travis, had promised to hold for fellow Rotarians – tickets for a performance of the musical *Out on the Town*. Travis was late for his shift. She had to wait. Uncomfortable at sitting there without ordering, she had asked for a glass of wine. While killing time, she was spied by good friends, Jack and Rita, who were walking past on their way to the restaurant section of the Water Trough.

"Hi Faith," they called in passing. "Nice evening."

"It surely is. Fall color's gone but the air's crisp." *They clearly don't know what to think of me drinking here by myself.* Faith smiled at their discomfort, but decided not to explain. *More fun this way.* Unsure what more to say, her friends moved on.

"Hi, beautiful." The words floated down the length of the bar from a bulky man sitting at the end, dressed in a flannel shirt and shredded work pants. He sported suspiciously black hair, a mismatch with his gray eyebrows. But his eyes… were a piercing blue. Not the handsomest guy around, but intriguing, nevertheless. Suddenly, Faith panicked. *Wait! What am I doing here as if looking for a pickup?* She quickly turned her back on the stranger to gaze out the window. She could see nothing but the black back of a red neon tube sign flashing "Budweiser" at folks passing outside. After a few more unsuccessful attempts to get a response from her, the fellow drinker gave up. While relieved to finally be left alone, she did, at the same time, sort of wonder if she was too old or not styling enough to hold his attention.

Travis finally arrived. With a hint of disappointment, she collected the two tickets, finished her drink, and no excuse to stay, slid off the stool and walked out, aware that eyes were following her.

She drove home to fix dinner for her husband Brad, watch TV, sleep, and get up again to leave for work at eight.

But she didn't return home quite the same as before. At the bar, a new notion had crept into her head. As the next few days went by, it tickled her defenses, begged to be released, to see the light. Faith fought back with all her puritan fiber, ignored the bothersome idea while at work. However, when night came, it emerged out of the dark to worry her sleep. She tossed and turned, looked for solutions – any but the most obvious. This went on for weeks, not letting up.

Until a month later, she finally gave in.

The very next day, on lunch break, she slipped into a beauty shop and tried on several wigs. The one with long, lustrous red hair transformed her completely. *Perfect*, she thought, with a blush of excitement. She bought it. Step one.

The next day at lunch time, she dropped in to check out the clothes at The Biker's Box. It was her first time inside the shop. She was astounded at the array of designs – everything from sequins and black leather to fringed jackets covered with wild colored pictures of eagles and American flags. There was even footwear: high-heeled black boots and flat riding boots with straps and buckles. *This is crazy* was her first thought; the next was, *What fun.* She began shopping, even buying sexy red underwear. Returning home before Brad, she carefully stashed her purchases under the bed.

When Brad readied to go out for his Thursday realtor meeting, Faith kissed him goodbye, closed the door, listened for his car to pull out of the driveway, then barreled upstairs to change into her disguise. Tonight…tonight she would go to the Rebel Roadhouse and get a taste of that other life. Fully costumed, she checked the mirror, laughed out loud, then decided she needed heavy dark red lipstick to complete the picture. *I'll have to pick some up tomorrow, I can't go out looking so pale.* Slowly, she took off her character, pushed it back under the bed and turned on the TV.

The following week, when Brad left for his meeting, it was a repeat performance. This time she was delighted with her new character, but suddenly realized she needed a new name as well. She hadn't thought about that before. *Sally? No, too ordinary. Betsy? Too suburban. Mary? Too old-fashioned. This is not so easy. Needs more thought.* So, she once more took off her clothes, got into her PJs and went online to google women's names. Sue,

Terry, none of it fit. She had worked through the alphabet to the P's when suddenly the name Pinkie jumped out. Ah! Pinkie! She would be Pinkie, the woman with the wild hair.

The third week, when Brad departed, Faith ran upstairs again, dragged her new wardrobe out from under the bed, pulled it on, took a look in the mirror and addressed her alter ego, "Not bad for a 40-year-old free range chick. Enough with the excuses, Pinkie. Pull yourself together. Time to go."

It was a good twenty miles to the Rebel Roadhouse, a safe distance from home and friends. There was plenty of time to think while she drove. *Brad's a good guy. I love him, but he's so predictable... realtor meetings on Thursdays, movies Friday evenings, golf on Sundays... A steady man, but I think a little more excitement could be fun.*

Arriving at the roadhouse, she pulled into the far end of the parking lot, out of sight from the road. *Don't stop now,* she told herself, then suddenly she remembered her wedding ring and pulled it off – the other rings as well– and shoved them into the glove compartment. Stepping out of the car, she locked the door and traipsed past the pickups and bikes lining the dirt lot. They looked a whole lot more at home there than her Volvo sedan. As she headed for the entrance, she reminded Pinkie, *Remember, you wanted to do this.* At the top of three steps, the wooden door loomed dark and forbidding. She pushed it open. Rock music and laughter came pouring out, nearly blowing her off her wobbly spike-heeled boots.

The small room grew quiet as Pinkie strode in with all the assurance she could muster. Making her way to the bar, she boosted herself onto a stool. Her tight leather miniskirt made it difficult, but with a bit of a wiggle, she made it.

"What'll it be, miss?"

"Got a Molson?"

"Sure. Coming up!"

Faith waited, then noticed Pinkie in the mirror – her crazy hair, her black fringed jacket – and thought, *No worries, that girl fits right in.* She let her gaze slide down the mirror toward a couple of other stool-perchers. A bald-headed man was slouched over his beer, his beefy hands clutching the bottle as he gazed at the surface of the bar in front of him. *He's a goner,* she thought to herself. Next to him sat a middle-aged man with a full head of hair, a carefully clipped mustache, and an obese, heavily made-up girl draped on his arm. *Surely he can do better than that,* she thought. As if she had spoken aloud, he suddenly looked up, caught her eye in the mirror and winked. *Oh Lordy, here it starts.* Rather than check out the other customers, she quickly shifted her gaze to the hockey game lighting up the screen overhead. A revved-up announcer was shouting out the plays of what sounded like exciting action, but which didn't seem to matter to the other customers. She suspected that for them, it was NASCAR or nothing.

The bartender set a Molson before her. "Want a glass?"

"No, I'm good," she said, figuring she would fit in better if she was a "bottle" girl. She reached in her purse for a bill when someone laid a hand on her arm.

"That's okay, I've got it," and a ten was smacked down on the bar. She turned to look at a hunk of a guy. He slid onto the empty stool next to her. His long black hair was caught back in a ponytail (she had always liked ponytails), his broad face seemed to be drawn together by a long, pointed nose (pointed noses, not so much). He was dressed in leather – a real animal.

"Haven't I seen you before somewhere?"

Pinkie laughed. "Oh, come on, can't you do better than that?"

197

"Okay, how's this? Want to talk?"

"That's more like it. What do you want to talk about?"

"You. You're new here. Sitting by yourself, I would guess you've been ditched. Who's the bore?"

"Some guy I met at a concert... stood me up tonight. He wasn't very exciting anyway," she replied while turning her beer bottle round and round on the bar. *Got to stay close to the truth or I'll mess up for sure.*

"Maybe I can help you out. Nice chick like you shouldn't be sitting by herself. What's your jam?"

"Fun. I like fun. Got some fun for me?"

"Sure do. I'll take care of that. Finish your drink and, for starters, I'll take you for a ride on my hog."

"Whoa. Not so fast. I don't even know you."

"Don't let that stop you. I don't know you either, but I'm taking a chance... inviting you to ride on the sweetest chopper you've ever seen. My Harley's a real tiger!"

"Yes, no doubt it is. Still, I need more time. What's your name anyway?"

"They call me Tractor," he said as he signaled for a beer.

"Tractor?"

"Yeah. Want to guess why?"

"I don't know, maybe cause you're overweight?"

"Don't get smart with me, girl. This here's all muscle," he said, pounding his gut with a beefy fist.

"Just joking. Really, what's with the name? Surely your parents never tagged you with it."

"Don't know what they tagged me with... Mother died when I was three... Dad took off... grew up in a foster home... good people, though."

"So, *they* called you Tractor?"

198

"Nah... my buddies do."

"You going to tell me why?" she asked, sipping at her beer.

"No. Not till you tell me your name."

"Pinkie."

"Pinkie! You're no Pinkie! Who gave you that handle?"

"A friend."

"Who's the friend? Some guy?"

"No... Faith," she said as she brushed at an annoying fly trying to share her beer.

"So, why does she call you Pinkie?"

"Because I wear my rings on that finger."

"You're not wearing them now."

"Nope. I have my reasons. Your turn, why do they call you Tractor?"

"Because I pull a lot of weight with the other guys."

"No kidding? What other guys?"

"The guys in my church. I'm chief there."

"Church? What kind of church? I'm almost afraid to ask."

"Don't be a smart ass. A bike club."

"Oh. So, what do you do in your bike club?"

"Lots of stuff... take trips, hang out with our chicks, a little charity work."

"So, why aren't you hanging out with your chick tonight?"

"'Cause I think I've found a better one: you." And he shot a long hungry stare from her head to her toes.

"Not too loyal, are you?"

"I was, she wasn't. We're on the skids."

"So, what makes you think we'll hit it off?"

"Look, you said you were out for fun, you're not a bad looker... and you're feisty. I like a challenge."

The bar was filling up, voices swelled, tables in the back taken over by lust-driven couples. Pinkie hardly dared to look their way. She swigged down a second beer, then a third. Her courage grew but it was getting late. She ought to be headed home before Brad arrived. "I gotta leave now," she said. Just then, the door swung open and a new couple staggered in. *I'll be damned! So, this is his realtor meeting!* It was Brad, a plump brunette clinging to him like a woman drowning.

Tractor saw her look that way. "That your stud?"

"Nah. Nobody I know. Hey, I think I'm ready for that ride now," said Pinkie, fury raging inside.

"Great. I've got an extra dome. First time as a back warmer?"

"A back warmer?"

"Yup... you can guess what that is."

"Sure. But I'm just up for the ride... nothing more."

"Yet," said Tractor under his breath.

Brad had not recognized her. The following week at home, each pretended all was normal. Brad kept up his side, Faith kept up hers. Breakfasts were finished in the usual rush before both set off to work. At night, suppers were eaten in front of the TV. Afterwards, they fell into bed, she too irate for anything but sleep.

The next Thursday, Faith kissed her husband goodbye, wished him well at his meeting, watched his car pull out of the drive, ran upstairs and changed into Pinkie. While driving to the roadhouse, she thought back to last week and her first ride on a motorcycle. *Sure was fun flying through the dark on Tractor's bike... moon bright, stars shining, hair streaming in the wind. Like a call of the wild... arms around a strange man... exciting. Better take care... not sure what I want. What the Hell was Brad doing there? A shocker having him show up. The frickin' liar! I'm not good enough for him? That rat! Unbelievable!*

When Thursday rolled around again, Pinkie drove into the roadhouse parking lot, hid her car in the back, walked inside. Tractor was there, waiting. She slid onto the seat next to him, unzipped her jacket. He grabbed it, then wrapped his arms around Pinkie, squashing her like a bug against his massive chest. *This guy stirs my coals for sure.* After a long steamy minute, he let her go and stepped back to hang her jacket on a nearby hook.

"So, you're here for more?"

"I'm here. Don't know what you mean by more."

"You tell me. A beer? A ride? A little fun?"

"Beer for sure. Molson. The rest... we'll see." *He really isn't bad looking. Not my type, but those high cheek bones, wide face, deep eyes, and what a build! I could get it on with him... if I dare.* Suddenly, the door opened. In walked Brad again. This time no woman slung about his neck. He looked around, then grabbed a stool at the far end of the bar. Pinkie sat very still, heavy mascara and false eyelashes disguising her face. She watched him in the mirror. He looked her way, his glance sliding right by as he continued to gaze around the room. *Perfect. He has no idea who I am.*

She turned back to Tractor, patting him on his tattooed hand. "So, tell me, what do you do for a living?"

"I'm a carpenter... skilled carpenter."

"So, what kind of things do you make? Like furniture, chairs and stuff?"

"No, I work construction. Build big, fancy-schmancy houses, like multi-million-dollar places. You can't believe how much money the owners have. They don't know what to do with it all."

"Well, they hire guys like you, for one."

201

"Right, but they expect us to build for peanuts. Generosity is not their thing."

"You don't look like you're doing too badly. Nice bike, expensive jacket," she said as she curled a strand of red hair around her finger.

"Are you going to start again?" He said, turning to inspect her once more, head to foot. "You sure are one cranky broad."

"If I'm so cranky, why are you hanging out with me?"

"Feel sorry for ya… drinking all alone. Nobody else seems interested."

"You're hanging with me out of pity? You got it all wrong mister. Think I can't find my own pickups? Just watch." Pinkie opened her purse, pulled out sunglasses and put them on. She slid off her stool and ambled over to Brad. "Hey buddy, how come's you'se alone tonight?" she said with a slur and gravelly voice.

"Guess I was just waiting for you to come my way, cutie. Have a seat," he said, patting the stool beside him. After a quick assessment, he added, "You're a looker, that's for sure. "

She plunked herself on the stool, turned to Brad and said, "Ya hang out here a lot?"

"'Bout once a week. Nice break from working all the time."

"What d'ya work at?"

"Making money."

"How's that?"

"Don't ask, honey bunch. Let's talk about something else."

"Bad stuff, huh? Don't tell me then."

"I've noticed you here before, with the guy down the bar. I can do better than that for you." *Wow! A side of Brad I've never seen before. Didn't know he had it in him!*

"He's okay. My kinda bad-ass guy," she replied. *Make him jealous,* interjected Faith, her inner voice. "I'm goin' back now. Jus wanted to check ya out. See ya," said Pinkie.

She returned to Tractor. "How's that? Still think I'm hard up? I hooked that guy real easy."

'Yah, but that guy's a nerd with his wire-rimmed glasses and wimpy mustache. I could kick his ass any day."

How dare he insult Brad like that. He's got more brains than all you guys together, thought Faith. Then Pinkie spoke up. "Maybe not sexy, but I bet he's a whole lot smarter than the people you hang with."

"Hey babe, I could show him a thing or two."

"Sure, sure. Take it easy, tough guy. Don't get hot under the collar."

"I've been known to take down a guy or two in my day. They don't mess with me. Okay Mama, this time I'll let it go, but don't be tryin' that again. We better get out of here, before I blow. Ready? I need my back warmer."

"Ready." And they walked out to the parking lot, climbed on his Harley and headed for the highway. Pinkie found it as thrilling as before. Tractor was a wild driver that night. He went too fast, stopped too suddenly, took the corners too sharply. She hung on for dear life. When he pulled over to the side of the road, she panicked.

"I agreed to ride, not stop…"

"What's with you? You're one cold chick. I can grab you right now and nobody would stop me."

Appeal to his decency, whispered Faith. *Think fast.*

"Listen, Tractor," said Pinkie as she slid a few inches back on the seat, "you look tough but underneath I think you're a pretty good guy. I'm sure you wouldn't force me into anything. I just need more time than some girls. I like to get to know a guy better."

"Son of a bitch.! What are you, a cock teaser?"

"Not at all. I think you're pretty damn sexy. I'll get it on with you and you'll not be sorry… promise. I'm just not quite ready." It worked. She managed to talk him out of it, but the ride back to the bar was even faster and more furious.

The next Thursday, she was torn about escaping to the roadhouse. *Time to give Tractor what he wants… and I want it too, if I'm honest with myself. What's the harm? Good-looking dude and he'd surely be exciting. On the other hand, there's Brad. I'm not sure what to do about him… never meant to more than flirt with another guy. But Brad lying to me… chasing other women … rotten of him. No doubt he's bedded down a few. He has it coming. My turn. Tractor, a hot hunk, think tonight's the night. No guilt.* She returned to her stomping ground. No sooner was she seated than the bartender came over. "Message for you, Pinkie. Tractor had to work overtime. He can't make it. He'll see you next week."

"Thanks," she said, and then wondered, *Is he really doing overtime or just punishing me?* She sat toying with her beer until she saw Brad walk in. *What's with him anyway? Think I'll push him a little.* She grabbed her shades and put them on before looking his way again. No floozy plastered on his arm… yet. She made her way down the bar and slid up on the empty stool beside him. "How's mister doin' tonight," she asked in an assumed voice. "All alone?"

"No, I'm waiting for someone."

"Oh, yeah? Who's that?"

"None of your business. Just a friend. She'll be along any minute. I'm saving that seat you're on for her." *Oh, but it is my business*, thought Pinkie.

"And what'll you do if I don't move?"

"I'll drag you off it!"

Wow. Awesome. That's more like it. I'll stay right here and see what he does.

Less than a minute had passed when the fur-coated, brunette entered the bar, spike heels clicking across the floor. She threw her arms around Brad's neck and, turning to stare at Pinkie, asked "What's with the redhead?"

"Not to worry," he replied, "she's just on her way." But she wasn't. She remained sitting where she was. "I said, it's time to go. Get up so my friend can sit."

"You heard the man. Scram!" huffed the hefty brunette. Pinkie stayed where she was.

"Playing tough, huh?" said her formerly meek husband.

Pinkie didn't answer. Brad slid off his stool, wrapped his arms around her and lifted her up off the seat. She kicked and wriggled but he only clasped her tighter against his chest. He had not held her that tight in a long time.

She's got spunk, Brad thought. *A redhead with possibilities!* Pinkie returned to her place but, watching the mirror, kept an eye on Brad and his pickup. He didn't look like he was having much fun. Every once in a while, Brad looked up and caught her watching him. Sparks flew back and forth. Potential there. Shortly after, Pinkie called it a night and headed home.

The following Thursday, Pinkie was back at the bar. So was Tractor… and Brad and the fur coat. *What to do?* Then Faith's inner voice, spoke up. *"You were looking for a little excitement,"* she said to Pinkie, *"but it looks like you're now in over your head. I can help. Follow me."*

They headed for the bathroom where they locked themselves into a stall. They stood there for a minute of quiet. Then, Faith began dismantling Pinkie, peeling off her wig, removing her large hoop earrings, pulling away her sunglasses. After that, Pinkie wiggled out of her blouse, unhooked her thickly padded bra, and hung it on the door while she put her top back on. They waited 10 minutes while the other stall doors opened and closed as beer flowed in a continuous tinkling stream. Finally, after everyone had left, Pinkie walked over to the sink where Faith removed her false eyelashes, her deep red lipstick, her dark blue eye shadow, and the rest of her makeup.

"Now, pull off those stupid stiletto-heeled boots and go in your sock feet. Ready?" It was Faith, not Pinkie, who walked back into the dark noisy room. She zig-zagged through the crowds of drinkers, strolling over to Brad and the fur coat.

"Fuck!" he burst out as he looked up to see his wife standing there. "What the Hell are you doing here?"

Faith threw Pinkie's baggage on the bar: the wig fetched up against Brad's can of beer like some wild mess of seaweed, her padded bra landed in his cheese/nachos, the earrings clattered across the counter to fall down on the other side, one making a neat ringer around a beer bottle by the sink. The sunglasses and cosmetics slithered down the counter. And the boots? She slammed them down so hard one of the heels broke off and speared the fur coat's sleeve.

"Just came to say good-bye," said Faith.

Tractor watched from several stools away, grinning. He recognized her by her voice. She looked his way, walked over and climbed in his lap.

"You are one crazy chick!" he said as he wrapped an arm around her, the other hand clutching his beer.

"Tractor, you did me a big favor," she said. "Here's to you and great memories." She grabbed his Budweiser, turned her head to look him in the eye, raised the can and took a long swig. Setting the beer back down, she gave him a long kiss, then slipped out of his lap and slid away.

"See ya!" she called out.

By this time, the room was beginning to buzz. The sound grew louder and louder as the drinkers caught on to what was going down. Finally, a wave of laughter broke out that swept Faith toward the door. In sock feet, tracking through puddles of beer, head held high, a free woman, she exited to wild cheers and whistles.

Mercy

"I hate him! I hate him! He doesn't answer my calls. He doesn't answer my texts!" yelled Trixie as she slammed the cupboard door. "He's stupid!"

"Don't you ever say that again," snapped Rose, her mother. "You're too young to know what you're talking about. After all, who do you think made it possible for us to move to this beautiful new town and live in such comfort. Your father did! So, knock it off."

Trixie, her curly blond hair framing a face contorted in rage, turned away, raced from the kitchen and up the stairs. A moment later the bedroom door slammed. Her mother, brown eyes narrowed in anger, mouth pursed shut, dark hair in need of a comb, dropped onto a chair.

"How long, Lord," she muttered "How long will this pandemic go on? How long must we isolate at home?" Distracted, she aimlessly turned the pages of a *Good Housekeeping* magazine. The kettle whistling on the stove demanded attention. She stood up to get it, then remembered the twins playing in the yard. Just as she looked out to check on them, they came bursting through the door with the jubilation of eight-year-olds.

"Guess what?" said Mark, straight hair falling in his face. "Our ball rolled under the hedge into the street. Someone picked it up, yelled 'catch' and threw it back. We couldn't see who it was, but we saw the ball coming and I caught it!"

"Yeah, but I was the one who saw it coming first," said Andy, his arms waving in excitement.

"Oh, my God. Give me that ball right now!"

"Why?" asked Mark, holding it behind his back.

His mother grabbed a pair of gloves lying by the sink, put them on and held out her hand. "Because I say so. Hand it over," she said. He did, reluctantly. She took the ball and threw it in the trash. Then, returning to the sink, washed off the gloves. *The poor kids,* she thought, *they just don't understand.*

"You threw out our ball!" howled Mark. "That's not fair. Why? We didn't leave the yard. We don't even know who threw it back. Why can't we have it?" And tears sprang to his eyes.

"You know why... germs! Now get over to the sink and wash your hands, both of you. Scrub them hard."

Meanwhile, upstairs, Trixie was on the phone to her good friend Patty who said, "A bunch of us are sneaking out at eleven tonight. We're getting together at Brookside Park. Bring a flashlight. We'll meet behind the maintenance building and have a party."

"Awesome! I'll be there. I'm sick of my mother... she's a real pain, doesn't want me going anywhere. She just thinks about herself. She's so afraid of catching this thing."

"Yeah," said Patty, "like our parents think we can be locked up forever. Crazy." And so, that night, after her mother and brothers were asleep, Trixie took off her pajamas, pulled on her shorts, t-shirt and hoodie, then tiptoed down the stairs and out the backdoor. She ran to the park. Ten kids were there. Some she knew, some she did not. They snacked on chips and soda, and played spin the bottle – until they heard the sirens.

"Let's do this again," one of the boys said, as they jumped to their feet.

"Run!" shouted another boy. They did. Each making his or her way home by a different route, sneaking along in the shadows, fearful of the cops catching them out breaking the rules. For the first time in her life, Trixie was really scared. However, she returned safely, and quietly let herself into the house and up the stairs to her room. *I'm not doing that again,* she decided. *That was too scary.*

The next day, it was back to the same old routine. "Trixie, I could use some help doing the dishes," or "Trixie, could you take your brothers outside and play with them?" Trixie wasn't having any of it. She was sullen, resistant... at times rude.

"Why do I have to do everything? I'm not their mother."

"That's right, but you *are* their sister and I need some help around here. Maybe you're fifteen but you act like you're five. Time to stop thinking about yourself and think of others," continued her mother.

"Where's Dad? Why doesn't he come home and help? He'd understand. It wouldn't be like this if he were here."

"I've told you before, he's straight out taking care of patients at the hospital. This virus is really hard on older people. The ER is overrun with admissions."

"So, why can't he come home to sleep? He could do that."

"I've explained already... he doesn't want to risk infecting us."

"He could at least answer my texts."

"Cut out your bellyaching," replied her stressed-out mother. Then, softening a bit, she added, "He loves you very much, you know, but his patients need him right now."

"What about us? I need him, too!" Trixie retorted as she retreated up the stairs to her room. There she pulled out her cell and began dialing Patty, but her mother was right behind her, grabbing the phone out of her daughter's hands.

"Enough! I'm keeping this until you start helping me out and spending more time with your brothers. You're being very selfish!"

Each day seemed a harder trial than the day before. Occasionally, Trixie reluctantly did a few chores, but only after a lot of grumbling and only when asked. The boys constantly begged for attention. Tension grew.

One night at 11 p.m., after the children were asleep, Rose's husband reached out by phone as he had done all along, though irregularly. "How're you doing darling? How are the kids?"

"Oh, Roger. How I wish you were here. I'm okay, but having the children stuck at home is taking its toll on me. Trixie seems dedicated to making my life difficult. She keeps asking why you don't answer her. All she wants to do is stay in her room and talk on the phone. I took it away from her for a couple of days. She needs to help but she does little at all. And the boys... they don't slow down for a minute. I can barely get them to do schoolwork. It's really hard controlling everything. I'm exhausted."

"Listen, Rose, these are tough times for everyone, the children as well. Tell Trixie I can't get back to her right now. I will as soon as I can. Tell those kids I miss them a lot, but I'm straight out with patient admissions. And darling, cut those kids some slack. Back off a bit. You don't have to control everything. Have some fun with them instead. I know this is stressful for you but buck up. Love you. Gotta go, I'm being paged. Courage."

The next morning, Rose told Trixie that her father had called. "He's under a lot of pressure and feels badly not being with us. He sent his love, said he'd get back to you when he can."

"That's unfair! You should've let me know so I could've talked to him. Why don't you think about me for a change?" Trixie slammed her fist on the table and ran out of the room, sobbing.

211

The boys had just come inside as their sister went banging up the stairs. "What's the matter with her?"

"Nothing serious," replied their mother. "Now wash up. Supper will be ready in a few minutes."

Mark and Andy, hungry from playing outside, wolfed down their food. "Can we watch a movie now?"

"Absolutely not! The teacher mailed another packet of schoolwork. Time to open it and start."

"Not now, Mom, we're too tired."

Mom was without mercy. "Don't talk to me about tired! You don't half know what tired is."

Rose was in despair, worry wearing her down. *I just can't go on. Oh Roger, when can we be together again? I need help, I'm not managing well.* The epidemic had forced schools to close. People were ordered to isolate in their homes, only to go out for emergencies and to wear masks anytime they left the house. Young people had to stay home as, even without symptoms, they could be carriers and infect others. It was the older folks who were dying, not the younger. Rose didn't tell her kids that – she didn't want to scare them. She had always depended on her husband to hold things together, to keep her calm. Now, it felt like everything was coming apart.

Trixie, warned to finish her school assignments, was sitting at the table frowning at her iPad. She looked up to ask, "Why do I have to keep my iPad down here? I work better in my room."

"Because here, I can keep an eye on what you do with it. So, let me hear no more on the subject."

"Why can't I see my friends? I'll be real careful. Keep my distance from them."

"You know very well why you can't."

"It's unfair and dumb! I think adults are just scaredy cats."

"You've got that right. We are, and with good reason."

"Can I have my phone back?"

"Maybe. Finish your homework first. And, I want to see it when you're done," replied Rose. It was a day like every other. Rose was increasingly weary from four weeks of managing the house by herself, keeping the twins occupied, and overseeing everyone's homework.

Until recently, Rose had had a house cleaner, but she no longer came due to isolation requirements. Occasionally, Mark and Andy asked when their dad was coming home, but seemed to be satisfied with the answer "soon". Rose eventually let Trixie have her phone back, but told her, "I'll take it away again if you don't behave. I want you to start spending more time with your brothers. I can't entertain them all the time. I have too much else to do."

One morning, Trixie came downstairs to find her mother sitting at the table, still in her robe and holding her head. "The boys have already eaten, but you'll have to fix your own breakfast for a change. I don't feel so well. It's my allergies kicking up again. I'm all stuffed up."

"How come you have these allergies all the time?" asked her rebellious daughter, with a teenage lack of sympathy.

"I wish I knew," answered her mother, "because it's no fun to feel like this."

Trixie banged around the kitchen, complaining she couldn't find the cereal, that the bananas were too black, and the dishwasher still full. She finally sat at the table, gobbled down her breakfast then jumped up and headed back to her room saying she had reading to do for school. Her mother doubted that reading was part of her plan.

In vain, Rose waited to hear from Roger.

The next day dragged on in much the same way. News about the epidemic grew ever worse. The twins mostly got along with each other, but were often bored. Trixie remained intractably difficult until the afternoon she came running downstairs in tears. She rushed over to her mother.

"Mom, Patty's mother got the virus and died! She was okay four days ago but got sick and suddenly died! Mom, why, why? I can't believe it. Poor Patty."

Rose spread her arms and gathered her daughter in while the tears flowed. "Mom, why couldn't they save her? Why couldn't Dad save her? I don't understand. Hospitals are supposed to cure people, not kill them."

Rose rocked her daughter as she used to do when she was a toddler. It was a sweet, though sad, moment for the mother, a harsh awakening for the daughter.

Trixie, tears spilling over, mumbled, "Mom, how do you know you don't have this virus, too? You're always sniffing and sneezing."

"I told you, it's just allergies. I'm not worried. I'd have to catch the virus from another person and I haven't been near anyone in over 4 weeks."

Trixie responded by burying her face in her mom's shoulder and sobbing even harder, not only with grief, but with the guilt of having possibly exposed her mother by sneaking off to see her friends.

After that, a little less complaining was heard and a little more help forthcoming. "Mom, I'll do the dishes," Trixie offered without prompt. She even found the vacuum cleaner, and with some difficulty, proceeded to clean the floors. "Which attachment do I use for the rugs? Should I move all the chairs? Where is the dust cloth?" Her mother felt a surge of relief. Her daughter was finally coming around. Trixie even began to take charge of the twins. "Mark and Andy, you sit right down and do your homework. No, you can't go out to play until this afternoon."

The boys wailed, "How come Trixie's suddenly ordering us around? She's not being fair. We're not listening to her," complained Mark.

"Yeah," said Andy, following the lead of his brother.

"Trixie's being bossy. Tell her to stop, Mom," pleaded Mark.

"Boys! She's trying to help. Quit your whining."

"We're not going to listen to her! Come on, Andy," Mark said as he pushed out his chair, stood up and tugged his brother's sleeve. "Let's get out of here." The two boys made a run for the back door, exploding outside into the glorious fresh air. "They're all being mean."

"You get back here right this minute," yelled their sister to no avail. "Mom, why don't you make them obey me?" complained Trixie in the silence left after the rambunctious twins were gone.

Rose, hearing Trixie give orders, suddenly heard her own harsh voice in her daughter's words. A moment of clarity came. *Oh Lord, she sounds just like me, too strident. Guess I'm not as collected as I thought,* Rose reflected in despair. *A bad example. I've got to pull myself together.* A moment of silence followed while all this ran through her head.

"Mom, you're not answering me."

"I was just thinking. This isolation is hard on everyone."

"It's not hard on you, Mom. You're used to being home all day."

"You'd be surprised," was all her mother said.

Trixie stared at her and said, "I think you should lie down and rest. I'll take your temperature."

"I'm not sick. It's just allergies and I don't need a rest," her mother replied.

215

Once more Trixie went stomping off to her room.

On overload at the hospital, Roger had asked Rose not to call. He would phone whenever he could. On the one hand, she felt engulfed with loneliness, on the other, frazzled by the constant demands of the quarantined children. An only child whose parents had died early, she had no one else to turn to. That night, she went up to her room and dialed Roger.

He picked up and before she could say a word began, "Rose, I was just going to call. Looks like I've caught something. I have a temperature and chills. They're waiting to wheel me up to a room as we speak. I can't hold them up, but just wanted to let you know I love you all. I'll call as soon as things settle down. Don't worry. Got to hang up now."

"Roger, wait! I'll be right over... won't take me more than twenty minutes."

"Sorry, Rose, visitors aren't allowed. I'll be in touch. Stay strong," and he hung up.

Rose sat like a statue on the side of her bed. A half-hour later, she jumped when the phone rang. It was their family physician, Dr. Smith.

"I guess Roger talked to you already? Good. We think he caught the virus. He's been admitted to the ICU. His fever is spiking, but we gave him something to bring it down. The nurses started an IV and hooked him up to oxygen as a precaution. He's been sedated and starting to doze off."

"On no, is he that bad? How did he get sick? I thought you all wore protection."

"We do. It's hard to know how he acquired the virus, but rest assured, he'll get the best of care. Roger's not able to talk right now but as soon as he feels better, we'll give him the phone so he can call."

"Can't I come see him?"

"I'm afraid not. He's in isolation and... as you know, the hospital is closed to visitors, including family. We can't take chances on spreading this thing. I'm so sorry."

Rose put the phone down. "This can't be," she said to herself, eyes brimming. She got up, went downstairs and made a cup of tea. *I have to be strong... can't tell the kids. They're too young. Oh God, I hope he pulls through. I've got to be strong like he said... got to get control of myself.*

As she sat at the kitchen table, she thought back to better days when the family had taken a camping trip to the Adirondacks: the orange sunsets over the lake, the loons yodeling, the children cooking hot dogs over the open fire. It helped briefly, but then the present came crashing back in.

Sinus congestion and worry combined to bring on a headache. *Maybe two aspirins will help.* Her throat felt constricted. She was barely able to get them down. Then she went up to bed to lie awake, headache subsiding but sleep impossible. She thought of calling the only people she had become friends with since their recent move to town. When morning arrived, she would phone her neighbor, Mary. Then she remembered that Mary was also trying to cope, not only with her children, but with an elderly mother in poor health. *I can't bother her. Maybe I'll call Cindy. I have to talk to someone.* But Cindy, her friend down the street, was caring for a disabled husband. She had her own worries. *I can't lay this on her. I don't know anyone else around here. I'm on my own.* Or so she thought...

Towards dawn, she dozed off for a couple of hours until the twins bounced into the room and jumped on her bed. "Mom, get up, its breakfast time!" Exhausted, she dragged herself from under the covers and downstairs to find Trixie had already begun making eggs. Her daughter's new attitude amazed her.

"Hi, Mom. You can just sit at the table and I'll fix you an omelet. How're you feeling? You look tired. Have you taken your temperature yet?"

"No, I haven't. Listen, stop worrying about me. I'll be alright. You've seen me with allergies before."

"Yeah, but you never looked sick before. Now you do. I *am* worried."

"Don't be. I'm tired. I didn't sleep very well, that's all."

The day passed slowly. Trixie spent some of the time in her room texting friends, but also made time to play games with the twins. Regardless, Mark and Andy were demanding. "Why can't we use the iPad like sis does?" they asked their mother.

"Because you're too young," she replied. Rose hated that her daughter and friends spent so much time on devices. She believed it was destroying family life. She also had an iPad but, trying to set a good example, only went online and read the latest virus updates after everyone had gone to bed. "Now get outside and play."

That night, after the children were asleep, she could hold back no longer. Sitting on the sofa, she finally broke down, weeping uncontrollably. Tears streamed down her cheeks, her body was wracked with spasms. Head bowed, handkerchief to her face, she let it all out. Suddenly she felt a soft touch on her shoulder. There was Trixie standing next to her.

"Mom, what's the matter?" she asked in a frightened voice.

"Oh sweetie, I'm so sorry. I thought you were asleep."

"No, I was awake and I heard you. What's happening?" Fear swept over her face as she stared at her mother.

Once again, Rose held out her arms and folded her daughter in. "I wasn't going to tell you, but now that you're here... it's your dad. He's sick."

Trixie, rejecting her mother's arms, sat up straight. "Why didn't you tell me? When did he get sick? Does he have the virus? You should have let me know!"

Rose, wiping away tears, tried to explain about their father.

Trixie blurted out again, "You knew this and didn't tell me?"

"I didn't want to scare you kids."

"Mom, you don't seem to get it. I'm not a kid anymore."

Not a kid? Of course she's my kid. She hesitated a moment, then opened her arms again. "Forgive me, you're right." This time, Trixie fell into her mother's embrace, tears filling her eyes. The two clung together. After a few minutes, Rose suggested they have a cup of tea. "We need to calm down."

They talked for a while before it occurred to Rose to ask why her daughter had still been awake. "Because I'm no longer a child who needs to go to bed at 9 p.m.. I always stay up late. Besides, I don't sleep that well."

"I guess you're right," replied Rose. "I haven't been fair to you, treating you as a child. Anyway, why don't you sleep well? Are you worried?"

"Yes. I'm worried about you. You look sort of sick and you have headaches and you're always stuffed up."

"I told you, it's just allergies."

"But why won't you take your temperature? It could be something more."

"Relax, sweetie. First of all, I don't know where I left the thermometer, we haven't used it in ages... and second, I've not been exposed, so no way could I catch this virus. Now, let's get to bed. We won't say anything about this to Mark and Andy. No sense getting them upset. Let's try to keep them happy."

Eventually, they shut off the lights and climbed the stairs to their bedrooms... but not to sleep. Each had worries, Trixie even more than her mother. *Dad's sick. What if he dies? Maybe Mom is sick, too. How can I tell her about sneaking out to that party? She'll get mad... never trust me anymore. I'll have to watch her closely. If she gets worse, I'll call the doctor. Wait, do I even know how to reach him?* Trixie still couldn't sleep for worry so she got up, tiptoed downstairs and looked at the list of names and numbers her mother kept on her desk. *Oh good, there it is. At least I know where to call if I have to.*

The next morning, the twins, now looking to Trixie for breakfast instead of their mother, came rushing into their sister's room and tumbled onto her bed.

"We're hungry. Get up and make us pancakes, please?" said Andy.

And so began another long day. She and her mother tried not to show how upset they were. The twins complained of boredom. When Trixie tried to play a game with them, they refused, saying they had already played it a thousand times.

"When can we go back to school?" asked Andy. There was a question never before heard in that household.

Rose went downstairs to be greeted by Trixie who told her their food was running low. Her mother sat down to make a list of what they needed, then handed it to Trixie. "Here's the list. Could you order online so we can get a delivery? I'm going upstairs to call the hospital."

When her daughter sat down to enter the order, she saw her mother had forgotten several essentials. Trixie added the items without saying a word.

Rose dialed Roger's number but got no answer. On calling the nurses' station, she was informed that her husband was "holding his own." Visitors still not allowed. Nothing more. She hung up and sat remembering their last call before he got sick. She suddenly realized that she had been so consumed with her own worries that she never once asked Roger how he was doing. *Next time we talk, I won't burden him with my problems but listen to him, ask him how he's coping... and tell him over and over how much I love him.*

Trixie, groceries ordered, came up to the bedroom where her mother was sitting, having just finished talking to the hospital. "How is he? Did you talk to him?"

"No, they won't let me. They just said he's holding his own."

"That's all? Maybe he's really sick?"

"I know, I'm sorry." Like a waterfall, sentiment suddenly tumbled from her mother as she thought back to her husband's recent words, 'You don't have to control everything. This is hard on them as well.' "Listen, dearest *(when have I last called her that?)*, I know I've been short on patience. I love you all very much, you know that, don't you? And recently, you've been such a help. It would be good if we could all find something different to do, but I just can't think of anything."

There was a moment's silence.

Then Trixie spoke up. "I know, let's all go for a drive in the country. Maybe we can find a place to take a walk away from everyone else. Do you feel well enough to take us?"

"Leave the house? I don't think we're supposed to do that."

"Yes, but they mean shopping and stuff like that. If we go for a walk in the woods, it won't hurt anyone."

"What a good idea," responded her mother. "I think I can manage to drive." And to herself she said, *Yes, I've got to pull*

221

myself together. I can at least do that for these kids. "I'll take the phone with me in case the hospital calls."

Two hours later, Trixie having packed a picnic, the family drove to Deep Caves Park. The children walked trails for over an hour, the boys running ahead to hide and jump out at Trixie, then scurrying off like squirrels, to spring from rock to rock. They left their mother waiting by a small pond. When the kids returned for lunch, Trixie showed them how to skim flat pebbles across the surface. Mark and Andy giggled and laughed. Rose actually smiled for the first time in weeks. They laid a blanket under the trees in the cool shade and munched on cheese sandwiches. When they piled back in the car for the trip home, the twins talked excitedly about the fun they had had.

Fun, thought Rose, remembering back. *Fun. Roger told me to have fun. He's right. This family needs more fun. I can't wait to tell him about this. He'll be pleased. Surely I can talk to him tonight.*

That evening, after supper, just as she was about to dial the hospital again, her phone rang. "Rose? This is Dr. Smith. I'm so sorry to have to tell you this, but things are not going well for Roger. We're doing all we can, but he's gotten worse. We had to put him on a ventilator." Rose stammered out a few questions, but he could answer little except to suggest she pray.

She hung up in tears. *Pray!* She thought. *Prayers won't cure him, only medicine will.*

"Was that the hospital?" asked Trixie.

"Yes. They're taking good care of dad," she announced to the kids. But Trixie saw her mother's red swollen eyes. Later, after the twins were in bed, she asked how her dad really was.

Her mother sat down on the sofa, patted the cushion next to her and said, "Trixie, dear, come sit beside me and I'll tell you everything." Trixie broke down as her mother put her arm around her, pulled her close and talked.

"Mom, what if he dies? Oh, Mom."

"We must hope for the best. Remember, no matter what, I'm here for the three of you. We'll manage, sweetheart."

Trixie, still sobbing, sat up straight. "There's something I never told you. I sneaked out to a party with my friends just a few days before Patty's mother died. I only did it once. I wish I hadn't. I never should have done that." The words came rushing out as she talked about the fear that she had caught the virus from Patty and brought it home. She thought her mother might have the virus. Then, she waited for her mother's anger to boil over.

Rose was stunned. "You did that? Really? I had no idea."

"Oh, Mom, I'm so sorry. If I'd known this could happen..."

"Why didn't you know? Didn't I make it clear enough? Didn't I explain about all that?"

"I guess I thought you were just being overly cautious. I didn't know that I was supposed to keep distanced from everyone else. I didn't really think people were actually dying from it. You never told me that."

"Oh, Trixie, I was just trying to protect you from what was happening in the outside world. Maybe I shouldn't have."

"Please don't protect me anymore. I'm old enough now. I need to know these things."

Rose sat there quietly. 'Cut them some slack,' she recalled Roger telling her, 'this is hard on them, too.'

"I guess," her mother replied, "I shouldn't have tiptoed around you. I know you wouldn't have gone out if you'd known how really dangerous it is. From here on, let's not keep things from each other. We need to be strong for... us and Dad and Mark and Andy."

223

It's true, her "allergy" was not quite the same as before. *Is it possible I am sicker than I want to admit?* thought Rose.

She was awake early the next morning. On her way down the hall, she paused to gaze into the boys' room. Andy had climbed into Mark's bed. The two were tangled around each other like young tree roots. Rose walked quietly to their bedside, smiled and blew them each a kiss. After that she headed for the bathroom to look for the thermometer. Taking her temperature, she was surprised to find it slightly elevated. She dialed the ER.

"It sounds like you have the virus. If your symptoms get more severe, call us back. For now, though, we suggest you stay home and continue self-isolating. We're overcrowded and can't see you at the moment."

When Trixie got up, Rose told her about the elevated temperature and about calling the ER. "This is not your fault," her mother continued. "It's mine for not being more open with you about how easily this thing is spreading and... who knows? I may still be just fine. Trixie, you are such a comfort to me. You and I need to be strong now, for your dad, for ourselves, and for Mark and for Andy."

Even as she spoke the words, she thought to herself, *Will Roger and I survive? Will the kids be okay? Funny, I don't feel alone anymore. Trixie is amazing. But still we are vulnerable, so vulnerable. We could all use a little mercy... please a little mercy... now.*

Power Outage

Winston, the country gentleman, hardly noticed the black clouds racing toward his home. After all, he resided inside a safe, luxurious estate. The outdoors was a place to observe from behind glass... not a place to actually experience.

A stocky man in shiny loafers, tweed blazer, and wool slacks, Winston stood looking out a plate glass window. He began, in a slightly British accent, to wax poetic.

"Oh, how I love the rural life... the wildness, the bloody sunsets, owls shrieking, stars like bullet holes in the black sky, and smoky wood fires on subzero nights. Not for the weak-hearted. You've got to know how to manage."

A large, long-haired galumpy dog, sprawled on the carpet, laid her ears back and growled. Winston scowled at the interruption, then continued, "Takes a lot of grit to live like we do. Our caretaker Joe has to shoot nasty woodchucks, fence the garden from marauding deer, clear out ugly trees, stack the cursed firewood, and plow the damned snow. It's all part of the scene, but we're used to the rough life. We just adapt."

His brother-in-law, Larry, was sitting on the leather couch. He stood up, stretched, and chuckled. "Doesn't sound too rough to me. Got a problem? Call Joe. How sweet is that! City's a lot harder: dragging to the laundromat, fighting cockroaches, moving the car – one side of the street to the other. Wish *I* could afford a Joe to do it all for me. The only kind of Joe I see is my morning coffee. But that's the life of a writer. Royalties suck, but I live with it." He walked over and joined Winston at the window. Larry, a young lanky guy in khaki pants, shirt hanging loose, and sock feet, stood beside his gray-haired host. He softened his remark by giving him a big smile. An ill-assorted pair.

Winston turned to Larry, his wife's brother, admonishing him, "Your situation is hardly frivolous. You might want to get a little smarter about the way you do things. No need to wallow in poverty. Stop letting others use you. Find your power, like I do. Learn to use *them.*"

Larry, ignoring the words of wisdom, responded. "Listen. I hear thunder. Wow! Did you see that lightning strike? The wind is starting to pick up."

Winston's young wife Deedee had been busy in the kitchen. On hearing the heavens rumble, she rushed into the room to join them at the window. The dog awoke and began to pace.

"Oh my, that's quite a storm brewing," said Deedee. "I've never seen it so black. Watching those trees rock back and forth makes me wonder how they manage to stay standing. Look at the trunks bend! You'd think they'd snap!"

"Hardly," said Winston. "They're flexible… like me… able to adapt. Uh-oh. There goes a shingle. Joe will have some repairs to do."

"Come here and watch," said Larry to his wife Linda, a petite blonde wearing a long cotton skirt, white blouse, and beads. "What a fantastic show!" he exclaimed.

"Uh-uh, I'm staying right here." She covered her eyes with her hand. "Storms like this scare me."

"Nonsense," said Winston. "They're nothing to get upset about." No sooner had he spoken than a loud clap of thunder shook the room. The lights went out.

"My God! Damned if we haven't lost power. That's not supposed to happen. What an outrage!" shouted Winston. "Where's that Joe? He's got to fix it right now. Can't have the little women all upset."

But one little woman was decidedly not upset. In fact, his wife Deedee was smiling, though no one there could tell in the dark. "Joe's left for the weekend." she said.

"He has no business taking off like that. Who gave him permission anyway?"

"You did," she reminded him.

"He probably knew there was a storm coming. That's probably why he left."

"Now, let's be reasonable," his wife urged.

"Reasonable, what would you know about reason? You, always half-distracted. If I didn't tell you what to do, you'd live in a cloud of confusion. Now, first thing, where is the flashlight?"

"There's one right here," said Deedee as she reached down to the windowsill, felt around, found it, and tried to switch it on. "Uh-oh, the batteries are dead."

"Damn it! That Joe," exclaimed Winston. "He forgot to replace them. Now, we're really in the dark. I can't see a thing."

"Surprise," chirped in Larry. "None of *us* can see a thing, either."

"There should be matches by the fireplace," said Winston, ignoring his brother-in-law's remark. He turned around, hands stretched in front and carefully inched his way across the room. First, he bumped into a chair, then tripped over a dog bone. "I've told you before, that damned Oya should not be allowed to chew her bones inside," he rebuked his wife as he bent down to retrieve the offending obstacle. Reaching the fireplace, he put it up on the mantelpiece. Then, sliding his hand further along, he found the match box. "Got them. By the way, aren't there supposed to be candles somewhere as well?"

"Hey," Larry said, "why don't you use the light on your phone?"

"Oh. Oh yeah, good idea," mumbled Winston who found the digital world a challenge. Even worse, he had to ask the younger man how to turn it on. Winston then found two candles on the far end of the mantle, lit them and carried them to the large table at one end of the room.

"There we go. Okay, everyone. I've solved that problem. Come over and take a seat where you can see."

"Perfect," said Larry, as they all pulled out chairs around the table.

"Well, not quite," said his sister Deedee. "Now I can't cook dinner. It will be a cold meal tonight."

"Won't be the first time," said Winston. "After fifteen years, I'm still hoping you'll serve me one that's hot. But, for God's sake! We shouldn't have to deal with a power outage! What's the matter with those people?"

"Wait, didn't you just say you were adaptable?" said Larry. "So, let's adapt. Actually, I think this is exciting. That wind and the driving rain!"

"If we can't eat, at least let's drink," suggested Deedee. "That always makes for a merry evening. Winston dear, could you pour us all another round?"

"Exactly what I was about to suggest until you interrupted me," replied Winston. He turned on his phone light and headed over to the bar. Falling back on one of his finer skills, he took delight in mixing and serving the drinks. Soon, everyone was nursing embossed crystal glasses filled with gin and tonic.

"I know what," said Deedee, "why don't I read you all a story while we wait for the lights to come on? I just found my favorite childhood book *Wind in the Willows*. The Mole and his friends, the woods and rivers... it's very poetic. I think you'll enjoy it."

"Another one of your silly ideas," said Winston.

Undeterred, Deedee retrieved the book from the coffee table. "Here it is."

Another loud clap of thunder rattled the house. The foursome jumped, despite trying to appear calm. The dog commenced growling.

"Uh-oh. Come here, Oya. She gets excited when the wind picks up," explained Deedee. The dog padded to her chair and laid her head in her lap. Her mistress stroked Oya, murmuring sweet talk in her ear.

"Oya? What kind of a name is that?" asked her brother.

"You don't want to know," said her husband.

"But I do. Tell me, Deedee."

"She's named for the African Goddess of wind, storms, death, and rebirth."

"Total hogwash," commented Winston. "Your sister is caught up in absurd spiritual nonsense! She's been bitten by some la-la mysticism from a godforsaken African country. She's forgotten how lucky she is to live in America. Why she has to get mixed up in this voodoo stuff is beyond me."

"That's not very nice, Winston," retorted his wife. "Anyway, it has nothing to do with voodoo. Nor is mysticism nonsense. It's very deep! If you opened up to it, you'd feel its great power."

"It's okay, Sis. It doesn't matter to me," said Larry. "If you find strength in the spiritual world, I'm happy for you. As for me, I can't be a writer without questioning spirits and everything else in the universe."

"Deedee, how fascinating," said Linda. "You do know the most unusual things." With that, she pulled out her cell and tapped in 'Goddess Oya'. Head bent, she started to read in the privacy of the long hair hanging in front of her face. After a minute she looked up, her blue eyes shining. Leaning close to Deedee, who was sitting next to her, she whispered, "Why she's also the protector of women! Did you know that?"

"I did. Oya is important." Deedee returned Linda's smile as she leaned forward and rested her cheek against Oya who had managed to crawl halfway into her lap.

Winston sighed, then warned Larry, "The dog is so spiritual she can't get outside fast enough when she has to go. Makes for a lot of accidents. I wouldn't walk around in your sock feet."

"If you let her out on time, that wouldn't happen," countered Deedee.

Oya slid down off Deedee's lap and paced about the room. She looked up at each person as they spoke.

"Winston, maybe don't speak badly of Oya in front of her. For all we know she understands every word."

"Maybe I'm imagining things, but I could swear she just nodded her head in agreement," said Linda.

"You are," responded Winston, "most definitely imagining things."

Taking her eyes off the dog, Deedee looked out the window just as a great streak of lightening hit the distant horizon. "Oh! Did you see that? The Gods are at it tonight. Beautiful!"

"But isn't it dangerous?" asked Linda.

"If you happen to get hit, yes," replied Deedee. "But if you don't... it's a privilege to bear witness."

Noting how nervous her guest was, Deedee opened *Wind in the Willows*. "There's nothing like a little magic to help us cope. This book is just the thing. Listen to the soothing words of Mole. '*...suddenly he stood by the edge of a full-fed river. Never in his life had he seen a river before ... this sleek, sinuous, full-bodied animal, chasing and chuckling, gripping things with a gurgle and leaving them with a laugh, to fling itself on fresh playmates that shook themselves free, and were caught and held again...*'

"I'm coping just fine without a *mole* telling me how to do it!" interrupted her husband. "Let's get practical. Somebody has to do something, and I guess it will be me... as usual." With that, he reached for his cell but managed to drop it on the rug. "Now, where did it go?" he said as he got down on his hands and knees and felt around. "It seems to be lost. Deedee, get down here and help."

"That's not all that's lost," mumbled Larry.

"Found it," Winston suddenly declared just as another clap of thunder cracked over their heads. Husband and wife returned to their seats. All resumed drinking.

"Let's just take it easy and listen to Sis read. This storm can't last forever," said Larry.

Deedee continued. "*The mole was bewitched, entranced, fascinated. By the side of the river he trotted as one trots, when very small, by the side of a man who holds one spell-bound by exciting stories...*'" Noticing Winston groaning, she finally put the book down. "Winston, dear, what's the matter?"

"Damned arthritis. Grabbed my back while I was on the floor."

"First storm casualty," commented Larry in an aside.

"Oh, I'm so sorry," purred Deedee.

Then, looking at the dog, "Here Oya, come to Mama." Oya paused by her chair and Deedee patted the dog's shaggy coat, scratching behind her pointy ears.

"Nice if you would give me as much attention as you do that stupid dog," her husband mumbled.

"What we need right now," Deedee said, "is to continue hearing the story. That will calm the spirit and strengthen the soul." She resumed reading. " '*The mole had to be content with this. But the Badger never came along, and every day brought its amusements, and it was not till summer was long over, and cold and frost and miry ways kept them much indoors, and the swollen river raced ...*'

"Blimey! Enough of that rot," declared Winston. "Deedee, you're not helping things. Clearly I have to do everything around here." With that he dialed 911. "Hello, hello, this is Winston Charles. We have an emergency out here!" he shouted into the phone.

"Tell me about it," came the calm words from the other end of the line. And so, he did. "Sir, that is not an emergency – you need to call your power company."

"Listen, you don't know who you're talking to. As I said, this is Winston Charles. We have tiles blowing off the roof and the power is out. If that's not an emergency, I don't know what is."

"I could explain, sir, but I don't have time. Call the power company," the voice repeated. "Goodbye."

"If that isn't the bloodiest stupidity I ever heard," he burst out. Then he dialed the power company. The others ignored him, spellbound as they were by mole, badger, and rat scurrying through the story which Deedee recommenced reading aloud.

Once again, Winston shouted into the phone, "Hello, hello! I need to report a power outage! What do you mean, you won't take my call? What's that? I have to go to your damned website and report it? This is ridiculous! What happened to good old customer service? Okay, okay. How do I find the website?" Hanging up, he steamed a little more, then continued in a loud voice, again drowning out his wife's attempt to bring calm into their midst. "Well, that wasn't much help. Now I have to find the website." Still holding his device, he switched to the internet. "Okay. Here we are. I've got it. Let's see, it's asking for our account number. Why can't they just ask for our phone number! All I want to do is report a power outage. Deedee, go find the electric bill." His wife's voice drifted off as she stopped reading and looked up from her book.

Used to obeying orders, she stood up, grabbed one of the candles and started to scurry off. "Wait," said Larry, "take the light on my phone."

The dog, suddenly abandoned, padded over to Larry and slumped against his legs.

A few minutes later, Larry remarked that his feet felt wet. "Could the roof be leaking?"

"No, the stupid dog is. I told you not to walk in sock feet," his host replied.

Deedee soon returned, a piece of paper clutched in her hand. She obediently turned it over to her husband. He took a look and exploded, "Bloody Hell, this is another one of your parking tickets! Smart, Deedee, really smart!"

"Oh dear! I didn't mean to give you *that*. I thought it was the electric bill."

Suddenly Winston slammed down the phone. "What a rigmarole! Now they're announcing that the power should be back on in less than half an hour. Why couldn't they have said that in the first place?"

"Got to love it! I should write a story about all this!" Larry pulled out his phone and his thumb took off.

"Now, just a minute, young man. What happens in my house, stays in my house. No lame-brained accounts of this evening." Winston, stuck in his old ways, still thought he could rule like a lord of yore. He failed to slow Larry down. The thumb kept going.

"Listen," said Deedee, "I have an idea. You're not listening to me read anyway, so while we're waiting, why don't we have a seance instead? This is the perfect setting for one."

"Oh, no. How can you believe in that claptrap?" came the predictable response from her husband.

"But my dear, it's not a matter of believing. It works. It's powerful. Sometimes I'm the medium for my group seances. We could try it."

"What a crock!" was his reply.

Larry, looking up from his device, heartily endorsed his sister's proposal. "Hey, why not? Come on Winston, it's all just good fun. Won't hurt us to go along with sis."

"Not *my* idea of fun but, to keep the little woman happy, I'll go along... this once."

Linda beamed, "What fun. Let's do it. Maybe a ghost will appear."

"So, one of you give me a question to ask someone who has passed to the other side."

"Okay, how's this? I had an old stinker of a grandpa... a real bastard... made my life miserable. Ask him if he's mellowed since he left us." suggested Winston.

"Are you sure that's what you want to ask? You don't want to provoke him."

"He provoked me for years. Why shouldn't I provoke him?"

"Because he might get mad, mess up your life."

"Right. And the moon is going to fall out of the sky. Ask him."

"Okay then, but I'm just saying, bad things can happen. What's his name anyway?

"They called him Clubby – a cranky president of the country club for too many years."

"Clubby. Alright. We'll start by holding hands and closing our eyes." Deedee reached for Linda's hand. Linda smiled sweetly and extended her other hand to her husband. Smirking, Larry put down his device and, after hesitating, took her hand on his right. He reached for his host's on his left. Winston gave a snort of exasperation, finally complied, grabbing both his wife's hand on one side and Larry's on the other.

"Oh, great spirits, please hear us on this special evening. We have a message for Clubby. Dear Grandpa Clubby, your grandson wants to know if you've mellowed since he last saw you." Suddenly the candles blew out.

"Strange," said Larry. "Where did that breeze come from? Is there a door open?"

"See?" Deedee's soft voice seemed to fill the dark. "The spirits *are* with us tonight."

Taking advantage of the dark, Oya's sniffer hard at work led her toward the fireplace, where she clambered up on a wide bench to retrieve her stolen bone from the mantelpiece. A few minutes later, suddenly all the lights came on. From Winston's place across the table, the bench was out of sight. The dog seemed to be standing in the air, nose pointed up, tail straight out behind her.

"Good God!" he burst out. "Levitated! How is that possible? I swear you're some kind of witch, Deedee." Winston began to tremble ever so slightly, at the same time letting go of the others' hands. Then, as quick as they came on, the lights went out again. When they came back up twenty seconds later, Winston's chair was empty.

"Oh no! Where's Winston? Winston! Where'd he go?" Larry cried as he ran out of the room, calling for his brother-in-law. "Winston! Winston! It's not funny. Where'd you go?"

Deedee still sitting, the glimmer of a smile on her pale face, stared at her husband's empty chair.

Spring on the Saranac

A warm day in early May, we relax on the deck sipping our morning coffee when the flick of a tail in the leaf litter beyond the railing gets our attention. A skinny weasel, dressed in her spring coat... brown back, white belly... scurries into a hollow tree trunk lying on the ground, which, for aesthetic reasons, we had thought of removing. We are reminded now why nature is best left alone. She scampers in one end and out the other, pauses to peek over the top, then undulates away into the woods.

We are inspired by this slinky explorer, decide to venture forth and see what other creatures are about on this sunny day.

In just twenty minutes, we arrive at the Moose Pond Road bridge. Kayaks unloaded, we launch onto the chilly waters of the Saranac.

Full of expectation, we paddle up the river. Birds are returning, courtship rampant, and everywhere new grasses and leaves are washing the shores in green. We are greeted by a tan and white bird, bobbing up and down as he runs along the mudflats. Spotted sandpipers are back! Flying to and fro, one bank to another, two comical woody-woodpeckers (aka pileateds) echo each other's raucous calls. The river is high, the current fast. Already we are being swept downstream toward the bridge and eventual rapids. Not for us, that kind of challenge; we were seeking a more peaceful trip with time to look and listen. We paddle hard, head for the quiet flooded areas upstream. A spring concert is in full voice: peepers shrilling out in ear-piercing chorus, an American toad joining with a deeper reverberating trill.

We arrive at calmer waters spreading wide onto a low area of reeds and bushes. I spy a straight line along the shore. I stare, unable to see what causes this divide: above, rosy-stemmed red osier shrubs and new lime alder leaves; below, a wintry scene of gray branches and flat dead grass. It takes a minute to realize this odd demarcation was caused by muddy flood waters. A few weeks earlier, the river had overflowed with melting snow. In fact, as I stare out toward the distant blue-gray peaks of the Moose and Whiteface mountains, I see they still display white fingers of winter streaking their flanks.

We paddle on. A dark furry beaver swims before us, then submerges with a slap of his great wide tail. That frightens a hooded merganser, which flies up out of the reeds and startles a great blue heron. The heron lumbers into the air, his body seeming too heavy for his long wings to bear him aloft. Instead of flying away, he flies before us, as herons do, landing just a few yards upstream. He resumes fishing, his long legs stepping carefully through the reeds, his snaky neck darting into the water in search of a meal. No sooner does he begin, then along we come to scare him up again. This hopscotching goes on for an hour. I feel guilty about our constant disruption of this elegant bird.

The river narrows, twists to the left, then turns back on itself. This is not the course to follow if in a rush. Though the village of Saranac Lake is a mere five miles away, we have no plans to go there. Today is for drifting and watching. I am delighted to find a tiny miniature sailboat catching the wind and heading our way. What child lost this charming vessel? It takes me back to the scenes of children sailing their model boats in city park ponds. But wait, this is no man-made structure. This, a scrap of birch bark, triangular corner turned up to make a sail, is as successful a model craft as ever I've seen. It cruises past and I lean over to bid it farewell on its 50-mile journey to Lake Champlain. How will you fare on those rough waves, little sailboat? I fear power yachts will not make way for such a small craft. Most will never see you at all.

Rounding a corner, we are dismayed to see a pile of brilliant blue and white feathers lying on the pine needle-covered ground, wings and tail spread, head cocked back. Whatever happened to this beautiful bird? We paddle closer, stare hard, when with a whoosh, he explodes in a flash of blue, flying off into the trees. A jay taking a sunbath? Or was he displaying his royal plumage for some star-struck female?

A host of birds sing us along. I recognize the "whichity, whichity, whichity" of the yellow-throated warbler; the sweet "Canada, Canada, Canada" of the white-throated sparrow; the chickadees' spring call "pheee-beee"; the endless serenade of a winter wren. But knowledge fails me as we float through a cloud of warblers with their ever-varied medley of songs. I listen and enjoy, but cannot identify. I have yet to learn the variety of notes produced by this twice-yearly migration of winged jewels.

A shimmer of young green leaves trembles in the bushes. Distant trees puff out in shades of emerald. Atop a distant hill, dark balsam firs, narrow and tall, point straight-up to touch the clouds. Down by the sandy shore, white pines spread dusty-green limbs to welcome passing birds.

Leaving the main channel, we veer off to explore the high water flooding the woods. We paddle between tree trunks, their branches overhead gifting us cool shade. Leaving the woods, a narrow, meandering corridor leads to more surprises: a frightened mallard rises helicopter-like; another stays motionless on her eggs;

239

a remnant of last summer, a tiny nest, clings to a bush revealing the skills of feathered artisans – reindeer moss woven into its walls – a yellow warbler? A flycatcher?

A red-winged blackbird creaks out his "cherr-ee, cherr-ee," reminding me of a song fragment: "Chim-chim, chim-chim chim-chim cherr-ee, a sweep is as lucky as lucky can be." I, too, am lucky. Lucky to be on this river.

We pass a small house tucked in the woods. A bench on the bank speaks of dwellers who savor the peaceful scene. I imagine them sitting quietly, after a long day's work, thankful to come home to this quiet spot.

Two hours later and the sun is blazing hot. We turn to head back downstream. Everywhere are beaver lodges. The birch and maple trees these industrious woodchoppers have felled lie waiting to be hauled away... material for their dams, houses, and meals.

In places, erosion has washed out the shore, leaving sandbanks and small damp beaches below, perfect for finding tracks. We see the webbed prints of beavers, the heart-shaped indents of deer, and the trails of peace-signs left by turkeys. Above, on the steep banks, are nesting holes. Kingfishers? Bank swallows?

Drifting with the current, we float by two vultures, shoulders hunched as they hunker down on flood debris lodged across the river. With their small heads and spring plumage they appear more red-brown than black, reminding us of large, overstuffed chickens. I am fond of these creatures, so graceful when riding the updrafts – sanitation crew, cleaning up life's detritus. Because of this, my husband thinks it would be fitting to designate them as the official New York state bird.

The current with us, we are soon back at the bridge. In this riparian landscape so close to home, winter melt gives rise to the poetry of blue forget-me-nots and yellow marsh marigolds.

Suddenly, we notice a distant rumble. What is that? A waterfall? But there are none nearby. Straining to make out the sound, we realize it is a river of traffic on a nearby highway streaming with cars flowing to unknown destinations. Folks impatient with the slow unfolding of spring are headed out... To shopping malls? Warmer climes? Sealed in their air-conditioned cars, enclosed in metal, blasting music, they follow a different course – dreaming of new clothes, furniture, a movie, or going to Disneyland. Their trips are fast and loud; ours, by the way, is slow and quiet. What gratifies them, does not gratify us. And yet, these two separate rivers flow so close to one another.

(Published in the Blue Line Magazine, Vol. 41, Potsdam, NY, Summer 2020)

About the Author

Caperton Tissot's writing life, preceded by years of work in healthcare, ceramics, and environmental advocacy, reflects an abiding interest in small communities and nature. Her work includes publications in journals and newspapers, plus several books of history, fiction, poetry, memoir, short stories, and a children's story. She and her husband live in the Adirondacks, where Tissot balances an outdoor lifestyle with an indoor writing vocation.

For contact and more information, visit
www.SnowyOwlPress.com.